"With *O Pioneer!*, Pohl once again demonstrates his special ability to evoke a sense of wonder. Pohl has scored again with this novel."

—*BookPage*

"Pohl shines, giving a wonderfully alien individuality to each species."

—*Booklist*

As Mayor Evesham Giyt walked in for his first meeting of the Tupelo Joint Governance Commission, all five of the other leaders rose to welcome him and there was an unexpected spatter of applause from the eight or ten people in the audience, almost all humans. The Centaurian female—the translator in his ear gave her name as Mrs. Brownbenttalon—made a speech of greeting. Giyt could make nothing of her squeaks and squeals, but the translation phone duly rendered it for him in English: "The total of us who are not from the planet Earth human are overcomely delighted, Large Male Giyt, to have you participate us in our unceasing struggle to ensure no hitting and the getting of along."

It wouldn't hurt to take a look at those translation programs, Giyt thought to himself.

"Pohl, whose nonfiction book *Practical Politics* is currently being studied with great interest by Russian democrats, clearly knows the political process and the character types it attracts. In *O Pioneer!*, Pohl's droll look at hands-on politics is made all the more amusing by his descriptions of the interaction among six very different cultures. Don't let the book's chatty tone fool you. This science fiction novel about civic virtue is something genuinely new."

—*Minneapolis Star-Tribune*

BOOKS BY FREDERIK POHL

The Age of the Pussyfoot
Drunkard's Walk
Black Star Rising
The Cool War

THE HEECHEE SAGA
Gateway
Beyond the Blue Event Horizon
Heechee Rendezvous
The Annals of the Heechee
The Gateway Trip

THE ESCHATON SEQUENCE
**The Other End of Time*
**The Siege of Eternity*
**†The Far Shore of Time*

Homegoing
Mining the Oort
Narabedla Ltd.
Pohlstars
Starburst
The Way the Future Was (memoir)
The World at the end of Time
Jem
Midas World
Merchant's War
The Coming of the Quantum Cats
The Space Merchants (with C. M. Kornbluth)
Man Plus
Chernobyl
The Day the Martians Came
Stopping at Slowyear
**The Voices of Heaven*
**O Pioneer!*

With Jack Williamson:
The Starchild Trilogy
Undersea City
Undersea Quest
Undersea Fleet
Wall Around a Star
The Farthest Star
**Land's End*
The Singers of Time

With Lester del Rey:
Preferred Risk

The Best of Frederik Pohl (edited by Lester del Rey)
The Best of C. M. Kornbluth (editor)

*denotes a Tor Book
†forthcoming

FREDERIK POHL

O PIONEER!

A TOM DOHERTY ASSOCIATES BOOK
NEW YORK

O PIONEER!

Originally published in a somewhat different form in *Analog*, October-December 1997. Copyright © 1997 by Dell Magazines, a division of Crosstown Publications.

Edited by James Frenkel

A Tor Book
Published by Tom Doherty Associates, Inc.
175 Fifth Avenue
New York, NY 10010

Tor Books on the World Wide Web:
http://www.tor.com

ISBN: 0-812-54544-3
Library of Congress Catalog Card Number: 98-9726

First edition: May 1998
First mass market edition: April 1999

Printed in the United States of America

0 9 8 7 6 5 4 3 2 1

To Betty Anne
for, among other reasons,
keeping me alive

I

Bal Harbor Residential Park. Low-cost Luxury for the Discriminating Few. Fully retractable private residences, 100 percent soundproofed, payments in cash accepted. Kitchen and all conveniences nearby.

—CLASSIFIED AD, "RESIDENTIAL DRAWER SPACE TO LET"

Evesham Giyt's mailing address was care of the Bal Harbor Residential Park, but he didn't use the address much. He practically never received any mail. He didn't expect to. He didn't even have a terminal, at least not one that anybody knew about. Certainly not one that had his name on it. Anyway, there wasn't anybody he'd ever known whom he had any interest in keeping in touch with. He had no living relatives. He had not retained any old friends.

Even if he had, Bal Harbor wasn't the kind of place you'd especially want people to know you were living in. Located in the industrial fringe of Wichita, Kansas, it looked more like a district of broken-down warehouses than anything you would call residential. About the only time Giyt mentioned that Bal Harbor was his home was when he was applying for a job as a bug-killer. That happened only when his money began to run out—maybe three or four times a year. That was because he had no choice, since employers always wanted to know where you lived. In this one rare case Giyt found that it was easier to tell the truth than to fake something.

What did have to be faked, of course, were his references. Giyt naturally wrote those himself, complete with net addresses that were keyed to divert any inquiries into one of his own programs.

However, Giyt's skills at bug-killing were very real, because Giyt was an absolute computer genius. In the first two or three weeks at any job he never failed to turn up and cancel a whole nest of the little nasties, some of them surveillance scout programs implanted by business competitors, some just the mischief of some harebrained hacker. Now and then, though, he turned up some really ugly time bomb that had been sneaked in by a bloodthirsty competitor or left as a parting gift by a disgruntled former employee—left, often enough, by the particular former employee Giyt was replacing. By the time that had been going on for a few weeks his bosses were invariably congratulating themselves over their good judgment in taking him aboard. So they always took it hard when, all apologies and sorrow, he told them the bad news about the sudden emergency in his family that made it necessary for him to quit and move to, say, Fargo, North Dakota, or maybe Key West. By then Giyt had also located some good and undetectable ways to divert a decent nest egg to one of his own six or seven untraceable dummy accounts. Thus solvency was assured for the next few months.

The cops considered that sort of activity seriously illegal. Giyt didn't agree. He didn't think that what he did was stealing. He thought of it as what it really was—namely, making sure he got the proper payment for the really very valuable services he had rendered. Who was in a better position to calculate the value of those services than the person who had rendered them?

Giyt never embezzled large amounts. He could have, easily enough. It would have been no trouble at all to reach into some megabank's files and siphon away a few million cues before they noticed—by which time the money would have disappeared into one of his untraceable ratholes—and then he would never need to lift a finger again.

Giyt didn't do that. In his view, that would have been dishonest. He *earned* everything he took, and he didn't need large amounts, anyway. It cost very little to live in Bal Harbor. He didn't need to keep on living in a dump like Bal Harbor, either, but the place suited him. Evesham Giyt had a very rich fantasy life. He spent a lot of time in the history net, with people like Julius Caesar and Adolf Hitler and the Spanish conquistadors and Alexander the Great. It would be a lot of fun, he sometimes thought wistfully, to conquer the world, or anyway some good-sized piece of it. Something about as big as, say, Canada would be nice, and he even spent a number of pleasurable hours rummaging through the secret defense files of both the United States and Canadian governments to figure out just how you could go about it. It didn't look all that hard. The only question was where to invade. Vancouver was a tempting beachhead. It would fall quickly, and then it would be hard for the Canadians to reinforce across the Rockies; but by the same token it would be a poor jumping-off place for invading the rest of Canada. He considered upstate New York, too; you could start by driving into Quebec, perhaps enlisting the more radical Francophones as guerrilla troops. But, taking one thing with another, he favored striking right across the northern tier into the prairie provinces, with their open terrain so marvelous for tanks.

It was fantasy, of course. Nobody fought actual wars any more, wars of conquest or any other kind. Especially not the kind that involved killing and maiming. The Earth's big battleground was commerce—an extra import tax here, some merchandise dumping there, a lot of juggling exchange rates everywhere. There were plenty of people who yearned for the good old glory days, but Giyt wasn't one of them. In old-style wars he could have been a Napoleon, at least a Patton, but he didn't want to fight. Not actually. Only in daydreams.

Anyway, all the places Giyt might have wanted to invade, given a few army corps to help the job along, were pretty well messed up by the inroads of civilization. Urban crime, drug cartels, street violence—who needed those kinds of problems? Not to mention that if you really wanted to physically conquer any sizable chunk of real estate in the way the old guys had, it would require a lot of—well—killing.

That was a stopper, right there.

Killing people had never been Evesham Giyt's style. He had no desire to hurt or enslave anybody. Not *any* person, much less the large numbers of persons that would die if you used those unpleasant mass-destruction weapons that made up modern warfare. The fact was that Evesham Giyt didn't like guns.

Guns, or at least one particular gun, were the reason why Giyt hadn't had any living relatives since his first year in college.

That was the year when his father had taken one of his carefully maintained guns from his private and highly illegal weapon collection and used it to blow his brains out.

That had been a traumatic watershed event for young Evesham Giyt. As a small child he had adored the old man, who was a skilled and highly prized technician in the field of parts assembly. The older Giyt was not just an important employee in the little boutique factories that hired his services. Often enough he was nearly the only one.

Sometimes when Giyt was little his father would take him along to watch him work. Evesham was fascinated by the way his father would sit there, patient and smiling, while his helpers dotted his wrists and fingers with tiny, almost invisible reflective patches. When he was fully marked he would sit before the bunch of parts he had laid out on the workbench and, as he had practiced, put them quickly together into the finished product—whatever the finished product for that day's run might be. Harriman Giyt only had to do it once. As he worked, the lidar scanners of the factory computer system registered each step. When he was finished the computers had only to repeat each step as many times as required for the run of the product—seldom more than a couple of thousand pieces, not enough to go through the bother of writing a program for.

It was a good living for the old man and his young son until the computers got a little more efficient. When all-purpose assembling programs had become capable of reverse-engineering a finished product and going back to work out the steps needed to put it together for themselves, Harriman Giyt abruptly found himself as unemployed as the piece workers he and the robots had replaced.

That was when he shot himself.

The effects of Harriman Giyt's suicide on his son were threefold. First, young Evesham discovered he had been left without enough money to finish college. He had to figure out a way of tricking the university records systems into believing that his tuition had been paid. He turned out to be pretty good at that sort of thing, which naturally led to his later career.

Second, he resolved never to find himself in his father's position, which meant he never intended to depend on a salary for his livelihood. And third, he acquired that lifelong distaste for guns—for, as a matter of fact, every one of the cunning devices human beings had invented to end the lives of other human beings. All of them, way back to the most primitive. Clubs were bad enough, swords worse. With the emergence of catapults and arrows things got worse still, because now humans could kill each other at a distance. And then, starting somewhere early in the nineteenth century, things got really bad. Rifles. Machine guns. Bomber planes. Guided missiles. Tricky devices like the bus that could fly around a corner and shower needle-pointed fléchettes on people who had thought they were perfectly safe from harm . . . Well, it was all nasty, and the thought that those were the tools of conquest took a lot of the pleasure out of some of Giyt's favorite daydreams.

Anyway, it wasn't their battlefield triumphs that he most envied about the great conquerors of the past. It was something quite different.

All those wickedly villainous heroes had something Giyt didn't have. They had attainable goals. They knew what they wanted to do with their lives—never mind that the way they did it would cause a lot of unhappiness for the people they did it to. While he really had very little idea of what to do with his own.

Military conquest, for Giyt, was only a daydream. He knew it. He would have settled for less—for example, for some untamed wilderness where he could buy himself an estate with some of the reserve money from his hidden accounts. *Buy* the estate. Not kill for it. And then he would clear the land and plant his crops and be a genuine pioneer.

Unfortunately, Giyt couldn't find the right kind of place. There were plenty of wildernesses on Earth, sure, but they all suffered from one (or more) of three disqualifying traits. Either they were already chockablock with people so desperately poor that the neighbors would take all the fun out of pioneering. Or they were burdened with unpleasant disease organisms. Or the climate was nasty.

So he contented himself with what he had.

Which, really, was not all that bad. Here in Bal Harbor he had a decent cubicle to sleep in and all the appliances he wanted and the finest food the city of Wichita had to offer any time he chose to go out to eat. He had his unregistered terminal. Sometimes he used this to roam the net or created a scout program to roam it for him, something armed with key words to check out and one of Giyt's own sniffer programs to watch out for defensive bugs. It was very easy to find secrets that way. Sometimes Giyt thought it might be interesting to write a book that exposed some of the political sins his scout discovered for him; but he never held on to that thought for very long. The secrets of the real world were actually pretty boring, and anyway the real world was what Evesham Giyt wanted to avoid.

Giyt liked his solitude. He kept it secure, too. Once or twice it had been threatened—most severely of all, long before, when he had been surprised by an intrusion on his screen: "Hey, warmonger! I liked your Canadian invasion plan. Ever think of doing it for real?"

Giyt didn't reply to the unknown hacker, of course. He didn't use those access codes again, either; he doubled his cutouts, and he never heard from that person again. He even thought for a little while of physically moving himself to some other town or even some other continent, but in the thoroughly homogenized world he lived in, what was the point? Giyt had no compelling reason to think he had to stay in Wichita, but even less reason to move.

Actually, in Wichita, Giyt had just about everything you could acquire that went to make life bearable . . . but that wasn't all.

He also had Rina.

Rina was a very big plus in Giyt's life. Rina was lively, pretty, and dark, a tiny woman almost half a meter shorter than Giyt himself but twice as energetic. She was smart. She had organized her life almost as efficiently as Giyt had his own. She was also crazy about Evesham Giyt and she was absolutely wonderful in the sack.

That last part, he supposed, was one of the fringe benefits

of her former profession as a hooker, although she had explained to him very soon in their relationship that she had specialized in whips-and-chains domination because that way you didn't actually have to screw any customer you didn't really like. Probably she thought telling Giyt that would ease any jealousy he might feel. She needn't have worried. Giyt didn't mind any of that. Rina's whoring was well in the past and had left her with neither a habit nor any STD. About the only trace of it in her present life was that sometimes Rina would shyly suggest that being handcuffed to the bed might be nice for a change, and once in a while he obliged her for old time's sake. He drew the line at the whips and chains, though, and usually it was nice, friendly, just-for-fun sex. They'd go out to have a good meal somewhere—Thai or Provençal for preference, because there were good places for both only a short autocab ride away. Of course it was generally Rina who paid the bill with her credit wristlet, and that was another nice thing about Rina. She never asked why Giyt didn't use credit of his own. She didn't have to. Obviously she figured out that Giyt didn't want to submit to being sniffed and thus identified in some databank somewhere. And of course, he always reimbursed her in cash, with a little extra rounded off.

Then when dinner was over, they'd go back to his slide and climb in, and when they'd retracted the slide and put on the privacy locks, they were all alone in their warm, pleasant, personal place with the minibar and the climate control and whatever kind of music suited their mood from his library of fifteen or sixteen thousand pieces, and maybe a light show or a porn disk to get them started. Once in a while he'd even invite her to stay overnight, because her own cubicle was really pretty spartan—Rina was living on savings while she finished her business-management courses at the Wichita campus of KU. Sometimes in bed Giyt would be lying on one side, putting himself to sleep by watching the story of Kamehameha conquering the island of Oahu, while she was trying to make sense of the difference between liquid versus colloidal nonconvertible debentures on her own screen on the other. Giyt sort of liked that. It was comfortably domestic. And did not represent a commitment.

Rina took her schooling seriously, too. She studied hard. She didn't really have to bother, because Giyt had showed her early how easily she could improve her grades by accessing the school's databank—for that matter, could award herself as many degrees as she liked, summa cum laude if she wanted them that way, and not go through the trouble of passing examinations at all. Rina caught on quickly. She had a natural ability for jiggling computer systems, but she wouldn't do any actual tampering with the school records and wouldn't let Giyt do it for her either. She didn't want good grades, she explained. She wanted to actually learn this crap. She didn't need to cheat anyway, really, because she was a straight-A student all down the line. There was a moral issue there for Rina, too. That sort of thing was like Peeping Tom stuff. Which was too much like business. The former hooker had no interest in invading someone else's privacy.

So there was Rina, and there were all his other little pleasures, and it was a pretty good life, if sort of lacking in any long-range objectives. Giyt could not see any practical purpose in trying to change it . . . until the Tupelo recruiters came to Wichita.

II

Once again, this year's Nobel Prize in Physics represents a major miscarriage of justice. No doubt Drs. Morchan and Weng have done notable work in the field of high-temperature antiquarks. Nevertheless, the grandest scientific event of this century is plainly Fitzhugh J. Sommermen's discovery of a means of faster-than-light transportation. It is here. It works. How can the august members of the Nobel committee continue to pass it over for the prize?

Dr. Sommermen has given us a hint of how the process works. It is, he has told us, related to the well-known Einstein-Podolsky-Rosen effect. In this litigious age in which we live, when scientists dare not speak freely about their ongoing research for fear that some less scrupulous person will appropriate the fruits of their work and even patent them, we cannot yet ask him to tell us more. To deny Dr. Sommermen the Nobel simply because he declines to make public all of the details of his work is shameful. Yet, truly, this great genius does not need a prize to validate his preeminence in his field. His work speaks for itself.

—EDITORIAL, THE NEW YORK TIMESNET

Evesham Giyt had heard of the Tupelo planet, of course. Everybody had. The story had been a headliner on all the news broadcasts fourteen years earlier, when the planet was first discovered by scout spacecraft operated by the Huntsville-based ET-DIXIE program and the word instantly flashed back to Earth by the amazing new Sommermen process. Giyt hadn't paid a lot of attention to the story even at the time. He wasn't actually much interested in news, but he hadn't been able to avoid seeing some of the stories when he was trying to check on the day's stock prices. Naturally, most of the interest in Tupelo had dried up fast when the next hot story came along to chase it off the headlines, but for some time now, Giyt knew, the Extended Earth Society had been doing their best to keep it alive with their commercials.

Of course, Giyt didn't pay much attention to commercials, either. When his blab-off cancellation programs slipped up and let one get through, he generally just ignored it. This one, though, caught his eye—nice graphics, good background music, probably Holst's *The Planets*, but jazzed up with a tricky rhythm. He actually listened to what the executive-looking man in the briefs and sunscreen was saying. "Tupelo," the man declaimed, holding up a string of thirty-centimeter trout. "An unspoiled world! Begging for people to come and enjoy its magnificent climate, its sports opportunities, its endless beaches, its balmy breezes! And Ex-Earth can take you there *now*. Absolutely without cost! All moving expenses met by the society! And you can begin the most wonderful vacation you can ever have, for the rest of your life!"

On impulse, Giyt pressed the key for the stats. The more he examined them, the better Tupelo began to sound. It was undoubtedly the very best of the extra-solar planets anyone had yet detected even telescopically, much less actually visited: very Earthlike gravity, air, and temperatures. It didn't have much land, of course. Only one piece you could call a continent in that immense, planet-wide ocean, and that one way up around the North Pole. But it had plenty of good-sized and comfortable-seeming islands.

And it was very nearly *empty.*

That was the part that intrigued Giyt the most. Tupelo was just about a perfect model of a world to conquer. Oh, not really *conquer.* Certainly not with guns and swords and armies. But still—

So before he could change his mind he set up an appointment, and an hour later he was in a suite in one of Wichita's best hotels, having coffee with a very affable man who was very impressed with Giyt's credentials. "You, Mr. Giyt," he declared, "are exactly the sort of person we want to send to Tupelo. Good health, no genetic negatives. And your socialization scores are, well, just *admirable.*"

Giyt nodded modestly. He had been quite creative with his personal stats. The man was going on: "We seldom get an application for somebody with degrees in both agronomy *and* business management, not to mention your building skills."

"That was a long time ago," Giyt protested. "Just summer jobs on construction projects while I was at school, but I did seem to have a knack for it."

"I'm sure you did. About the only other thing I could wish for is a medical background—"

Hell, Giyt thought to himself. He could have set that up too while he was inventing the other credentials, if only he'd thought of it.

"—but, good lord, what can we expect from a single colonist? No, Mr. Giyt, you're perfect. I can inform you now: you're definitely accepted for the program. More coffee?" Then, almost as an afterthought, "Of course, we'll have to know something about your wife, too."

"Wife?" Giyt repeated cautiously.

"You do have one, don't you? You see, Ex-Earth doesn't just want *tourists* to come to Tupelo. What we want is *families.* I don't mean you can't come right back to Earth if you decide you don't want to stay on Tupelo," he added hastily, "but we don't think you will. We think you'll want to live your whole life on Tupelo, and your children and your children's children after you. Now, when can you bring her in?"

So when Giyt left the hotel he didn't go back to Bal Harbor. He walked around Wichita's decaying business district, thinking. Street people thrust scanners at him for a handout, dope dealers whispered in his ear. He didn't hear.

Then he made up his mind. He crossed the street to a Kinko-WalGreenMart superstore and rented a terminal. He had an hour before Rina got out of her class, and that was plenty of time to do what he had to do. When he was finished the clerk goggled at Giyt as he pushed the ID-sniffer away and offered actual money in payment. But Giyt had a stock explanation ready for using cash: "Don't want my wife to see the bill," he said, smiling.

When Rina emerged from the school building, loaded down with palmtop and disks, looking like a very pretty schoolgirl, she was astonished to find Evesham Giyt waiting there for her. "Hey, Shammy," she said good-naturedly, "this is an unexpected pleasure. What's the occasion?"

"There's something I want to talk to you about."

"Really? What?" Then her expression changed. "Oh, Shammy," she said unhappily, "you're not suddenly *jealous*, are you? Sure, I have lunch with one of the guys now and then, but that's as far as it goes, and that's no reason for you to come down here to *spy* on me."

"No, no, it isn't anything like that. I just wanted to ask you something. How would you like to get married?"

She almost dropped the palmtop. *"Married?"*

"That's right. Married. You and me." To prove the point he displayed the printout of the backdated license he'd got from the county clerk's program, absolutely indistinguishable from the real thing, even in the unlikely event that anybody would ever take the trouble to check back into the database.

She studied it for a long minute, standing on the street

corner with the breeze whipping her hair. Then she looked up at him. "My God, Shammy, I never thought— I don't know if we're really ready for . . . It's a big . . . Tell me the truth, Shammy, no shit, do you really mean it?"

"You bet I mean it. And listen, I have a really great idea for the honeymoon."

Rina said she wouldn't be nervous about being shot from one star to another in this newfangled Sommermen transportation thing, but Giyt thought she really was. *He* was. He got in and closed his eyes—and then, wonderfully, it was over as soon as it had begun. You stepped in the chamber on one world and stepped out of it on another, and that was all there was to it.

And Tupelo was just as promised. It was an Earth-sized planet, with perfectly breathable Earth-style air—which was what it more or less had to have, because none of the ET-DIXIE probes had ever found a life-bearing planet that didn't. And it had a *lot* of water. Just as described, it was mostly ocean, with the colony on a Sri Lanka–sized island that was part of an archipelago in its temperate zone.

Giyt wondered about living on an island. He'd never done that, and it sounded—well, sort of confined. He had to admit that it was a nice island, though. It had everything the recruiter had promised. The island was built like a sombrero, with huge central peaks, the remnants of ancient volcanoes (but now, they swore, thoroughly dead), and the town they were to live in was on one of the series of broad plateaus that descended to the sea. Streams with pretty waterfalls raced down the mountainside to make Crystal Lake. The climate was ideal, sort of like a coastal Oregon spring. Their new home was within easy walking distance of the pretty freshwater lake that had, as promised, already been stocked with Earthly game fish. There was a fully functioning net, with a prime database that had been copied from the North

American nexus itself; one subset was the complete Library of Congress base, so Giyt would not have to be without his favorite entertainment. There was a hypermarket, well stocked and promising to special-order from Earth anything they wanted that wasn't already on the shelves; there were beauty shops and an office depot with everything the Earth superstores had and five or six small but nice-looking restaurants and bars . . . and all those things just in the services Ex-Earth had provided, with all the wonders of an alien planet to explore as well.

And then there was their home itself.

It had been a long time since Evesham Giyt had lived in anything that didn't pull out of the wall, like a file drawer. He was a little uneasy as they prowled their six rooms with one of the Ex-Earth resident agents. She was a woman named Olse Hagbarth, and it was her job (and, she said, her pleasure—and that of her husband-slash-colleague, too) to make all the new colonists welcome. "Of course," she said, looking around at the furniture with some disdain, "this stuff belonged to the previous occupant. Pity about her. She went back to Earth—homesick, I guess. You don't have to keep her furniture. If you want to replace it we can get you just about anything you want from Earth. And listen, don't worry about spending your resettlement grant. There's more where that came from; Ex-Earth is *loaded.*"

But Rina was happy with the furniture supplied, was happier than Giyt would have believed with the house itself, and with the queer, un-Earthly plants that grew in its modest garden, and with the kitchen and the bathroom that was all their own, and she couldn't wait until the agent left and they could try out their huge and comfortable new bed. "Shammy, Shammy," she murmured into his ear, "don't you think this is *wonderful?*"

It probably was, he agreed. Tupelo was everything they'd been promised.

The only thing was, in one or two unexpected ways it was somewhat *more* than they'd been promised, because the recruiter in Wichita hadn't said anything about the fact that five rather odd-looking races from other star systems were also doing their best to colonize it.

III

Come on, guys! Let's all give a big Tupelo welcome to Ms. and Mr. Evesham Giyt, just joining us in our little heaven in the heavens. Ms. Giyt was a college student back in Wichita, while Mr. Giyt was a network systems analyst and consulting agronomist. We're glad to have you here, Evesham and Rina! And listen, folks, don't forget that Maris Bretweller's square-dance treat is on this afternoon in Sommermen Square.

—Silva Cristl's siesta-time broadcast

The funniest thing that happened to Evesham Giyt on Tupelo was when he got elected mayor of the human portion of the community.

It was, Rina told him fondly, quite an honor for somebody who'd been on the planet for only five weeks. Giyt didn't think it was actually a *great* honor. There were only about eighteen hundred Earth humans there to be mayor of. Nobody else seemed to want the job, and the previous mayor, Mariam Vardersehn, flatly refused to run again, because she wanted to stay home and take care of her newborn twins.

Still, it was an odd turn of events for the man who for all of his thirty-four years had resolutely paid very little attention to the problems of anyone but himself.

Getting elected mayor was pretty much Giyt's own fault. When Hoak Hagbarth, the male half of Ex-Earth's team of on-site facilitators, happened to complain that the tax, license, and record-keeping functions of the government were in a terrible mess, Giyt incautiously volunteered to fix the programs. After that Hagbarth pointed out that it only made sense for the man who understood the system to be in charge of running it. "But I don't know anything about politics," Giyt protested. "Back in Wichita I didn't even vote."

"Well, who did? Who could vote for those snot-nosed, bleeding-heart politicians—'cept the president, of course," Hagbarth added loyally. "I'm not talking about him. Walter P. Garsh is a real kick-ass go-getter that wants to make America strong again."

"I guess so," Giyt said, not mentioning certain reservations. President Garsh was the one who had called the prime minister of Canada a pitiful pip-squeak and threatened to punch the Chinese party secretary in the nose if he didn't repeal the import tax on American rice. Garsh's status as a kick-ass-America-the-Greater was, in fact, the principal reason Giyt would have voted for almost anybody else, if he had ever voted at all. But Hagbarth was punching his shoulder in a friendly way.

"When Mariam got elected she didn't know anything about politics either," he said soothingly, "and she did all right. You'll be fine. Anyway, you look like a candidate. Got that friendly dumb face—not too handsome, not really ugly, either. You look—I don't know, I guess I'd have to say you look *honest.*"

"Yeah, thanks," Giyt said, rubbing his shoulder. Hoak Hagbarth was a big man, even by Giyt's own standards, and he was as strong as he looked. Giyt knew that he looked honest; it had been one of his most useful traits in the pursuit of his career as a crook, but Hagbarth didn't sound as though he meant it as a compliment.

"Tell you what," Hagbarth said, winding up the conversation, "why don't we just let the voters decide? Now I've got work to do."

As it turned out, the voters loved the idea. There was one vote for Albert Einstein, one for George Washington, and five for, succinctly, "Me." All the remaining nine hundred and seventy-six adult members of the Earth-human electorate cast their ballots for Evesham Giyt. It was a wonderful display of democratic consensus at work.

Mayoring didn't seem to be a very difficult job at first. Since Giyt had straightened out the fiscal programs, they pretty much ran themselves. For the first bit of time his only real duties were more or less honorary. He was expected to speak to the graduating class at the human school; that worried him a little, as he had had no previous experience in public speaking. However, there were only eleven students graduating, so Giyt's public-speaking debut wasn't really all that public. Then, come Christmas, Giyt was the one who put on the Santa Claus suit and descended from a gyrocopter onto the soccer field, where the giant community tree was winking its eighteen hundred (by then eighteen hundred and eighty-five) instrument lights, one for every human being on Tupelo. It happened to be a very sultry and rainy day, not Christmasy at all, but the human part of the colony was still resolutely sticking to the Earthside calendar. Giyt kept his ho-ho-hos short and got a big hand when he was finished, since everyone was grateful to be allowed to get out of the rain.

It wasn't bad. As a matter of fact, Giyt surprised himself by actually enjoying that sort of thing, once he got used to the idea of being *known* by everybody around. He liked the fact that all the humans greeted him as they passed in the streets—yes, and a good many of the eeties, too. At least Giyt *thought* the extraterrestrials were giving him friendly greetings, though unless he remembered to wear the earpiece translation phone, their various slurps, squawks, chirps, and gargles could have been anything.

Getting used to a new neighborhood—actually to a whole new *planet*—was pretty much an unprecedented experience for Evesham Giyt. He had never paid much attention to his physical surroundings. His real environment had always been electronic and global, and didn't change simply because the location of his body had. But here he felt a real need to explore. Giyt had never spent so much time out-of-doors since the long-ago college days when his girl of the moment persuaded him to try jogging. He found he liked it. Liked to wander the streets of the town, enjoying the sight and scent of a human bakery next to a Kalkaboo soup brewery—two very different smells—and watching work crews digging new sewers and putting up new houses. It didn't disturb him that so many of the workmen—well, the work things—weren't at all human. He even enjoyed going to the hypermarket with Rina to pick out towels and bed linen and kitchen appliances—Giyt hadn't even known that his bride knew how to cook—and that *really* surprised him about himself.

The other big advantage of being mayor was that it solved the problem of stalling Hoak Hagbarth, who had been getting increasingly insistent that a man with Giyt's impressive (if fictitious) background in agronomy would be a treasure on the community farms. Not that farming required any very demanding physical work, because Ex-Earth was very good about providing automatic machines for all the colony's really hard labor. Nevertheless Giyt, who had never once in his life had the experience of working with his hands, was just as well pleased to be spared the prospect of beginning it now.

There was one part of his job, though, that he hadn't been prepared for. That was the weekly meeting with the heads of the five other Tupelo communities in the Planetary Joint Governance Commission.

The evening before his first meeting Giyt was sitting on his tiny front porch, overlooking the "decorative" clumps of spiky flowering plants, with a drink in his hand. From next door were the distant sounds of Lupe and Matya de Mir trying to get their brood ready for dinner. Apart from that, it was more quiet than Giyt had ever known.

That was one thing you had to say about Tupelo. Other than the occasional whir of one of the electric carts going past, bumblebee drone for the ones he and most of the races used, mosquito whine for the roller-skate-sized ones used by the little Petty-Primes—well, and also the New Day firecracker ceremony from the Kalkaboos every morning, and of course the once-or-twice-a-week thunder of the suborbital rocket taking off for the polar continent—well, at least *generally,* it was fair to say, Tupelo was wonderfully noise-free. Certainly it was not at all like Wichita. Once you got used to its awkward thirty-four-hour day and the occasional drenching rain (and Giyt was pretty sure he would get used to them, sooner or later) it was actually not bad. Giyt wasn't prepared to go much farther than that. Rina evidently was, though; from inside the house he could hear her singing to herself as she made dinner.

The singing got closer and stopped as Rina came out, wiping her hands on her apron. "The pot roast'll be ready in about an hour," she announced. "Who's that coming?"

One of the electric carts had rounded the corner and was drawing up in front of their house. A man emerged from it, consulting his memo screen. Giyt had seen him before when they arrived: as big as Hagbarth, with a spade beard, named—Tschopp? Wili Tschopp? Something like that. "Got your order from the hypermarket, missus," the man said, looking Rina over in a way that Giyt was surprised to find he didn't like. And then he turned to Giyt. "You weren't at the terminal today when the new people came in," he accused.

"Was I supposed to be?"

"Of course you're supposed to be. You're the mayor, aren't you? So who's going to welcome them and all if you're not there?" He shook his head reprovingly, then returned his attention to Rina. "Where do you want me to put your towels and stuff, honey?"

Giyt answered for her. "Just leave them. We'll put them away ourselves." He hadn't meant for his tone to be quite so sharp. After the man got back in his cart and drove away, Rina looked at him curiously. "Are you feeling nervous or something, Shammy?"

"About what?"

"About this Joint Governance Commission thing, maybe."

"Of course not. What is there to be nervous about?"

She nodded, then said, "Listen, maybe we should stretch our legs before dinner's ready. I'd kind of like to watch the sun set over Crystal Lake," and he couldn't come up with a reason why not.

As they strolled, Rina looked up at him. "You don't really have anything to be nervous about, Shammy dear," she told him.

"That's good, because I'm not nervous," he said.

"Of course not, hon," she agreed, and began telling him the funny thing the eldest neighbor boy, eight-year-old Juan, had said about his mothers. At the shore of the lake they hesitated, then turned right, away from the town, heading toward the farm plots. Rina did all the talking. She had plenty to tell him, because Rina was blossoming in their new home; she had made several dozen instant friends, not only human but all over the community; had been offered a job she liked as receptionist in the beauty shop; was a volunteer Gray Lady at the human hospital when she was needed (which wasn't often, because the human community was a healthy lot and most of the hospital's beds stayed empty); was glad to take the neighbor kids to the beach when their mothers were busy. There was a time when Giyt would have found her steady stream of gossip irritating, because, really, what did he care if the General Manager of the Delt colony had made a fool of himself by getting excessively high on hallucinogens at the Delt High Mass? Or that Lupe and Matya had weathered a serious strain in their marriage just a year ago, when Lupe thought for a time that Matya was getting a bit too involved with one of her coworkers at the Public Works office, who not only was clearly sexually attracted to Matya but was unforgivably a *man?* Now, though, he didn't mind Rina's chatter at all. He didn't really listen to it all, either, but he went so far as to pretend he did, for no other reason than that these things gave her pleasure.

It occurred to Giyt, as they strolled past one of the human farm plots (harvester machines neatly slicing ripe tomatoes and yellow peppers off their vines and trundling them to the storage building in town), that their relationship had changed since they arrived on Tupelo. He caught another glimpse of what that change had been when they reached the Petty-Prime allotment next along the shore. (Properly those particular eeties were called Petty-Primates by the human colonists—never mind what they called themselves—because they were little and they were definitely primates, more or less, but Giyt had already learned to drop the extra syllable.) One of the little pink-skinned, monkey-like creatures stopped his work of grafting a new branch on a juice tree and chattered a greeting to them. They had no translator with them so Giyt had no idea what the thing was saying, but he automatically bowed to the creature in response . . . until Rina, by his side, chattered a few syllables back and he realized the greeting hadn't been meant for him but for her. "Hell," he said, wondering, "when did you learn to speak their language?"

"Oh, Shammy, I never will learn it, really. Just a couple of words like 'I hope you're having a nice day.' That's their chief agronomist who just said hello; his kids were playing with the ones next door and we got friendly. Are you feeling more relaxed now?"

He was more amused than annoyed. "Are we on that again? I'm not nervous."

"Of course not," she said comfortably. "After all, Mariam Vardersehn did it for two years, and anything she can do you can do better. . . . Oh, and Shammy? Did I tell you? I want to see if I can finish my college courses."

"Here?"

"Oh, yes. Olse Hagbarth says there's an extension program I can use, and Ex-Earth will pick up the tuition. Olse says I can even quit my job at the beauty shop because they'll throw in a stipend."

She looked as though she expected congratulations, so Giyt provided them. "That's wonderful," he said, patting her arm.

"Isn't it? I think I'll switch my major, though. There's not much call for a business-management degree here."

"Good idea," Giyt said approvingly, and squinted at the sun now just at the horizon. "I think it's time we turned back." He put his arm around her shoulders as they started home, silent again while he tried to analyze just how he felt about all this. Rina had never before asked his opinion about anything she chose to do before she did it. Was that part of what it meant to be "married"? And did it mean that he was expected to consult her, too?

After dinner Rina fixed him a hot toddy and went off to her studies. Giyt sat down at his terminal for some real relaxing.

But although he sampled some of his favorite programs—a really good documentary on Genghis Khan; another on Alexander's father, Philip of Macedon, almost as impressive a conqueror as his better-known son—what he was really thinking about was Rina. Rina, who had always got straight As in every course she took and was evidently on her way to getting more. Rina, who was a model mayor's wife, making friends among all, or almost all, the varieties of weird eeties, and for that matter humans, who lived in this place. Rina, who had never been a mother but was already a well-loved honorary aunt for the kids of the couple next door. Rina, who had never been a housewife in her life, either, but had mastered immediately, almost instinctively, the operation of the dust-sucker that whooshed their house clean and the cryptic settings of the dishwasher, the washing machine, and the stove . . . and while she was doing all these things, nevertheless still had time to do all the other things that were needed to keep Giyt himself content.

Rina. Who had suddenly become so big a part of Giyt's life that he could no longer imagine a life without her.

Giyt had trouble diagnosing this new feeling he seemed to be having about her. It wasn't exactly "love." There was no change there. He had recognized some time earlier that he probably loved Rina, more or less, within the general meaning of the term as he understood it.

This new feeling was something else. It wasn't merely friendship, either. He came to the astonishing conclusion that it was largely, of all things, *pride*. He was proud of the way his, ah, his *wife* was coping so wonderfully and rapidly with the demands of this bizarre new place he had brought her to.

It took him a while to identify the feeling, because it was so unfamiliar to him. Giyt could not remember that he had ever before been proud of any other person in his life.

IV

The institution of the Joint Governance Commission was older than the presence of Earth humans on Tupelo—or on the Peace Planet, depending on which race was doing the talking. In the pre-Earth days there were only five races to jointly govern, and the commissioners met in a five-sided building. That structure was now downgraded to serve as a storage facility for farm produce, as the admission of Earth humans required a new building. Not all the Earth humans were happy about what had happened. It seemed to some of them, especially the most patriotic of the Americans, that there was a subtle insult concealed in the fact that the Pentagon had been turned into a root cellar.

—Britannica online, "Tupelo"

The Hexagon—the place where all six of the colonizing races, human and eetie, got together to talk over whatever interests they had in common and, in particular, to stop disagreements before they got started—was larger and fancier than Evesham Giyt had expected. Each species had its own special place: chairs for the bipeds, a pretty little artificial tree for the Kalkaboos to perch in, a kind of couch for the Centaurians, and a two-meter-long cushion, with internal plumbing to keep it warm and damp, for the use of the Slugs.

As Giyt walked in for his first meeting, all five of the other leaders rose to welcome him—the ones that were physically able to rise, anyway. There was an unexpected spatter of applause from the eight or ten people, almost all humans, sparsely occupying the chairs and chair equivalents that were set aside for the use of the audience, whenever there happened to be one. The Centaurian female—the translator in his ear gave her name as Mrs. Brownbenttalon—was taking her turn in the regular rotation as president for the week, and so she made a speech of greeting. Of course Giyt could make nothing of the squeaks and squeals that came from her pursy little mouth, but his translation phone duly rendered it for him in English—well, more or less English: "The total of us who are not from the planet Earth human are overcomely delighted, Large Male Giyt, to have you participate us in our unceasing struggle to ensure no hitting and the getting of along." *To ensure peace and friendship,* Giyt corrected for himself, thinking it wouldn't hurt to take a look at those translation programs.

She went on from there, giving Giyt time to look around. He had never before seen all six of Tupelo's colonial races in the same place. Mrs. Brownbenttalon, whose Centaurian title was Divinely Elected Savior, looked more or less like a curly-haired anteater, nearly two meters long as she crouched on her cushions. Mr. Brownbenttalon, her main husband, was a tiny thing the size of a chipmunk, and he was crawling around in her fur and whispering in her ear as she spoke. The Delt General Manager was listening intently, sucking on his fingers—maybe, Giyt thought, because of embarrassment over his recent behavior at the mass. In the doll-sized armchair of the Petty-Primes their Responsible One was lackadaisically sprawled and staring uninterestedly at the ceiling. The High Champion of the Kalkaboos was tucked into a fork of its tree, but listening intently with its immense elephant ears. And the Principal Slug was, well, a slug; and if it was showing any sign at all of what was going through its mind, Giyt could not detect it.

When Mrs. Brownbenttalon finished her speech Giyt, feeling foolish but nevertheless obliged to do so, offered a few words in response. All he said was that he was honored to be selected and hoped he would do credit to this body that was responsible for maintaining order on Tupelo. Giyt knew it wasn't a particularly great speech. He didn't expect an ovation, but all the same he was surprised at the chill of the response. The Delt took his fingers out of his mouth to peer at him reprovingly, and even the Slug twitched.

But no one said anything, and then Mrs. Brownbenttalon got down to business. She reported to the commission that the power plant on Energy Island, six kilometers across the strait, was going to need expansion, and each home planet would be required to supply funds and materials for the job. Additional farmland had been cleared on the far side of their own island, and each race was entitled to 3.962 hectares for its own purposes, the particular allotment for each to be determined by a random drawing—after which, of course, they could swap back and forth as much as they liked. The weather satellites had detected no approaching storms large enough to require special precautions for at least the next few weeks. All this information, she pointed out, was in their datastores already, so if they would simply move to accept the reports as rendered? They did. Then she paused, while Mr. Brownbenttalon whispered urgently in her ear, and twisted around to look at Giyt. "Great misery I have," she declared, "for necessity disimproving your nuptial night participation here with irritating complaints, but Delta Pavonis guys raise problem of conflicting interests. You speak now, Delta Pavonis guy."

The Delt took his fingers out of his mouth again and

began to bark at Giyt. Giyt was willing to do his best to get along with these alien freaks, even the Slugs. But he couldn't honestly say that he cared much for the Delts. For one thing, he thought they were unnecessarily ugly, with pop eyes that stared out in all directions from the top corners of their inverted-triangle heads. (Did the first humans call them Delts because of the name of their star, or for the Greek-letter shape of their faces? Giyt didn't know.) The Delts also smelled, well, distinctly *rancid*, even in the thoroughly air-conditioned confines of the Hexagon. And they had the reputation of being a nuisance.

Which last trait the General Manager demonstrated for him now. The Delt translation program was little better than the Centaurian, but Giyt was able to figure out what the Delt was complaining about. It seemed that those steelhead trout Ex-Earth had stocked into Crystal Lake were eating the copepods the Delts had planted there, and no proper Delt could enjoy his dinner without a copepod garnish to give it taste. Something had to be done, the General Manager declared. Instantly. If not absolutely at that very instant, then certainly pretty damn soon, because all the Delts were suffering greatly from their deprivation.

The Delt was doing his best to make Giyt suffer, too, because he went on and on about it. Giyt took some comfort in the fact that the other commissioners were paying very little attention to the Delt's complaints. Mrs. Brownbenttalon was whispering cozily to her principal husband as he perched just above her nose, the Kalkaboo was scratching its shiny pelt absorbedly, the Petty-Prime was studying its readout of reports, and the Slug was simply being a slug. And then, when at last the Delt was finished—or came to a breathing space in his oration—Giyt quickly promised to look into the matter, Mrs. Brownbenttalon immediately declared the session adjourned, and the audience applauded again as they all got up to go.

"You were wonderful," Rina told him at the door. "See? I told you it would be a breeze."

"Yes, sure," he said, abstracted, "but you go on home and I'll get there when I can. Right now I need to talk to the Hagbarths about this copepod business."

Hoak Hagbarth wasn't in his office, which was also the Hagbarth home, but Olse was there. "You did fine," she told him at once. "Want some lemonade? I make it myself, bring in real lemons from Earth. Oh, the meeting? Sure, we both watched you on the screen, but Hoak's gone fishing. The copepods? My advice is, forget it. The damn Delts try that on every time there's a new mayor, but really, it's all Delt crap. There's no problem. We've got sonic barriers to keep the trout out of the copepod breeding places—you know, the wetland shallows in the lake's bays—and if they do eat a few of the cruddy little things every now and then, who cares? There's always plenty left over for the Delts. You sure you won't have some lemonade?"

But that last question came from the kitchen, where Olse Hagbarth was already pouring him some. "Yes, thank you," Giyt called to her, accepting fate as he looked around their place. It wasn't any fancier than his own house. They did have a grand piano in the living room, but the rest of their furniture was, if anything, cheaper and less attractive than the stuff they'd furnished the Giyts. Nor did the Hagbarths have nearly as nice a location, half a kilometer away from the lakeshore, with no real view out their windows—unless you counted the rather hideous shape of a towering Petty-Prime barracks next door. So whatever else the Hagbarths might do, no one could say they were pampering themselves at the expense of their charges.

When she came back with the lemonade Olse settled herself on the couch to face him, looking motherly and hospitable. "There's one thing," she said. "You called the planet

Tupelo, but the eeties don't call it that. They call it the Peace Planet. They get bent if we don't."

"Oh, right," Giyt said, remembering. "I thought at the time I might've said something wrong—"

"Not *wrong,* for heaven's sake. That's what the ET-Huntsville people named it when they discovered it, and we can call it what we like, can't we? But the eeties get antsy if you don't go along with their name. As I guess you noticed. How's the lemonade?" When he had reassured her that it was fine, she added, "Listen, Hoak was thinking about something, if you're interested. Hoak thought you might want to take a look at some of the off-island facilities. You know, the power plant on Energy Island, that sort of thing? Or even the mines and things on the polar continent. He said he'd order you a chopper any time you want to go to the island. You'll have to take the suborbital to visit the mines, but you could go along when the next shift goes there. Or we could order a flight up there for you. Take Rina if she'd like to go; probably you'd both enjoy seeing more of Tupelo than this one island."

"Maybe so," he said, dazzled at the thought of having a high-speed suborbital transport ordered up for him any time he wanted to fly a few thousand kilometers away. "I'll talk to Rina."

"You do that, hon. And listen, Hoak and I just want to say that you're doing a wonderful job, fitting right in the way you're doing. But that's our way, isn't it? I mean the Earth humans here. We pitch right in, don't make waves, don't start trouble for anyone—"

"Like that Delt, you mean?"

"Including the Delts," she said, nodding vigorously as she stood up. "They're all eeties, so what do you expect? Anyway, come see us again, won't you? Maybe we'll have a little dinner party. Now I'd better get busy and try to catch up on our reports back to the home office."

On the way back home, Giyt thought about the trip to the polar continent. He had no idea what it would be like. Cold, yes. According to the pictures he'd seen it was almost as ice-covered as Earth's Antarctica, and just as bleak. When he told Rina about the invitation, sure enough, she was thrilled. She was standing in their front yard, talking over the fence to Lupe from next door, with a couple of Lupe's kids splashing in their wading pool. "I'd love it, Shammy!" Rina cried, and Lupe confirmed:

"You will. Matya worked up at the Pole a couple of seasons, before the kids began to come, and I went up sometimes for weekends. It's nice. Great accommodations, and they have a really good health club—in the Earth-human part, I mean. I guess the other people have all that stuff, too, but I never got around to seeing it. And speaking of the kids coming . . ."

She looked inquiringly at Rina, who shook her head. "I haven't had a chance to tell him yet. Come on inside and have a cup of tea, why don't you? You can watch the kids through the window."

What it was that Rina hadn't told him didn't get told just then, either, because Rina disappeared into the kitchen to make the tea for the guest, leaving Giyt to be the gracious host. Since Rina liked the woman, Giyt made an effort to be hospitable. Rina had told him all sorts of stories about the de Mirs. She had been charmed by the fact that they had invented a new surname to replace their old ones—so that, Rina said, they would all have the same name, and the kids would always be reminded of where they came from. So they had taken a word from each of their ancestral languages and made de Mir—from Earth.

Well, all right, that was somewhat charming, Giyt admitted to himself. But he had never been alone with either of the de Mirs before, and by the time Rina came back with the tea tray he had run out of subjects that did not touch on sexual orientation.

Lupe, too, seemed oddly embarrassed. She greeted Rina with relief. "And your stove's all right now? Shura used to have a lot of trouble with it, among other things, and Hoak Hagbarth just wouldn't get it fixed for her."

"It's fine. I think they put in a new one after your friend moved out."

But Giyt was not interested in a friend who had moved away; he wanted to know what it was that was hanging over his head. "There was something you wanted to tell me?" he prompted his wife.

Rina looked at her guest for an answer. "Well, it's just that I'm pregnant again," Lupe announced, flushed becomingly rosy. "We always wanted six, so we're almost there."

"Congratulations," Giyt said, since that was what she seemed to be expecting; thinking that for a pair of same-sex females they were certainly remarkably fecund, courtesy of Ex-Earth's sperm bank.

"Thanks, but what I wanted to say is that all of a sudden Matya is after me to quit being a volunteer fireman. Too much physical activity for a pregnant woman, she says. Which is nonsense. We don't have that many real fires, and even if we did . . . Well, that's between Matya and me, isn't it? Anyway, I'm going to quit, just to please her, and what I was thinking is that that means there'll be a vacancy in the fire company. So what I was wondering was whether you wanted to join."

He blinked at her. "Be a fireman?"

"Only if you want to," Lupe said quickly. "It doesn't take much time—hell, how often does anything burn around here? Not counting brush fires, I mean, and you only get those in the dry. In a couple of weeks we're having our annual firemen's fair. We're calling it 'The Taste of Tupelo' this year, and that'll take everybody in the company to man all the booths. But—"

"But you really ought to, Shammy," Rina coaxed. "As mayor. Set a good example. What do you say?"

Well, what could he say? He said yes. And on their evening walk that night, did little talking, because he was wondering how it had happened that, without warning, the lifelong career computer thief and con man, Evesham Giyt, was suddenly turning into a model citizen.

V

One thing about Tupelo that took some getting used to was its inordinately prolonged day. It wasn't quite 34 hours long, but the Earth-human clocks said it was—it was easier to deal with an "hour" that was only 59 and a bit minutes long than to try to handle an odd fraction of an hour every day.

Sunrise was at 10 hours. That's when Earth humans usually had a breakfast (actually, their second of the day) and started their day's work. At 16 hours was lunch, then siesta until 19 hours. Then the afternoon's work went until 22 hours, when it was customary to have a break for afternoon tea. Evening work was from 23 to 27 hours, which was sunset. Dinner at 28 hours; nighttimes free for whatever the persons wanted to do until 32 hours; then sleep. Since Earth humans could hardly ever sleep for more than 8 hours at a stretch, they generally rose at 6, had their first breakfast while it was still dark, and then were on their own until sunrise at 10. It made for a long day, to be sure. But because of the midday siesta, it wasn't an exhausting one.

—"GETTING ALONG ON TUPELO,"
EX-EARTH GUIDE FOR NEWCOMERS

Time was, back on Earth, when Giyt might hear someone refer to an elected official as a "servant of the people" and take it as a joke. It wasn't a joke here, though. Here his constituents took it seriously. They called him on the net. They showed up on his doorstep. They buttonholed him in the street; and they all wanted something—sometimes a transfer to a different job, perhaps an increased line of credit at the hypermarket, even some private tutoring for the child that wasn't doing well in school. At first most of the requests struck Giyt as easy enough to handle—"Actually," he would say, "that's not my department; you'd better talk to Hoak Hagbarth"—but then it turned out that a lot of the petitioners had already talked to Hagbarth, and Hagbarth had said no.

Hagbarth even said no to Mayor Giyt when Mayor Giyt asked him about some of the petitions. "Take Kettner off the farm and transfer him to the Pole? Hell, no! Listen, don't pay any attention to that bad back he keeps talking about; he just wants to sleep away his shift in a factory instead of running a cultivator. And how can we raise Gottman's credit limit past what the computer says he can pay? We plug in his income; we plug in his present debt balance; we plug in his past payment record. The rest is just arithmetic. Cripes, Evesham, you ought to know that for yourself; you're the guy who rewrote the programs."

It all made sense once Hagbarth explained it. It was just a little surprising to Giyt to have Hagbarth say no to him, since he'd never said no before.

On the other hand, Giyt realized, he had never asked Hagbarth for anything before.

It wasn't just the endless demands for favors he didn't know how to give, either. The real time destroyers were the endless extracurricular duties of a model citizen mayor. For instance, he was expected to show the flag when the Slugs had their annual eisteddfodd. That meant two hours of squirming in damp, uncomfortable seats in Slugtown, pretending to enjoy the sounds of the Slug choir baying and moaning at the bright Tupelovian stars. Well, it was interesting to see how the Slugs lived, in their mud huts just below the old dam on the far side of the lake. It made him wonder why they chose to live by themselves instead of bunking in higgledy-piggledy with all the other races, the way everybody else did. (But then the Slugs liked the climate moister than anybody else.) Rina sat loyally beside him at the sing, showing no signs of concern that her brand-new boots were getting all muddied up. But she did mention to Giyt her interesting observation that, although half a dozen other Earth humans had gamely showed up for the event, neither of the Hagbarths were among them.

Then there was the business of the volunteer fire company. Lupe insisted on taking him to the station herself so he could meet the others. Unpleasingly, the fire chief turned out to be that general handyman and admirer of Rina Giyt, Wili Tschopp. Giyt knew that it was unreasonable to take offense at the way the man looked at Rina. Lots of men had looked at her that way back in Wichita, and it had never bothered him. Still, it made him uncomfortable in Tschopp's presence. Then, as soon as he entered the firehouse, one of the other men buttonholed him to ask why he and his family couldn't be transferred to the north polar mines on a permanent basis; it was cooler there, the man explained, and his wife really hated hot weather, and what was the use of having a damn mayor, and one, he pointed out, that he personally had voted for, if he couldn't get a little help from the man now and then?

Giyt promised to think about it. He knew he would, too, because he was already thinking, a lot, about these endless requests.

The firehouse was interesting, though. Giyt was impressed, not to say amazed, by the mass of heavy-duty fire-fighting equipment the company possessed: three great tankers, four pumpers, and a chief's car. "But what burns here?" he asked the chief. "I mean, everything I see is fireproof, isn't it?"

"Brush," Chief Tschopp said succinctly, opening a beer. "Want one?"

Giyt didn't want any beer, exactly—he would have preferred a decent white wine—but he took the beer and listened to the chief's stories about how when the droughts came, they turned the chaparral and the stubble in the farmlands on this side of the mountain into tinder. That made sense, though it had never occurred to Giyt that the island could ever suffer droughts. But the important thing was that Tschopp seemed to be doing his best to be friendly; and when the company voted Giyt in that night (Lupe told him later), it was Chief Tschopp himself who made the nominating speech. All the same . . .

All the same, although each of the little new drags on his time was reasonable enough, and maybe even kind of fun—Giyt was actually looking forward to the time when he himself might be driving one of those huge pumpers to a fire—there were a *lot* of drags on his time.

Giyt wasn't used to that. He'd devoted his life to making sure nobody would ever be in a position to tell him that he had to do this or that at such and such a time. He'd made it happen that way, too, if you didn't count the times when he rented himself out for a few weeks as a master debugger. Even then those times were short and he could quit when he liked.

Here it was different. Here there was always some duty he was supposed to perform, and some of those duties took actual *work*.

The fact that it all took time meant there wasn't much time left over for his former hobbies. Rina noticed that was true when, digging through the datastores for her schoolwork, she stumbled on an old TV series that she knew he would like. It was so old that it was just flat pictures, and black-and-white at that, but it was a documentary of Oliver Cromwell subduing the rebels in Ireland. But then, a day or two after she'd given him the locator data, she asked him how he'd liked it. "Haven't had a chance to look at it," he confessed.

"But I thought I saw you . . . Never mind," she said sunnily. "What would you like for dinner?"

She really had seen him sitting before the screen, watching something or other; but it wasn't his usual fare. For the first time in his life Evesham Giyt had become a news addict; it was the only way he could hope to understand what his constituents were going to ask of him. Tupelo news came over the net and it was delivered by a sharp-faced, homely-featured woman Giyt recognized; her name was Silva Cristl, and she was a lieutenant in the volunteer fire company. Tupelo news wasn't much like the stuff he'd avoided in Wichita. There were weather reports, introductions of new arrivals, personal messages (the Dunbay teenagers offering babysitting services, the Carlyles wanting to know if anyone else was interested in Zen chanting), once in a great while an obituary, details of who was in the hospital, new births, standings in the bowling league—well, there was all sorts of stuff there, delivered in Silva Cristl's hokey jes'-folks dialect. It didn't matter if you got interrupted in the middle of it. Giyt hated having someone bother him when he was in the middle of a good story of some exciting conquest, but with this stuff there was no problem.

When he found out all five of the other races had their own equivalent news programs he tried to access them as well. It didn't work. He got only garbage. Each eetie race had its own transmission codes, and none of them were in the least like Earth's.

That was a tough technical problem to solve, or would

have been for anyone else. For Evesham Giyt, however, it was just a matter of decryption, and that was the thing he was really good at. It took him a while to solve the basic protocols that went into Petty-Prime electronic communication, but he did it . . . and was rewarded with what appeared to be an installment of an interminable Petty-Prime soap opera. And then, while he was trying to puzzle out just why the two young males were refusing to mate with the older female—who already seemed to have several husbands, all of whom were urging the males to take her on—he heard Rina call his name. "Shammy? Aren't you supposed to chair the commission meeting today? You don't want to be late for it, do you?"

He wasn't late in arriving at the Hexagon. But he wasn't really ready for it, either. As he called the meeting to order he realized he hadn't read over all the department reports so he could summarize them for the other commissioners. Besides, he was still a little worried about the Delts' copepod problem.

But the Delt General Manager accepted without demur Giyt's promise that the matter was being looked into, and actually, it was the Kalkaboo High Champion who made the only fuss of the day.

Even in this whole zoo of weirdly designed extraterrestrial beings, the Kalkaboos struck Giyt as being pretty much excessively weird. They were vaguely primate in shape. That is, they had two arms, two legs, and a head, though the head looked truly bizarre with those enormous ears flapping around it. But they looked more like skeletons than people. They seemed to have no body fat at all; and their skin glittered with metallic scales.

Which, Giyt learned, were actually some sort of photovoltaic cells, and what the Kalkaboo High Champion was pissed off about was that their perfectly reasonable requirement for a new and larger radiation house to soak up ultraviolet in was being deferred because of the need to conserve power. It wasn't anyone's fault that Tupelo's sun was deficient in the intense far-UV radiation they liked, the High Champion admitted. On the other hand, it was definitely everyone's fault that they were wastefully burning up so much electrical power for their own frivolous purposes that none could be spared for this urgent requirement of the Kalkaboo horde. The most wasteful people of all, he pointed out, were the new immigrants, of whom so *many* continued to flock in.

As one of the new immigrants, Giyt knew who the creature was talking about. What he didn't know was what to do about it. It was the Principal Slug who came to his rescue with a proposal. Each race, he suggested slobberingly, should make a survey of its power consumption and at the next meeting come in with plans for reducing their demand. On a strictly temporary basis, of course. Until the added generating capacity was on line. He expressed confidence that there were plenty of reductions that could be made without seriously discommoding anybody, and then perhaps the Kalkaboos could have their new radiation chamber right away.

Moved, seconded, and passed; and then, surprisingly, the meeting was over.

Giyt hurried out of the Hexagon before anybody could raise any more problems, feeling he had dodged a bullet. He didn't like the feeling. He needed to get ahead of these problems, and the way to do that was to have a talk with Hoak Hagbarth.

He found Hagbarth at the EPR terminal in Sommermen Square, but—Wili Tschopp explained—if Giyt wanted to talk to him about this power-conservation matter, he would have to wait. "It's Cargo Day, for Christ's sake," Tschopp told him. "Hoak has to be in the control loop."

"Control loop?"

Tschopp looked at him without patience. "The keys to the portal. Every race has a key. The portal can't operate unless all the keys are used, didn't you know that? So you'll have to wait. Just stay out of the way."

Giyt had seen the great portal before, of course; in fact, he had come through it himself with Rina, because how else could you travel the vast distances from Earth? But he'd never seen it from outside with power on, when it was already wreathed in the golden glow of what he had learned to call the Einstein-Podolsky-Rosen field and thus was ready to receive a transmission from Earth. Inside the chamber Giyt could see crates of merchandise ready to ship. He knew what they had to be. At the polar factories the Earth colony had a small production line that turned out various kinds of toys, trinkets, and knickknacks to export to the home planet—nothing very valuable, but, Giyt supposed, every little bit that helped offset the cost of the Tupelo colony was worth having.

The thing that struck Giyt as curious was the number of nonhumans at the terminal. Five of them—and Hagbarth—were seated or slumped at workstations around the terminal. That made sense. As Wili Tschopp had explained, there was this rule requiring all six races to be present whenever the terminal was operational. But there were at least one or two others present of each race, and what could interest them about a purely Earth matter?

He got the answer in a moment. There was a blue-and-white warning flare; then a faint hand-clap of air as the stacked merchandise disappeared; a moment later a gentle puff as the export crates were replaced with others. At once the nonhumans descended on them, opening every crate and peering inside. It looked like a customs search to Giyt, and then recognition clicked in his mind. It *was* a customs search. The nonhumans were looking for contraband, and they were being damned thorough about it. Wili Tschopp was protesting vigorously, but the eetie representatives were insisting on opening every carton.

Hoak Hagbarth abandoned his post at the controls and, yawning, strolled over to where Giyt stood. Giyt blinked at him. "That doesn't bother you, what they're doing to the shipment from Earth?"

"Naw. Those guys are always like that. Look, Wili said you wanted to see me about something."

"Oh, right." Giyt was still staring at the commotion before him; a Kalkaboo had opened a crate of chiplets, the microcontrollers that ran most devices, and Wili was profanely urging him to be careful, while the Slug and a Delt were pawing through containers of personal goods meant for various human residents. "It's this power-rationing thing. The Kalkaboos say—"

Hagbarth sighed. "I heard all about what the Kalkaboos say. Same old crap; don't sweat it. I'll cook up some kind of an airy-fairy program for you before the next meeting. Nothing that we need to take seriously, of course."

"But if the Kalkaboos really need the power—"

Hagbarth chuckled unpleasantly. "Need it? Do you know what they need the power for? They use UV radiation to get high. You see how they go around naked here, with all those little photocells on their skins? Well, they don't do that on their home planet. They'd be buzzed from the radiation all the time, so there they go covered up totally. When they have a party they take off all their clothes and get smashed from the ultraviolet."

"Oh," Giyt said, abashed. But as he turned to leave, Wili

Tschopp came toward him, grinning, an opened carton in his hands. "Might as well take this with you, Giyt," he said. "It's for your wife. I always said you were one lucky guy."

Giyt looked after him, puzzled, as the man walked away, chuckling. Then he looked into the carton and understood. It was a selection of chains, handcuffs, and a fancily pink-wrapped packet of what the label called "marital aids." And yes, the whole box was addressed to Mrs. Rina Giyt.

VI

We have established that both the so-called Centaurians and the so-called Slugs come from planets that orbit the star Alpha Centauri, and that the so-called Delts come from the system of the star Delta Pavonis. The provenance of the other two extraterrestrial races remains unknown. They decline to respond to any questions on the subject, nor have our searches turned up any data that would resolve it.

It is a noteworthy fact—it cannot be called a coincidence—that the automatic probes dispatched by the Huntsville Group to both of the above stars have lost contact even before they established circumstellar orbits. Analysis indicates a very high probability that these losses were not due to equipment malfunctions or accident. This leaves only one reasonable explanation.

—INTERNAL COMMUNICATION, EXTENDED EARTH SOCIETY
MARKED: DO NOT DISSEMINATE OUTSIDE OF SOCIETY.

When Giyt gave Rina the package she was a little irritated, a little amused, and a little bit hurt, too. She stood there with her palmtop in one hand and her shoulder bag in the other, just getting ready to go out, looking both startled and disappointed. "But I didn't get those things for *us*, Shammy!" she said. "I wouldn't try anything like that on you, would I? I know how you feel about them. I ordered them for Lupe."

"Lupe next door?"

"Do you know any other Lupe? She was afraid that when she gets real pregnant, you know, Matya might not be so interested in her anymore."

"Oh." Giyt cast around for something to explain his jumping to a wrong conclusion. "I just didn't know that women went in for this, ah, this dominatrix kind of thing."

"Well, they do," she said firmly. "Anyway, some women do. When I was in the game I had quite a few female clients, you know. It was pretty hard work sometimes, but they were mostly good tippers." She went back to stowing her gear in the bag, and when she spoke again the subject was clearly changed. "I think I'll see if Lupe wants to take a run down to the store and see what came in this time. Do you want to come along?"

Giyt didn't. He said he wished he could, but he had work that he had to do, which was no more than a faint tincture of truth in a solid lie. The main truth was that he did not want to see Lupe just then, because he did not want to find himself speculating on just what it was that she and Matya did in the privacy of their bedroom. Much less on what Rina had had to do, in the old days, to earn those good tips.

The tiny tincture of truth was that he did have a good many things to do, and nowhere near enough time to do them all in.

Giyt had never in his life wished for more hours in a day. He certainly didn't wish for them here, either, because the long Tupelovian day already possessed nearly ten more hours than the Earth norm. That was one of the problems. The daylight hours were easy enough to deal with, especially because they were quite pleasantly interrupted by the after-lunch siesta. It was the night that was disorienting. You went to sleep in the dark and, because you couldn't sleep much more than eight hours at a time, no matter how hard you tried, you woke up in the dark, too.

Still, those four or five hours between wakeup and sunrise were precious. People didn't call each other then, or come to visit. The official workday didn't begin until the explosion of Kalkaboo firecrackers announced the dawn, and so Giyt had those hours for his own.

He used them for uninterrupted work. For trying to read all the reports that no one bothered to read at commission meetings, and then for trying to catch up on all the things he didn't know about Tupelo and his new life.

There were enough of those things to use up a good many of those valuable morning hours—things like learning the planet's geography, identifying the various kinds of work that kept the Earth-human community occupied, trying to figure out the nature of all those bizarre extraterrestrials who had suddenly become his townies. Well, learning *everything*. All that stuff was in the databanks, of course, but it was still a lot to try to learn in a hurry. And then there was all the new information that kept coming in every day, four times a day, from Lt. Silva Cristl's news-chat programs on the net.

The trouble with the lieutenant's news broadcasts was that almost everything she said raised new questions faster than it answered old ones. Like the late-night roundup when she announced, with almost a wink and nearly a grin, that she and a deputy had arrested four teenagers for being drunk and disorderly on the lakefront beach. Well, fine. The wink and grin were because Silva Cristl liked gossip, no puzzle there. But what was a fire-company officer doing arresting anyone? Giyt had to go back to the datastore to find out that, as the volunteer firemen were the closest the Tupelo humans had to a law-enforcement agency, they were also charged with performing what few police duties were ever necessary.

That made Giyt's eyes go wide. He himself was a volunteer fireman. So that meant that he had power to arrest wrongdoers—a most unusual situation for a man who had for most of his life been more likely to have been the one who was arrested.

Trying to keep all this new information straight was a lot of trouble. The things that Giyt felt he had to do kept getting in the way of the things he wanted to do, and Evesham Giyt wasn't used to that. It wasn't the work he minded. Giyt thrived on work, but the kind of work he thrived on was the heady challenge of matching wits against the best security programs anybody had devised, or solving some tricky problem in the net someone else had given up on.

Of course, there were a few tricky problems waiting for him if he ever got around to them—fixing up those crappy translation programs, for instance, or maybe taking the time to solve the protocols for the Slug and Centaurian and all the other alien communications systems. But that was just another kind of drudgery. Protracted drudgery, too, because any of that would take a *lot* of time; just writing a conversion program for the net belonging to the Petty-Primes had used up several of those priceless pre-dawn mornings.

Giyt almost longed for the old days in his Bal Harbor slide, when he could daydream or scheme about the conquest of Guatemala or Thailand in as much detail, and for as long, as he liked, with no constraints on his time except the ones he imposed on himself.

Actually, Giyt did manage a little of that daydreaming. It came from his tap into the Petty-Prime system.

The things that Giyt saw when he looked in on the Petty-Primes weren't all that interesting in themselves; in fact, they were almost always either hopelessly confusing or terminally dull. The Petty-Prime local news programs were even less interesting than the humans'. Perhaps the Petty-

Primes themselves thought so, too, because most of their transmission time was spent on those interminable soap-opera things or on sports events or on horrible cacophonous music. The dramatic programs he couldn't figure out and the music he couldn't stand at all, but the sports kept him interested for a while. He tried to deduce the rules of the games—the one, for instance, in which two teams of eighteen or twenty Petty-Primes confronted each other in an arena. Each of the players carried a little live reptile the size of a shrew, and when they released them the creatures streaked for the opposite team, which did its best to stomp them into mush. That much was clear, but how the game was scored or who won, Giyt could not tell. Or the other kind of contest in which two Petty-Primes engaged in bare-handed combat—but had their work cut out for them if they wanted to do each other any real harm, because they were tied to each other, back to back. Or the one—

Well, they were all pretty weird, but then, Giyt thought, probably the Petty-Primes would feel the same way about, for instance, ice hockey or sumo wrestling. What the Petty-Prime sports events did for Giyt was to give him a feeling for the funny little creatures as real people, with all their own habits and faults and relationships and interests.

That was where the new varieties of daydreams started. Giyt wondered if the Petty-Primes had their own history of wars and invasions and conquests. And then he began to think of how you might go about conquering the world of the Petty-Primes.

Thinking of it purely as an intellectual enterprise, it didn't seem that it would be all that hard to do. There didn't appear to be any large military forces among the Petty-Primes, though to be sure, a sports arena was not the most probable place to look for them. But even if they had combat-ready troops and an arsenal, surely Earth weaponry could take them out in a fair fight.

He considered how you could go about getting Earth forces to a place where that fair fight could happen. The first thing to do, he decided, was to transmit some heavy-duty mass killer weapon through the terminal to wipe out all the Petty-Primes nearby, then a couple of divisions of fast-moving armor to establish a beachhead. What sort of weapons for that first blow? That took some thought. Maybe chemical, maybe biological; you didn't want to use anything nuclear because that would wreck the terminal, too. The best thing of all would be to find something that would kill Petty-Primes but not Earth humans. For that you would need to know a lot about Petty-Prime biochemistry.

It took only a moment to check that out, and he was pleasantly surprised to find that there was, in fact, a considerable store of such data already in the banks.

Of course, before you could get that sort of operation off the ground you would have to secure your staging base on Tupelo itself. That would involve neutralizing all the other races on the planet, but that should be pretty straightforward: arrest the leaders, evacuate the area around the EPR terminal, bring in the weapons from Earth and the assault troops to follow—

But Tupelo's eetie leaders would probably resist, and that would mean killing. Not just killing creatures on another planet a zillion kilometers away, but murdering actual neighbors. Nonhuman neighbors, sure.

But even theoretically, even in this mind game, did he actually want to kill, say, Mrs. Brownbenttalon and her husband?

It occurred to him that the commanders of some expeditionary force from Earth, assuming anyone on Earth were crazy enough to want to try anything like that, would have no such compunctions: eetie freaks would be just eetie freaks to them. (But that, of course, wasn't going to happen; it was precisely to prevent any such lunatic effort that all six races had to be present to allow transmissions to come in.)

Then it occurred to him that one of those eetie freak races might, just possibly, be crazy enough to want to try to invade Earth in the same way; and then he understood why there had been all those soldiers with their machine guns around the EPR terminal on Earth when he and Rina had come through it to get here.

That made Giyt thoughtful in a different way. It seemed that somebody had been thinking about the prospects of invasions before him. Not just as a daydream, either, but as a real-world possibility.

That was not an enjoyable thought. The human race on Earth had pretty much got over its addiction to wars. Talk, sure. But no action. Nobody had the armaments for real war any more. Like most of his predecessors, the current American president followed the policy of speaking as loudly and offensively as possible, but carrying no stick at all.

But what did this stuff in the files mean? Was the cycle going to start again in space? Maybe right here on Tupelo?

Giyt shook his head at his own folly. Not a chance! That was ridiculous. There were no signs of that sort of pre-battle tension, and even if there were, there just weren't any weapons on the planet to carry out such a scheme.

That was when he heard the rat-a-tat-tat-*boom* from outside.

That startled him, and it almost felt for a moment as though it was those machine guns firing. It wasn't, though; he realized that at once. It was only the dumb thing the Kalkaboos did with their firecrackers every morning to greet the dawn. But it told him that sunrise had come. His private time was over. Any minute now Rina would be coming in to find out if he wanted pancakes or cereal for breakfast. And he hadn't made a dent in his real work.

He sighed and went back to the dreary business of trying to understand the commission reports. Briefly he wondered if he had made a serious mistake in trading his idyllic life in Bal Harbor for the irksome constraints of this new existence on Tupelo. He couldn't honestly say that he had any good reason to be happier here.

The funny thing was that he actually was happier. Not for himself. For Rina. There was no doubt that the woman was blossoming by the hour here on Tupelo; and how strange it was, Giyt thought wonderingly, that he found himself happy simply because she was.

VII

There is only one inhabited island on the planet Tupelo. It occupies the center position in a thousand-kilometer-long island arc, like Maui in Earth's Hawaiian chain. Like the Hawaiis, the chain on Tupelo was formed as a chunk of ocean crust dragged itself over a deep hot spot, producing volcanoes that ultimately produced islands; like the Hawaiian chain, too, this one is situated close to the planet's equator in the middle of an enormous sea—Tupelo's even vaster than Earth's Pacific Ocean. The island's soil is fertile. There is plentiful water arising from springs and streams on the central mountainous massif. However, as all the islands are of volcanic origin, they are singularly poor in exploitable mineral ores and completely lacking in fossil fuels. There are three other similar island chains elsewhere in the ocean; they also are mineral-poor. The only rich ore finds are on the planet's one Australia-sized continent, which lies near the planet's north pole.

Extraction of useful ores from the continental deposits, including petroleum, was begun by the nonhuman races before Earth was admitted to the planet. Most of the ores are worked and refined on site. Then the raw materials are fabricated into goods of all kinds by largely automatic factories.

—Britannica online, "Tupelo"

While Evesham Giyt was dressing after his post-siesta shower he turned on Silva Cristl's early-afternoon news broadcast. There wasn't much news that day, only a couple of announcements. The polar rocket was due in at 1950 hours; one family had given up on Tupelo and was heading back to Earth; the Bassingwells had had another baby, their fifth. Giyt listened with a feeling of comfortable lassitude. He and Rina had fallen into the pleasant custom of making love twice a day—at least twice a day; once at bedtime, but also once at the time of the midday siesta, because, as Rina said, "What else is a siesta for?" It certainly made the afternoons nicer. When Rina looked in to announce that she was taking the younger de Mir children to the beach, because Lupe had to go in for a checkup, Giyt surprised himself by volunteering to walk along.

The day was warm and the beach was crowded, not only by Earth humans. A pair of Kalkaboos, as near naked as made no difference, lay soaking up as much sunlight as they could extract from Tupelo's inadequate star. Even the Responsible One of the Petty-Primes was there. He wasn't alone, either. Rina was greeting two of his mates, and at least half a dozen of their little kits were running energetically around and kicking sand in one another's faces. When Rina greeted the little creature, he responded at once, the translator phone in Giyt's ear doing its job as well, and as poorly, as ever. "A misfortune that cannot remain," the Responsible One apologized, throwing his head back to face the giant Earth human. "Second eldest daughter just presently returning from first-ever duty tour at polar complex, must go meet rocket to greet." He waved one tiny arm in the general direction of the landing strip across the lake, and Giyt nodded.

"Yes," he said, awkward with the problem of talking to someone who only came up to his thighs. Giyt wondered if he should kneel, but the Petty-Prime didn't seem to mind. "I'd like to see that myself."

"Can be nothing more simple, you come with ourselves," the Petty-Prime declared hospitably. "Plenty of room on skimmer for even large person."

And Rina looked up from trying to rub sunscreen on the back of one of the squirming de Mir toddlers. "Yes, Shammy, why don't you do it? You've been stuck in the house too much. Get out and blow some of the stink off."

Giyt had never been in a skimmer before. Even on Earth he had rarely trusted himself in any kind of waterborne craft, and he wondered if he would get seasick in the fast drive across the lake. But the water was calm, the spray cast up by the skimmer's racing progress was pleasing enough on a warm day, and it was a nice change from sitting before his screen. The Responsible One chattered away, pointing out the things of interest along the far lakefront: the crude road that led through the jungle down to the cargo-submarine port; the ancient dam, originally built by the Slugs for hydroelectric power back in the days when only the first two races had come to live on Tupelo. "Entire lake," he piped up, "is due to existence of dam Slugs built, was not here before."

Then they were approaching the rocket's landing pad. There were three or four other skimmers moored to its floating dock, a variety of races sitting in the craft and talking idly among themselves. He was surprised to see that Hoak Hagbarth was among them, which triggered a reminder in his brain: where was the energy-conservation plan Hagbarth had promised to give him for the Kalkaboos?

It was a good chance to remind him, but apparently the chance for that was not going to happen right away. "Must not debark out of skimmer craft yet," the Responsible One cautioned as his children scurried about, tying the skimmer to the dock with cords the thickness of packing twine. "Not given permission. Requirement to wait for rocket to land, thus minimizing risk."

In fact, Giyt could see the suborbiter coming at them, high up to the north. It was no more than a glint of metal and a flickering flare of red flame and white as its thermal shield ablated. They had left their arrival to the last minute; as Giyt watched the craft was visibly settling lower and growing larger. It passed directly over the island, no more than a couple of thousand meters up. Then it reversed course and, dropping rapidly now, touched ground, the flames from its main rockets almost blinding Giyt. When it stopped, it was directly in front of the waiting group at the dock.

Chittering wildly, the Petty-Prime kits started to romp toward the rocket, with only their parents reining them in. A low-slung vehicle Giyt hadn't noticed before began to roll in the same direction, one end of it tilting upward as it moved to form a flight of steps. Almost at once the rocket's doors began to open—first the heat shield, far too hot to be touched; then the inner door. The passengers began to disembark, stepping carefully over the hot metal of the exterior shield.

Then the Petty-Prime kits broke loose. First off the polar rocket was a pair of Petty-Prime females, one of whom hopped agilely down the steps to throw herself into the arms of the Responsible One. Cheeping and squealing, the kits were doing their best to swarm over them both, and not cautiously. A Delt was coming down the steps in a hurry. He tried to dodge around the Petty-Prime family and didn't quite miss them all. One of the kits wound up under the Delt's foot; it squealed shrilly and began to whimper.

The situation quickly developed the makings of a nice little squabble, the Responsible One chirping belligerently up at the unrepentant Delt, others gathering around to take sides. Giyt observed that the infant wasn't really hurt; in fact, it and all its siblings had already taken themselves away from this argument of the grown-ups.

But Hoak Hagbarth wasn't in the group.

It took Giyt a moment to find the man, off under the lee of the rocket, taking something in a woven-fabric satchel from a man who had just disembarked. They didn't linger over it. Hagbarth said a few words; the man nodded and turned away to head toward another skimmer, drawn up on the beach, while Hagbarth returned to his own.

Giyt caught up to Hagbarth just as he was putting the satchel into the skimmer's locket and taking a beer out. He looked up as Giyt approached along the dock. "Evesham," he sighed. "How're you today? Care for a beer?"

Giyt took it for the sake of avoiding a discussion. "How're we coming with that energy-conservation thing for the Kalkaboos?"

Hagbarth showed no sign of remembering what he was talking about, so Giyt patiently went through the whole thing again. Hagbarth listened with only minimal attention, which was annoying. But then the man was always annoying. Giyt controlled his temper. Hagbarth wasn't the first person in authority Giyt had had to get along with—briefly, at least—in his infrequent spells as an employee of some large concern. Experience had taught him patience, even when you knew that to almost any question there would be only two probable responses: either "Don't worry about it" or "Forget it."

This time Hagbarth expanded slightly on the stock reply. "Don't worry about it," he said. "I'll flange something up. Anyway, when you get to the next commission meeting you can tell the Kalks there's a high-powered expert coming from Earth to look into the problem."

"Really? What's he going to do?"

"He's a she, and what she's going to do is study the problem, what did you think? Listen, Evesham, you worry too much. Just take it easy. Have another beer."

Giyt, who hadn't touched the first one, repressed a sigh. "Thanks, no." He looked around at the Petty-Prime Responsible One, still engaged in unfriendly conversation with the Delt who had stepped on his child; evidently he would have to wait for his ride back. To make conversation, he offered: "This is the first time I've been here. Do you always come down to meet the rocket?"

Hagbarth looked at him with a cautious expression. "Not always."

"Just to pick up that package this time, I guess?"

He meant nothing by it, but Hagbarth seemed to consider it a significant question. "Oh, that. Well, sure. Sometimes there's a shipment coming down from the Pole that has to be met, that's all. You know how it is. Most of the stuff comes by cargo sub, but there are some goods people are more in a hurry for than others." He sighed and stretched, then looked over Giyt's shoulder. "I promised to give the damn Delt a ride, but I didn't say I'd wait all day," he complained, then began to grin. "Look at those silly little Petty-Prime buggers; they're nuts, you know that?"

Giyt turned around to look. The Responsible One was still arguing with the Delt, but his kits were playing their childhood games. One pair had turned itself into an animated wheel—each kit holding the ankles of the other and rolling across the mossy ground. Another pair was standing back to back, trying to flail their arms around to strike each other. "I've seen grown-up Petty-Primes doing that one," Giyt announced. "It seems to be a big sport on the home planet."

Hagbarth gave him a questioning frown. "How do you know what they do on the home planet?" So, of course, Giyt had to tell him how, just for the fun of it, he'd gone to the trouble of figuring out the Petty-Prime protocols so he could listen in on their transmissions.

That seemed to impress Hagbarth. He said, "Huh." Then he reached into the cooler and pulled out two more beers. He popped them both open and handed one to Giyt, without asking whether he wanted it or not.

"You know," he said, "I forgot how good you were at that stuff." Giyt shrugged modestly, but Hagbarth persisted. "I wonder if you could do something important for me."

Giyt got cautious. "What's that?"

"Well, you know how we handle transmissions at the portal? There's six of us, and each one has a switch; if we turn it off, the transmission fails. Only that's a pretty dangerous situation, you know? What I'd like, if you could do it, is to figure out how I can cut the other guys out of the circuit."

Startled: "What the hell for?"

"So as to prevent accidents," Hagbarth explained. "This whole six-switch business doesn't make any sense. They just have it because they're scared, but what could happen? Who would try to sneak anything really bad through the terminal, for God's sake?"

Giyt said cautiously, "Well, you can't blame them for not taking any chances—"

"Sure, but, the way it works out, this 'safety' thing might actually *cause* an accident, don't you see? Something could go wrong. Hell, something did, once."

He stopped there, but Giyt's curiosity was piqued. He persisted. "What did?"

"It was a while ago," Hagbarth said moodily. "One of the keyholders turned off his key in the middle of a transmission. A bunch of Slugs were coming in and—well, they got lost. You know what happens to somebody like that? They were transmitted. They weren't received. So they're gone forever."

"You mean they're *dead*?"

"I mean they're *at least* dead. Maybe something a lot worse. Like something I don't even want to think about. Now, we don't want that happening to the energy lady from Earth, do we? Not to mention there's a six-planet meeting coming along."

"Six-planet meeting?"

"Oh, didn't you know? Twice a year all six of the races get together here on Tupelo to talk things over—it's like your commission, you know? Only these people represent their whole home planet. Now, we wouldn't want anything going wrong with them, would we? We're talking about some of the most important people there are. So if you could manage to dig out those codes for me—"

Giyt thought it over for a moment, then temporized. "I thought you'd have all that stuff. I mean, you must have access to the portal design."

"Must we? We don't," Hagbarth said bitterly. "The goddamn eeties won't tell us how the portal works, and if we try to take it apart to find out for ourselves it'll blow up. I mean, a *big* blowup. They've probably got the thing booby-trapped with nukes or something."

"I don't understand," Giyt said plaintively. "Wasn't it this man Sommermen who invented the portal, based on what they call this Einstein-Podolsky-Rosen thing? Aren't all those guys human beings?"

Hagbarth shrugged. "I'm just telling you the way it is. So what do you say? Can you figure out those codes for me?"

"Maybe, but you've got me confused. I don't understand what you're telling me about the portal."

"Oh, hell," Hagbarth snarled, losing patience, "what're you asking me about all this stuff for? Maybe I misunderstood—and look, those Petty-Primes look like they're getting ready to go. Don't miss your ride."

* * *

Giyt got away without promising anything, but he didn't stop thinking about the portal codes—and most of all, about the portal itself. After dinner he sat down to stare at his terminal.

For starters, he was pretty sure he wasn't going to work out a system for bypassing the other controls for Hoak Hagbarth—not, anyway, until he convinced himself that Hagbarth was smart enough and responsible enough to be trusted with that kind of power. But what about the bigger question Hagbarth had planted in his mind? Was there something that no one was being told about the portal's provenance?

It occurred to him that a good place to look might be in some of the other species' data stores. Anyway, it might be worth a little time spent at the terminal to see if he could find them.

He started with the Petty-Primes, and an hour's hard work later he had to admit he had drawn a blank. However unreliable the damn translation programs were, Giyt was pretty sure he'd converted every possible name for the terminals into the dots and strokes of the Petty-Prime script and all he'd had for his pains was a lot of garbage about the numbers of immigrants and the volume of goods shipped back and forth.

It had seemed like a possible shortcut, but it wasn't working. Giyt sighed and went back to the human data files.

But even the Library of Congress store was less than illuminating. Yes, somehow or other, long ago, Huntsville Inc. had pried a grant from some foundation or other to finance the airy-fairy project of interstellar exploration. Yes, they'd launched a dozen or so miniature ion rockets, one to each of the most promising nearby stars. . . .

But then what? How did they get from the tiny, slow, unmanned probes to the instant transportation of the Sommermen portal?

That was where the story clouded over. Dr. Fitzhugh Sommermen worked for Huntsville, that was definite. He had been conducting researches on the Einstein-Podolsky-Rosen simultaneity effect—and doing it very expensively, in Low Earth Orbit, paid for by another of Huntsville's free-flowing grants. The reason for his being in orbit, the report said, was that it was necessary to avoid interference from Earth's surface gravity. Then somehow—this was when it all got misty and uncertain—he had come back from one session in orbit with the prototype of his portal device in his lander.

The rest of the story, for security reasons, was classified secret. But what "security reasons"? Military? But military security implied an enemy, and what enemy was involved here?

The questions were not getting answered, they were proliferating.

The obvious next place to look was in the Tupelo files of the Extended Earth Society, but when Giyt accessed them he was no farther along. Maybe there was something there, but every interesting file turned out to be secured. A password was needed.

That was neither a surprise nor a problem; not for Evesham Giyt, who had a hundred ways of getting past such obstacles. The first was to check every terminal on the island that might have access to the protected system to see if someone might have been stupid enough to leave his password in its default setting—its extension number, his name, something like that. He wasn't surprised when that didn't work; even Wili Tschopp wasn't quite that dumb. Another way of gaining entry was to select a terminal that was privy to the closed file and flood it with extraneous messages. That was how Giyt had financed his college education, going through the university president's terminal to enter the financial files; they would normally have questioned his status, but with the president's terminal bogged down it could not give the reply that would have denied Giyt access.

On Earth that no longer worked; net users had become a good deal more sophisticated since Giyt's college days. But here on Tupelo—

It took less than five minutes for Giyt to get into the closed files. But when he was there he was still nowhere.

The trouble was that even the secured files were still unreadable for him. He found plenty of entries that concerned the portal or the Sommermen terminal or any of the other variations he could think of on the term, but, just as with the Petty-Primes, they dealt only with what particular shipments had arrived or departed on particular days. And even those were enciphered.

What did it mean, for instance, when an entry read: "President TARBABY stocks: 1533 JUNIORS, 114 GRABBAGS, 11 SUPERS"? Or "Need 16 gross additional HAIRNETS"? Not to mention the wholly incomprehensible transmissions like "GREEKS 53 FLYSWATTERS, COPTS 2600-plus RUTABAGAS all sizes, others not identified."

Giyt blanked the screen and sat back. He could, of course, ask Hagbarth what all this stuff meant, but that would mean telling Hagbarth he'd snooped into the files . . . and, anyway, the mere fact that it was all encoded meant that it probably was something Hagbarth wouldn't want to talk about.

Giyt hated to admit defeat, even when only curiosity was involved. He knew that if he were on Earth he could probably get into the master system there. But he wasn't. Here on Tupelo there was no continuous contact with Earth, only the burst transmissions that went to and from Earth when the EPR portal was open. He had no firsthand knowledge of that stuff, since neither he nor Rina, of course, had any reason to communicate with anyone back on Earth.

But as it turned out, about that he was wrong.

VIII

The climate of the planet Tupelo is uncomplicated, if sometimes drastic. There are relatively few major hurricanes, perhaps because of the lack of large landmasses, which means relatively few collisions between dry, continental, high-pressure air masses and humid maritime lows. However, disturbances from the planet's intertropical convergence zone may from time to time drift north or south and propagate some severe storms. Generally speaking, Tupelo's one inhabited island, which lies quite close to the planet's equator, avoids hurricanes because there is relatively little Coriolis force at those latitudes. There are, however, exceptions.

—BRITANNICA ONLINE, "TUPELO"

Giyt discovered that his wife had been communicating with Earth when she asked him for a favor. "Shammy, hon, I have to go to the store. I'd appreciate it if you'd come along."

That was a little surprising, because Rina knew that her husband wasn't fond of shopping, but then she went on. "It's a nice day for a walk," she wheedled. "Anyway I need you to help me pick out a birthday present for my sister's husband."

Then he was really astonished, since he hadn't known she had a sister. Rina was curiously defensive about it, too.

"Oh, yes," she said, "she's living in Des Moines. So I dropped her a line, just to let her know where I was and what I was doing."

"You sent a message to Des Moines?"

"Well, sure, Shammy. She's the only sister I've got. Wasn't that all right?"

Giyt wasn't quite sure of the answer to that. It had been his belief that they had cut their ties with Earth entirely—that is, not counting his private stashes of mad money, available any time he chose to draw on them. "Anyway," she went on, "there was an answer from her in the last transmission—wait a minute. I'll show you."

She poked at her terminal, and in a moment her sister's face appeared. The woman on the screen didn't look a lot like Rina, Giyt thought: older, sterner, sharper-featured. But she was smiling as she said, "Well, Rina, you could have knocked me dead. Imagine you settled down at last! And married to an important man, at that—a mayor, for heaven's sake!"

Rina stopped it there. "The rest is just personal stuff," she said, sounding embarrassed. "We had a lot to catch up on because, you know, she didn't much care for my, uh, lifestyle. So we sort of lost touch for a while. Anyway, her husband's birthday's coming up. I'd like to get him something. The trouble is, I don't know him well enough to know what he'd like, so if you wouldn't mind . . ."

Giyt didn't mind. He did have a pretty full afternoon ahead of him—the commission meeting first, and after that there was a scheduled transmission from Earth, but with live people coming in this time so that he would have to go to the terminal to greet them. No problem there, though. Giyt had become very relaxed about the commission meetings, now that he'd actually read up on the reports ahead of time. And even better, he had a tangible announcement for the Kalkaboos.

The store wasn't crowded. There was a knot of people in the food section, picking over the fresh vegetables and the wrapped cuts of meat, with another handful sorting through the video displays for things to order from Earth. None of that was what Rina was after. "I'd like to get him something from Tupelo if I can," she said, doubtfully fingering the sleeve of an anorak. "How cold do you suppose it gets in Des Moines?"

"Cold enough," Giyt told her, looking under the collar of the coat. He was a little surprised to see cold-weather gear in this balmy place, but no doubt it was for anyone unlucky enough to have to work in the polar factories. Then he found the label. "I think that one comes from Earth, though."

She sighed. "I know, but the ones they make here are all plastic." As they were. As were most of the locally produced garments, because there were these oil wells at the pole, and there was no need for the oil as fuel. The nuclear plant on Energy Island took care of all the town's energy needs, so most of the oil not burned at the pole itself got turned into plastic and fabricated in the polar factories into—well, face it, Giyt thought, mostly into junk.

The biggest export item on display was the doll collection. The dolls came in six varieties, one for each race on Tupelo, and they all squeaked out a friendly line of patter from their interior chiplets—"Hi! I'm a Slug! I like wet places and I can sing!" But Rina's brother-in-law, a forty-year-old insurance broker in Des Moines, Iowa, was not likely to want a doll of any kind. Nor did any of the locally made kitchen appliances seem like a good bet, however smart they were with chiplets of their own. Rina finally settled on a mantel clock. It was a fairly nice-looking thing, and it had two faces side by side, one displaying each hemisphere of the planet—not that there was much difference between them, unless you know what island groups to look for. One face told Tupelovian time, the other displayed the twenty-four-hour Earth clock. "I guess it could be a kind of conversation piece," Rina said doubtfully, hefting the thing in her hand.

"You bet," Giyt encouraged. "Anyway, he sure couldn't get one of those in Des Moines. Let's get them to ship it."

Giyt enjoyed walking around the town when he had the time for it. He liked seeing the new buildings going up—Delts installing the electrical connections, Slug crews running the machines that dug trenches for the sewer and water pipes. There was a human bakery cheek by jowl with a Kalkaboo brewery, offering two distinct smells, both interesting. He passed the human ecumenical church, reminding him that, since he was the mayor, after all, probably he and Rina ought to go there once in a while, and a Centaurian home with the little males bossing children around.

But the day was no longer fine. It had clouded over while he was in the store with Rina, and he wasn't halfway to the Hexagon when he heard thunder. The storm came on fast, and it was a big one, thunder crashes like artillery fire and startling displays of lightning flashing through the clouds. The rain had already begun and he was drenched by the time he got a cart. He got drenched again when it let him out at the Hexagon. So as the meeting of the Joint Governance Commission started, he was soggy and no longer had the feeling of being entirely comfortable about it.

He was right about that, too. The meeting was a mess. The Petty-Primes' Responsible One was in the chair, and he appeared to be having a private feud with the Principal Slug. The meeting got off to a late start because the Principal Slug and the Petty-Prime were off in a corner squeaking and slobbering furiously at each other; and then, when finally the Responsible One climbed into his doll-sized chair and declared the meeting in order, Mrs. Brownbenttalon seized the floor to complain about the delay. "Have wasted expensively irreplaceable time of important and very busy persons here most shockingly," she declared—or so the translation button in Giyt's ear made her say. "Personally possess great forbearance or would propose immediate motion of censuring!"

It went on like that. The Delt General Manager complained that the Slugs had damaged some of the electrical connections in digging sewers for the new houses; the Principal Slug announced the Delts were unreasonable, almost as bad as the Petty-Primes; the Petty-Prime in the chair declared the Principal Slug out of order. They were all at one another's throats—even the Centaurian, Mrs. Brownbent-talon, whom Giyt had regarded as the most sensible of his colleagues on the commission. He could not imagine why. Even the audience, surprisingly numerous this day, seemed restive, chattering among themselves. He caught a glimpse of Olse Hagbarth sitting with her arms folded over her chest, looking amused and unsurprised; she winked at him, as though at a shared joke. But Giyt didn't know what the joke was. So he sat there, listening in wonder, until the Kalkaboo High Champion got his chance to say that the proposals of the other races for reducing their wasteful use of power were totally unacceptable. Then Giyt managed to get in his announcement that the Earth humans had an expert coming to study the whole question of the power plant, the Petty-Prime declared the meeting adjourned, and everyone flocked for the door.

By the time Giyt got to the exit the rain had slackened off to a steady drizzle and most of the waiting carts were already taken. Olse Hagbarth was waiting for another in the shelter of the doorway and she grinned at him. "Real catfight today, wasn't it?"

"What was it all about?" he asked.

"Oh, didn't you know? It's the six-planet meeting coming

up. They're all antsy because they want to look good for the VIPs from home—ah, here's my cart," she finished as one last vehicle rolled up to the curb.

She was heading for it before Giyt could react. He hastened after her. "Look, Olse," he said, "I need to get to the terminal."

"Of course you do," she said sunnily, one hand on the cart door. "Have a nice time."

"Well—what I mean is, any chance you could give me a lift?"

She looked surprised. "I wish I could help you out, Evesham, but I'm going the other way. Anyway, it isn't that far to walk, is it? And, look, it's hardly raining at all anymore."

Actually the rain had almost stopped by the time Giyt got to the Sommermen terminal and so he was only mildly soaked this time.

What surprised Giyt was to see how many people, and nonpeople, had gathered at the terminal, most of them sitting warm and dry in the cars that had brought them. (Which explained how so few cars had been available at the Hexagon.) He caught sight of Hagbarth and Wili Tschopp standing by Hagbarth's portal control, but before he could go there, squeals from one of the carts attracted his attention. He turned to see the Divinely Elected Savior of the Centaurians, Mrs. Brownbenttalon, poking her long nose out toward him. The translator in his ear piped, "Apologetics, Mayor Large Male Giyt. Should have to offered the sharing of transportation from Hexagon. Trust you scurried well through raindrops."

"Thanks. Actually I was glad for the exercise," he lied.

It seemed to Giyt that Mrs. Brownbenttalon was giving him a skeptical look—as much as a curly-haired anteater could manage a look of that kind—but Wili Tschopp was shouting at them to stand back. The golden glow was beginning to surround the terminal. Almost at once it began to flash blue and white.

The transmission from Earth was arriving. No, had arrived; the portal lights went out as the sharp puff of displaced air startled Giyt. He blinked, and when he opened his eyes again, fifteen or twenty large crates were stacked in the bay. A woman was sitting on the edge of one of them, tapping her feet and frowning impatiently, and behind her were three other rather worried-looking adults and a small child, all of them holding suitcases, purses, and each other's hands.

It was time for Giyt to carry out his mayoral duties. He advanced on the newcomers, hand outstretched. "Welcome to Tupelo," he said. "I'm your mayor, Evesham Giyt, and this gentleman over here"—waving toward Hagbarth, hurrying in their general direction— "is your Ex-Earth representative, Hoak Hagbarth. Hoak will arrange for your housing, and all your other needs, so if you'll excuse me—"

Hagbarth gave him a scorching look. "Stay here, Giyt," he ordered. "Keep these people company while I take care of Emissary Patroosh."

"How?" Giyt asked, but Hagbarth was already most obsequiously greeting the woman on the box.

So Giyt found himself doing the tour-guide thing for the new arrivals, while out of the corner of his eye he saw all the nonhumans getting out of their carts and swarming over the cargo. Mr. Brownbenttalon had leaped off his mate's back and was running the fabric of some new garments through his tiny paws; four or five of the Petty-Primes were concentrating on the luggage belonging to the immigrants. One of them sniffed at a bunch of grapes suspiciously, then bit one of them in half, stared at the interior and then spit the thing out. The woman Giyt was talking to cried out, "My basket of fruit!" They all abandoned Giyt to protect their belongings as Wili Tschopp came up behind him.

"When they've got their stuff," he said, "you can take them to Olse's house. She's sorting out places for them to live."

"I never had to do that before," Giyt remarked suspiciously.

"No, of course not. Usually Hoak does it for you, but this time he's got the energy lady to take care of. And listen"—smirking again, in the way Giyt had learned to hate—"you be sure to give my regards to that really good-looking lady of yours."

By the time Hoak Hagbarth had shepherded his VIP guest's luggage past the inspection—with much argument and raising of voices over the scientific instruments she'd brought with her—he escorted her to the waiting cart, pausing to introduce her to Giyt. "Dr. Emilia Patroosh, Mayor Evesham Giyt. Listen, Giyt, you'll have to take the new people to my place so Olse can—"

"I know," Giyt said, politely shaking the hand of the energy expert.

"Fine." Hagbarth started to get into the cart with his VIP visitor, then paused. "Hey, listen. I've got an idea. You were wondering about the power situation? Why don't you go along with Dr. Patroosh to take a look at Energy Island tomorrow? I'll have a chopper ready for you in the morning. Take your wife; it'll give the two of you a chance to see the sharks."

"Sharks?" But Hagbarth only shook his head, grinning, as the cart sped away.

IX

The geological and paleontological history of the planet Tupelo is not well understood, due to the paucity of land areas available for digging. No fossils have ever been discovered. However, it is generally believed that sometime in the relatively recent past, perhaps circa 2 to 4 million years BP, the planet underwent an extinction event similar to the ones which on Earth ended the Cretaceous and other ages. The causative event—whether a bolide impact, an episode of very large-scale vulcanism, or something unique to Tupelo—is not known. However, the result is clear. Whatever large land animals existed on Tupelo disappeared at that time. Life in the ocean, however, is quite another matter.

—BRITANNICA ONLINE, "TUPELO"

It was a sparkly dawn day, with dew beaded on the "grass," the sun still hidden behind the great mountains to the east, the air cool but comfortable. Altogether it was just the right kind of day for a chopper trip to Energy Island . . . except that there was no chopper. Hoak Hagbarth apologized profusely to the VIP woman from Earth. The gyrocopter, unfortunately, was in the shop. So if Dr. Patroosh didn't mind, they would have to take a Delt skimmer to the island. Either Dr. Patroosh really didn't mind or she was being a good sport about it. "Let's just do it, all right?" she said.

When they reached the lakeshore the Delt skimmer turned out to be a much larger ground-effect vehicle than the one that had taken Giyt to see the polar rocket land. Giyt's first look at it made his eyes pop. Startlingly, the thing was gleaming in metallic gold and ten or twelve meters long. It came complete with a Delt pilot sitting on the rail, impatiently tapping his long fingers on his knee. When Rina politely thanked him for agreeing to transport them, the Delt turned one wandering eye on her, the other wavering between Giyt and Dr. Patroosh, and gargled something that the translator turned into, "Imposition no greater than expected, happening at all times without considerateness. Board now. Sit. Strap in for bumps."

There weren't any bumps, though, at least not at first. The skimmer lifted on its air cushion and slid out onto the surface of the lake, heading swiftly for the hills at the far side. Giyt was glad for the moving air, which diluted that Delt aroma from the driver. Rina didn't seem to mind the smell. She was squeezing Giyt's hand in excitement, staring around at everything—back at the low buildings of the town; at the approaching hills; at the barely visible rim of the old Slug dam that long ago had created Crystal Lake for their own first colonists; at the fittings of the Delt skimmer. Those were pure nonhuman technology, all right: corrugated seats that pressed cruelly into human buttocks, double view screens for the pilot—one for each eye?—and an instrument panel that kept whispering and beeping constantly. Even the safety straps were woven of some kind of glass-like fiber, and where they rubbed against the bare skin of Giyt's throat they scratched.

Then they were across the lake, the skimmer gliding easily onto the shore and entering the rude roadway through the woods Giyt had seen on his previous trip. There was plenty to stare at there.

Ground-effect vehicles worked splendidly on flat surfaces,

but they did poorly on grades. In order to ease the slope on the far side of the dam the skimmer roadway was a series of switchbacks, and yes, now there were plenty of the bumps the pilot had warned against. There was no real road there at all, just a bulldozed track littered with knocked-down logs. Every time the skimmer crossed one the jolt relayed itself to the bruisable bottoms of the human passengers.

But it was a small price to pay. These were not the woods Giyt had seen on the slopes of the mountain. There were flickers of color darting about among the trees—barely glimpsed before the skimmer had left them behind; birds? insects? The trees themselves were not of any variety Giyt had ever seen before. Some were almost branchless until they expanded into an umbrella of fronds at the top, almost turning the roadway into a tunnel as they met overhead. Some hardly looked like trees at all; they resembled the stumps of even huger trees, four or five meters thick, no more than half a dozen meters tall. When Rina exclaimed over them, the VIP woman looked up from the palmtop she had been intently studying and said, kindly enough, "That's how they grow. It's what you get when you don't have any large animals to knock them down; there are trees like that where my grandparents come from, on the Indian Ocean islands of Earth."

"That's right," Rina said sociably. "There aren't any large animals at all on Tupelo, are there?"

"Not on land," the woman said. "But if you want to see large animals, wait till we're crossing the strait."

Then they reached the bottom of the slope. The skimmer left the roadway to slide onto the surface of the river below the dam. A pair of huge steel whales were moored at the side of the stream. Though Giyt had never seen one before, he recognized them. They were the submersible cargo vessels that carried goods to and from the polar complex. The skimmer pilot, who had ignored his passengers as he concentrated on making the turns in the road, jerked a long thumb back upriver. "Place where Slugs live, under dam. They like wet." He thought for a moment, then added, "Slugs not so bad, though. Not like damn Petty-Primes, get all crazy when somebody comes near damn tiny young. Just the other day my ex-brother have much abuse from Responsible One—you know, you saw whole thing, right?"

"I guess I did," Giyt admitted.

"So you know. Totally without warranted crapola, right? Kit not hurt. Purely accidental stepping-on, anyway. Sure, he only ex-brother, but still kind of family, you know? So must stick up for." He shook his head judgmentally, the eyes wandering in all directions. Then he added warningly, "Gets stinky now."

Giyt twisted his neck to peer behind them, but caught only a glimpse of igloo-shaped mud structures, far back. He was turning over in his mind the curious fact that a Delt would describe anything else as stinky. Then the odor hit them. "Christ," he said, gasping.

Dr. Patroosh gave him a tolerant smile. "See that pipe?" she offered. It was a meter across, jutting out into the river, with an ooze of foul-looking sludge coming out of it. "Sewage. It comes from the town. Whatever you do, don't dabble your fingers in the water."

At least on the river the ride was smoother than on that terrible jungle trail. Slowly the appalling stench dwindled to bearable proportions—or else, Giyt thought, they were getting used to it. The stream broadened. The woods surrounding it diminished and then disappeared. The skimmer left the channel that had been dredged out for the cargo subs and glided out onto a broad beach.

Rina gasped in alarm, and Giyt saw why. The great waves of Ocean were pounding in on the pebbly shore. Creatures were riding them, like surfers on a Hawaiian beach. Big creatures. *Nasty* ones, some that looked like the "sharks" that Hagbarth had mentioned, letting themselves be thrown up on the beach and floundering around on their pectoral fins for a while before lumbering back into the water; some like lizards that dug in the pebbles with their long, sharp-toothed jaws—looking for something to eat?—and were careful to stay as far as possible from the sharks.

"It's the sewage that brings them," Dr. Patroosh said, without pleasure. "You always see them here."

And the pilot called, "You bet! Mean bastards. Eat you up, one bite, quick-quick. Get bad bellyache after, sure, but what you care? By then you dead. Now everybody shut up, must catch wave."

He had throttled back the skimmer's thrusters, though keeping the fans that raised them above the water level at full power. They idled for a moment in the shallows where the river broadened out to enter the sea. Then he poured on the power, the skimmer leaped ahead, and they slid over the froth deposited by one breaking wave and climbed the next before it crested. Finally they were in deep water.

Nonchalantly the pilot stood up, swaying easily in the motion of the sea. From a compartment in the wall he took out a thing that looked more like a pocket camera than anything else and held it to one eye as he began to study the sea. Something in the control board began to hum and stutter; Giyt hoped it was an autopilot of some kind. At least, though the pilot was paying no attention at all to what the skimmer did, they seemed to be moving steadily toward a smudge on the horizon. Giyt supposed it was Energy Island.

As the skimmer rose and fell over the vast Ocean swells, Rina began to look uncomfortable. The pilot took the thing away from one eye long enough to stare at her. "You think you going to puke? Okay, over side, Ocean don't mind; only don't lean over too far, Christ's sake. Got no way to pull you out before, you know, gobble-gobble."

* * *

By the time they reached Energy Island—sliding right up into a dock as behind them a great steel-wire gate closed to keep the shore animals out—Dr. Patroosh had explained why she preferred the skimmer to the gyrocopter. Under its gold skin the skimmer was built of a sort of foam plastic, so light that if anything went wrong the vessel would simply float until rescue arrived. The chopper had its own flotation devices, but swells would overwhelm them quickly enough. Then it would sink like a rock, and, she said positively, nodding toward the hungry creatures on the far side of the gate, "You can see why you don't want to go swimming in Ocean."

Whoever built the power plant seemed to like gold as much as the builder of the skimmer did. The plant was a collection of hemispherical golden domes. There was a twenty-meter-tall giant hemisphere in the middle and there were smaller ones, which gave off a sound of big engines running, nested around it. Every one of them was bright with a golden skin. The difference was that what the power plant's skin covered wasn't foam plastic. It was something hard and solid. Cement, maybe. Steel, more likely, Giyt thought.

The Delt pilot was watching him. He tapped Giyt on the shoulder with a long-fingered hand and said with pride, "Good electric, true? You know who build plant? Us. Not stinky Slug, Centaurian, Kalkaboo; when we come they have zero but damn pitiful hydroelectric dam for power. Delts laugh and laugh. Too tiny. Us build good one here. Fuse atoms, fine Delt designings. Then plenty electric, you bet, except now so many immigrants coming in need more. Oh," he added quickly, not meaning to give offense, "not just you Earth-creature guys, you understand? Damn Petty-Primes even worse."

Dr. Patroosh scowled at him. "Wait for us here," she ordered; and to Giyt and Rina, "Come on." And a moment later, when they were out of earshot, "You know what they want? They want us to dig the damn *foundations* for the new plant, while they supply all the high-tech stuff that we don't even get to look at. Like we were some damn Third World country that doesn't know anything about technology." She shook her head gloomily. "Anyway," she said, "I've got to talk to the head controller—he'll be another damn Delt, of course. You two can look around. There ought to be a few Earth people on the shift; maybe you can get one of them to show you what's what."

Evesham Giyt had never been in a power plant before. He had never thought much about what one might be like, either. Electricity was what you got when you turned a switch. Here inside the belly of the plant it was something else, something that shook the walls with low-frequency rumbling and hurt the ears with high-pitched whines. And those, he knew, were only the sounds of the turbines that turned steam into electricity. The source of the infernal heat that distilled Ocean's water and then flashed it into steam to spin the turbines was silent. But it was there. Somewhere no more than a few dozen meters away, Giyt knew, incalculable numbers of hydrogen nuclei were madly coupling with each other to make helium. It was the same nuclear fusion that made the old H-bombs so terminally lethal—no, it was scarier than any H-bomb, because what was happening inside the biggest dome wasn't a single explosion. It was a process rather than an event, and it went on and on.

It did not seem to Giyt that this was a thing that should be left to run itself, however good the automatic controls. But there seemed to be nobody in sight. As he and Rina walked along the golden corridors they passed a sleeping Kalkaboo, curled against a wall. He woke up long enough to glare at them, then returned to sleep. It was only after a ten-minute search that they heard a whirring sound. It came from where a human shift worker was watching a porn film on his handset as he followed the cleaning machines around.

When Giyt asked the man for guidance he gave Giyt an injured look. "You don't recognize me, do you? Colly Detslider. I'm the relief driver on Pumper Three in the fire company."

But after Giyt apologized and shook his hand, the man was happy enough for an excuse to leave the machines to do their job on their own. Yes, he told them, there was a full shift on duty—thirty persons, five of them human like himself. No, he didn't know where the others were. Sure, he'd show them around, although it was only fair to warn them that his own job here was janitorial and he didn't know much about the machinery.

He knew enough, though, to keep them from going near the central chamber where the tokamak held its fusing plasma in an unbreakable magnetic grip. They saw the pumps that sucked cool water in from Ocean, to make steam and then to condense it when spent; they saw the gratings that kept the creatures of Ocean from being sucked in along with it; they saw the remarkably slim cables, wrapped in the chilling jackets that made them superconducting, that carried the power plant's output down under the strait to the community that used it. They even peeped into the control room, every wall a mosaic of screens and signals, where they saw Dr. Patroosh furiously arguing with a pair of uninterested Delt controllers. They would have seen more, probably, but Detslider was watching the time. He was due for his lunch break, he informed them, and they were welcome to come along if they wanted to.

Lunch was machine-served in a large room filled with tables, couches, and Kalkaboo tree-rests, sparsely occupied by beings who paid no attention to the human visitors. To Giyt's displeasure the human lunch menu turned out to be creamed chipped beef on toast. "It's always something the machines can dispense. Real crap," Detslider told him. "Come on. Take your plate and we'll go someplace that smells better to eat it." A Delt, sipping some thick yellow liquid from a shallow bowl by the door, turned one eye to glare at Detslider as they left, but the man ignored him. Five meters down the corridor there was a smaller room, with two human women and a man playing pinochle at one table and space for the visitors at another. While Giyt doggedly ate his lunch Rina made polite conversation with all of them. Detslider came from Pasadena, he said, but left it for Tupelo because there was too much crime in California. Like his job? Well, it was all right, but boring. The others, respectively from Tucson, Pottsville, Pennsylvania, and Boston, agreed, the woman from Pottsville adding, "The damn Delts push you around here, like they owned the place." But it wasn't just the Earth humans that suffered, she conceded; the Delts acted superior to everybody.

When they went back to the control room Dr. Patroosh spied them, snapped some final argument at the Delt controllers, and swept past them at the door. Over her shoulder she called, "Come on, we'll go home. I'm not doing any good here." And crossing the strait in the skimmer she was silent and morose. When Rina asked her sociably how her mission had gone, Dr. Patroosh snapped, "Lousy. They've got this whole fusion section locked up, nobody but Delts allowed in—because of radiation danger, they say, but for Christ's sake we know all about radiation danger." She glanced at the Delt pilot, who seemed to be paying them no attention, but lowered her voice. "I'm going home to report. We'll see what happens . . . but I'll bet we'll cave in again and dig their damn foundation for them." Then she was silent. So were Giyt and Rina until their pilot, sweeping the surface of Ocean with his glass, cried out joyfully and began pulling something heavy and harsh-looking out of a locker. With one hand he steered the skimmer toward dimples of disturbed water; with the other he was locking the object from the locker to a mount on the skimmer's rail.

"Now what?" Dr. Patroosh demanded irritably.

Giyt had no answer for her, but Rina piped up. "Do you know what that looks like, Shammy? That long gold thing with the barbs on the head?" And then of course he did. It was a harpoon, and the Delt proved it a moment later by firing it at the little whirlpools—no, at something under the whirlpools, something red and many-eyed that gasped and snorted as the shaft struck home and it rose briefly to the surface.

The pilot shrieked in exultation, something that the translator did not even try to put into English. The creature sounded, pulling a hundred meters of supple, braided cable out of the harpoon's reel. The pilot made an adjustment on the reel, darted to the controls, and started the skimmer at high speed toward the coast. Then he turned to his passengers, grinning. "Good eating, you bet! But maybe too far out for any good."

"Too far out for what good?" Rina asked, but the Delt had already turned away. He was talking rapidly on the communicator to someone ashore, keeping one eye on the skimmer's wake, where the cable was stretched out almost horizontally. At the end of it Giyt could see the quarry flailing about for a moment, then it disappeared below the surface. Ominous whirls appeared all around it, and then something else was in the water. Blood?

It was blood, all right.

By the time the skimmer reached the river's mouth a Delt vehicle built like an armored car was waiting for them, but it was too late. When the pilot hauled his catch in to retrieve his harpoon most of the creature was gone, slashed away by the horde of predators.

The pilot laughed and spoke into the communicator; the

tanklike thing lumbered away as he turned the skimmer upstream toward the town. He said philosophically, "Too far out, you understand? Too bad. Wonderful to eat, only not just for Delts." Then he pursed his everted lips, as though trying to remember something, then brightened. "Hey, I know Earth thing! You know Earth-human liar Kepigay?"

"Who?" Giyt asked, and the Delt tried the name several times more before Rina said, "Oh, do you mean Ernest Hemingway?"

"Yes. Excellent liar, Kepigay. Greatly enjoy Earth-human lies; Earth humans such excelling liars. You know Kepigay old Earth romance lie, *Man Approaching Death in Relationship to Ocean*?"

"I think he means *The Old Man and the Sea*," Rina offered. "We had it in American lit in Wichita."

The pilot nodded enthusiastically. "Yes, I had volume also in aboriginal folk lie study. Damn good lie, that one. You see? Same thing here; catch fish too far, sharks eat. Aboriginals have much native lore which persons can learn from, I say always—though not," he added, with one eye wandering over to fix on Dr. Patroosh, "on subject nuclear fusion."

And all the way back to the town their pilot entertained them with stories of his fishing exploits while Dr. Patroosh glowered silently into space. When the pilot let them out on the shore of Crystal Lake, he said cheerfully, "Survive well until dark."

Rina giggled. "I think he means have a nice day."

"Yes, exactly. Do not shoot brain fragments all over house like famous Earth-human liar Kepigay."

They dropped Dr. Patroosh off at the Hagbarth home. Then, in the cart going to their own house, Rina said thoughtfully, "You know what's funny, hon?"

"What?"

"Well, Colly's from California, right? We're from Kansas. Matya comes from a little town on the Jersey shore, Lupe from just outside of Albuquerque, those other guys—"

"What's funny about that? Everybody has to come from someplace."

"Well, sure, Shammy, but they're all from *America*. Wouldn't you think there'd be some people from South America or Asia or somewhere?"

He thought for a moment, then brightened. "What about Dr. Patroosh? She said she was from some island in the Indian Ocean."

"No, not exactly. She said her grandparents were. She's an American, all right. So I just think it's funny that there isn't anybody from the rest of the world, that's all."

X

The celebrated inventor of the faster-than-light transmission portal, Dr. Fitzhugh Sommermen, remains in a coma after suffering a major stroke. The attack occurred while the scientist was being interviewed on European network television. His physicians have declined to offer any prognosis for his recovery, saying only that he is resting comfortably and that all possible measures are being taken. In a related story, U.S. President Walter P. Garsh interrupted a news conference this morning to deliver a typically outspoken attack on the European reporters who were questioning Dr. Sommermen at the time. "When will they stop badgering this poor man?" the president demanded. "No one can pretend that it is only scientific curiosity that continues to impel them. They want secrets, and they want them for their own use. Well, they won't get them. These secrets belong to America, and we aren't giving them away."

—Earth news transmission to Tupelo

Once his wife had called it to his attention, Giyt began to ponder the question himself. It seemed to be true. There weren't any Tupelovian humans from anywhere on Earth but the U.S.A., and why was that?

The person to ask, of course, was Hoak Hagbarth. The Ex-Earth man shrugged it off. "America's where our funding comes from, right? So I guess that's where they do the recruiting, too. Probably they'll get around to the rest of the world sooner or later. Make sense?" And when Giyt nodded, Hagbarth pressed on. "Listen, Giyt, I need to talk to you about something else. I wanted you to take that trip to the island for a reason. You saw those monsters in Ocean, right?"

"Yes?"

Hagbarth gave a rueful sigh. "Mean-looking bastards, weren't they? I have to admit, every time I take the chopper over there they scare the crap out of me. Can you imagine what would happen if the chopper broke down over Ocean and had to come down in the water?"

"I think it has flotation devices," Giyt said.

"Sure it has, if they work. But can you imagine what it would be like to be waiting for rescue out there? With the damn shark things doing their best to climb aboard for dinner? They're *big*, Giyt. They'd probably swamp the thing, trying to get at the passengers—and lots of women and children take that flight, Giyt. And there'd be the damn monsters, tipping the chopper over and everybody screaming and—"

"Yes, yes. I get the picture."

"So what we need," Hagbarth said, getting to the point, "is some kind of protection. A couple of guns for the pilot to carry. To shoot the animals so they can stay alive out there waiting for help."

He paused, inviting a response from Giyt. "I guess that makes sense," Giyt said cautiously.

"Only the trouble is, the eeties have this damn rule against importing weapons. So what I think you should do, at the next meeting of Joint Governance, you could make a motion to let us import one or two guns for the pilots to carry. For defense against the sharks. Do you think you could do that?"

Giyt considered the question for a moment. It didn't sound entirely unreasonable. It didn't sound entirely kosher, either. He said cautiously, "I guess I could try."

"Good, Evesham! I knew we could count on you. And listen, try not to be too specific about the number of weapons, all right?"

If there was one thing Evesham Giyt had learned in his time on Tupelo, it was that he had a lot to learn. So whenever he found a moment—which is to say when he wasn't asleep or doing his household chores or fending off the demands of his constituents—whenever there was a crumb of unbudgeted time at Giyt's disposal he used it to work on Tupelo's immense database.

His best time for that sort of homework was first thing in the morning, when an Earth-conditioned human being would have slept his full eight hours and still had the remainder of the long Tupelo dark before the sun rose and the workday began. Those were the hours Giyt spent filling the voids in his knowledge—some of the voids, anyway. Prohibition against importing weapons? Oh, yes, there was one. As far as Giyt could tell there had never been any exceptions allowed, though he supposed it could do no harm to ask. Electric power? Yes, the Delt pilot had spoken truth: When the Delts discovered the planet they earned their way into the communality by building the fusion plant. Utilities in general? There were surprises there for Giyt, who had not given much thought to how the various races divided up the chores of building and maintaining the community's infrastructure. It turned out that Petty-Primes handled waste disposal, at least until everything solid had been mulched and diluted and the resulting sludge poured into the sewage lines, which were Slug. Power was Delt, of course. Building and maintaining the little carts everyone used to get around was a Centaurian task. Kalkaboos controlled the weather satellites and the polar rocket.

And the Earth humans?

Giyt was somewhat taken aback to discover that the only communal task reserved for Earth humans was clearing land and preparing it for agriculture. Every species had its own farm plots, of course. Humans had cattle and goats, some of the other races maintained fish farms, while the Delts and the Kalkaboos alone occasionally fished in Ocean. The Kalkaboos also practiced a sort of vermiculture, maintaining flocks of wormlike creatures that lived and grew underground and returned to the surface only to spawn—and to be captured for food. But the drudgery of digging out places for the fish farms or chopping down the trees to make new farmland—that was for human beings. Dr. Patroosh hadn't been out of line when she complained. It was true. The other races treated Earth as a kind of Third World planet.

The whole question of infrastructure was unfamiliar to Giyt. Just as you got electricity by turning on the switch, the way you got food, for example, was to take an autocab to the nearest restaurant. It didn't matter whether the food originated in a garden plot next door or on some agrotech industrial farm ten thousand kilometers away. All you needed to get the food was money, and the way you got money was by holding a job. Or by living on the government grants, like most of the people in Bal Harbor. Or, in Giyt's own case, by milking it out of some corporation's files.

Thinking of money made him think of the spendthrift way the Delts treated gold. That, the datafiles informed him, was a consequence of their home planet's geology. The Delta Pavonis planet was unusually well endowed with heavy metals in general. There was plenty of uranium, for instance, rich in its fissile isotopes—so no wonder they were good at nuclear power—and an inordinate amount of precious metals, including gold. The Delts didn't prize the gold for its beauty, it seemed, but because it was so easily worked and so unlikely to corrode. And, of course, so plentiful.

Giyt grinned to himself. Cortés, he thought, would have had a hell of a fine time on the Delt planet. He probably wouldn't even have had to hold the Delt General Manager in a cell, as Cortés had Montezuma, to force him to cough up his treasures. He probably just could have picked up all the precious metal he could carry as chunks of street litter.

Which led Giyt to wonder what the Delt planet was like, exactly, and that was when he got the greatest surprise of all.

No human being had ever been allowed to visit the Delt planet.

Nor had any human ever set foot on the home planet of any of the other races on Tupelo; and none of those other races had ever visited Earth, either. The races never had any face-to-face contact at all except what occurred right here on Tupelo when, every one hundred and thirteen Tupelo days, representatives of each of the six planets came together here to talk.

And the next scheduled meeting of that sort was only a few weeks ahead.

The Kalkaboo dawn racket made him realize that it was getting light outside. He winced as a particularly loud firecracker went off somewhere nearby—some Kalkaboo was expiating some particularly nasty sin by blowing it to bits—and went looking for Rina to tell her his discovery.

He found her in the kitchen, carefully feeding some sort of mashed vegetable to the baby from next door. Matya was at work, she explained, and Lupe had taken the older ones to the lake for an early-morning swim. The conference of the six races? Oh, sure, she told him, that was what Matya was doing this morning, overseeing construction of new and better quarters for the dignitaries from Earth. She thought Giyt must have known about that. Everybody did. And listen, as long as he was here, what would he think if they invited Lupe and Matya over for dinner some evening soon?

He paused in the middle of lifting the lid of something that was simmering on the stove. Here was another surprise; they had never had dinner guests before. "With the five kids?"

"Maybe after the kids are asleep; they get one of the Donar girls to babysit for them sometimes. Or we could bed the kids down here, for that matter." She picked up the baby and held it to her shoulder, gently massaging its back as she studied Giyt's face. "I'm just thinking we ought to get to know more people socially. Of course, if you don't want to—"

"No, that would be fine," he said hastily. "Maybe we should invite the Hagbarths, too."

The baby emitted a moist burp; satisfied, Rina replaced it in its chair and resumed the feeding. After a moment she said, "Maybe . . . Well, to tell you the truth, I'm not that crazy about the Hagbarths."

"Oh?"

"We can have them if you want them, but—well, I've known guys like Hoak Hagbarth. When I was hooking, you know? There was this one guy, good-looking, nice body, good manners; it made you wonder why he wanted to pay for it. We didn't just jump in the sack. He made it like a date, brought a bottle of wine and everything, and when we got to bed he was sweet and so, well, loverly that I almost didn't want to charge him. And then before he left he beat the shit out of me."

"Oh," he said again, though this time his tone was quite different—having nothing more useful to say. He got up and walked aimlessly to the door, pausing to kiss the top of Rina's head on the way. Among the other things he didn't know, he reflected, was much about Rina's life before she turned up in Bal Harbor. She certainly had concealed little from him, but he had not encouraged her to talk about it beyond the simple synopsis: poor family, no future, prostitution the easiest way to make a living.

He stood on his little porch, gazing unseeingly out at the street. Down the road a pair of Slugs were running a digging machine, checking some problem with the drains. One of them turned an eyestalk on Giyt, who waved a greeting, admiring their dexterity with the tiny limbs usually concealed inside their slimy integument. He wasn't really paying attention. Something had changed about his relationship with Rina. Was it just the fact that now they were "married"? He hadn't thought very much about that before he popped the question, and maybe—

He turned, startled. From the kitchen Rina was screaming his name. "It's the baby, Shammy! He's choking! Come help me, please!"

It wasn't really a big problem. From high school days Giyt remembered the old Heimlich maneuver, remembered to be gentle with the baby's tiny body, on the first try got the child to cough a plug of something wet and nasty halfway across the room, and then he was fine. But Rina wasn't satisfied. Was overcome with guilt, in fact; begged Giyt to help her rush the baby to the hospital for a checkup. Then she got on the communicator and told Lupe what had happened, wringing her hands until Lupe arrived and the doctor had reassured them both. "Ah, no, Rina," Lupe said consolingly, "it's not your fault. I made the damn goo; I must've left some lumps in it. But you did just the right thing, Evesham, and Matya and I owe you."

And on the way out of the hospital Rina paused in front of the nursery—two tiny infants in the twenty beds for newborns—deep in thought.

"The baby's fine," Giyt informed her, holding her hand.

"Yes, I know," she said, and then looked up at him. "Shammy? I might as well tell you now. I hope you won't get sore. I'm pregnant."

That stopped him in his tracks. "You're *pregnant?"*

She looked embarrassed. "What can I tell you? I guess I forgot to renew the patch." Then she corrected herself bravely. "No, Shammy, that's a lie. I didn't forget. I threw the damn things away a month ago."

XI

The first sentients to visit the planet which Earth humans call Tupelo came from a moon of the sixth planet of the star Alpha Centauri. It appears to be inevitable in the development of any technological civilization that sooner or later it will explore space for other habitable worlds. The Centaurians, however, had a stronger motive for such projects than most. For more than five centuries they had been intermittently at war with the inhabitants of their sun's fourth planet. The casualties had been great, the costs enormous. In desperation the Centaurians sent probes out to every nearby star in search of a habitable world that they could make their new home. Most stars had no suitable planet. The first four planets that might have been livable were ruled out because races of sentient beings already lived there; the Centaurians did not want to flee one war to risk fighting another. When they discovered Tupelo it was everything they had dreamed of: thoroughly habitable, totally uninhabited. But their colony had just begun to feel at home when another race appeared, with the same designs.

—BRITANNICA ONLINE, "TUPELO"

For Evesham Giyt the news of Rina's pregnancy took considerable thinking over. He had dreamed many dreams in his life, but not one of those dreams, ever, had been about fatherhood.

Giyt didn't find the prospect overwhelming, quite, but it was certainly well and truly *whelming*. It contained so many consequences and ramifications: The raising of a kid. The changing of its diapers. Teaching it the facts of life. Teaching it how to throw a ball. Carving the bird at the head of the table at Sunday dinners, with the wife at the other end and the kid in between (or might it not be the *kids*, plural? because once you started on that track, didn't it get harder and harder to stop?). Babysitters; school; helping with homework; nursing through usual childhood diseases. The list was endless, because this baby business wasn't one of those things you could just grit your teeth and get through. It entailed a total reconsideration of your whole life, and it was *permanent*—or at least it was likely to last as long as Giyt himself did. What it came to was a whole and totally demanding new career, and Giyt was a long way from sure how he felt about it. Sometimes he glowered dismally at the wall as he thought of all that time taken up. Sometimes he felt a curious and wholly unexpected thrill of excitement.

He wasn't even really sure how Rina felt about it. Oh, she was conspicuously *happy* about being pregnant, sure. She smiled a lot, kissed him a lot, went out of her way to find excuses to mind the neighbor kids for Matya and Lupe a lot. But how did pregnancy *feel?* He kept stealing glances at Rina when she was looking the other way to see if she showed any signs of—of what? Of morning sickness? Of strange food cravings? Actually, of being different in any detectable way at all. He couldn't find any such signs. Except for this boundless affectionate cheer—not all that different from her usual state—she was just the same as ever. She kept right on with her studies and her volunteer work at the human hospital and her attempts to coax the bizarre plants in their front yard to produce flowers. She hadn't changed a thing.

That fact puzzled Giyt quite a lot. He was sure that if he had some organism growing inside of him he would spend a lot of time staring into space and trying to feel the damn thing grow.

But Rina didn't seem to be doing that. As far as he could tell she simply went on with her life just as before, as though this business of pregnancy were something, well, *normal.*

When it came time for the next Joint Governance Commission meeting, Giyt greeted it with pleasure. It was tangible work to do, and thus a relaxing change from worrying over the perils of approaching parenthood. Besides, he had some actual business to propose.

As he took his seat, the Petty-Prime Responsible One was already in the chair—well, in his tree—and fussily chirping for order. The Responsible One ran a tight meeting. All in favor of the municipal reports accepted as read, yes; all old business continued for next meeting, yes; then, if there is no new business—

That was when Giyt hastily put his hand up. "I have some new business, honored chairperson," he said, and launched into his sales talk.

It didn't go well. The other mayors listened tepidly, or more likely hardly listened at all, to his graphic description of the predators of Ocean. But when he reached the point of formally requesting permission to import a few weapons for the protection of downed chopper crews he had the commission's instant attention. There was a mumbling from all five of the other seats, too low-pitched for the translator to make sense of, but the Slug had two limbs in the air before he finished speaking. "Is against all rules!" the Slug declared, slobbering at maximum volume. "No one imports weaponry to Peace Planet ever anyhow, for sure!"

Hagbarth's briefing had prepared Giyt for that. "It is not a case of *weapons*, Principal Slug. It is merely for protection in case of accident. It is precisely analogous to the harpoons the Delts carry."

And of course that got the Delt into it. "Not to be compared! Harpoons vital accessory for skimmers, for purpose providing protein to feed hungry persons."

Giyt had an answer ready for that, too; surprisingly, someone else made it for him. It was the Petty-Prime chairperson who spoke up: "You have of skimmers, General Manager, only three in total. You have of self-launching harpoons more than one hundred eighty."

"Needed! For spares in case of losses or damages, which are frequent! And, repeating remark already spoken here, are also used for fishing purposes, not merely protection, same as Kalkaboos."

The Kalkaboo High Champion jumped in: "Kalkaboo practice is primarily using of nets for fishing purposes."

"Oh, yes," the Delt sneered. "Poison nets! Also harpoons as well."

"Very small harpoons, very few in number," the Kalkaboo protested; and then it got worse. Several of them were talking at once, the translation phone in Giyt's ear totally unable to cope. Not only Giyt's phone, either. Nobody's translator was making any sense of the chorus of gurgling, baying, moaning, chirping, and screeching until the Petty-Prime rattled his doll-sized drumstick on his doll-sized drum. And kept it up until all the others had quieted down and the Petty-Prime declared the subject deferred for future study and the meeting adjourned.

The funny thing was that, through it all, Mrs. Brownbenttalon hadn't said a word. She simply crouched there, eyes half closed, looking almost as though she were asleep; but from his position on her shoulder her tiny husband was raised up and staring. He never took his eyes off Giyt. And when Giyt said good-bye to them as everyone was leaving, neither he nor his giant wife replied.

When Giyt got home a message from Hoak Hagbarth was waiting for him on the net. "You made a start, at least," Hagbarth told him consolingly. "Who thought they'd go along right away? It's a big decision for them. They need time to get over their outmoded prejudices and face up to the real needs of the present day. So we'll bring it up again next time. Then we'll just keep on bringing it up until they say yes. And listen, Giyt, you haven't forgotten about the safety codes for the portal, have you?"

When Giyt hung up he stared glumly at his screen for a moment, considering what use to make of the rest of his day. What he needed to do was to try to catch up on his homework. He had a lot on his plate, and figuring out how Hoak Hagbarth could circumvent the portal's safety circuits was low on the stack. He had to read all the reports nobody had read at the joint governance meeting. Or he could tackle some of the accumulated petitions that kept silting up in his file. That particular part of the job was even tougher than it looked, because a lot of those requests dealt with questions Giyt still didn't really know much about, and so he had to educate himself first. For instance, the guy who had been turned down on moving to the polar mines was now demanding to know why at least the mines couldn't be located just as well on one of the neighbor islands so he wouldn't have to travel so far. Was that a sensible idea? Giyt had no way of telling. Probably he should begin to look it up . . . and at the same time repair the other gaps in his education, too. The history of Tupelo. The reason it had so many islands and so few continents. Et one damn cetera after another.

But first, and most of all, there was one special subject he could not put off learning more about. So what he began accessing on his screen wasn't any of the problems of Tupelo and its people. It was medical files, the ones that dealt with the dangers and problems associated with pregnancy. Of which, it turned out, there were a lot more than he was really prepared to face. When he got to the part about teratogenesis and how every once in a while a seemingly normal fetus would fail to develop a head, or turn out to have a partly developed Siamese twin, he shuddered, closed the file, and went looking for Rina to reassure himself.

She was cooking him lunch, and Lupe was in the kitchen with her. When Giyt came in Lupe beamed up at him. "Congratulations, Evesham," she said as she got up to kiss him chastely on the cheek. "The little monsters're a hell of a lot of bother, but, you'll see, they're worth it."

"Thanks," he said, giving Rina an accusing look. It hadn't occurred to him that she would tell some outsider about their new problem—their *situation*, he corrected himself.

But neither Lupe nor Rina seemed to think there was anything odd about it, and Lupe had something on her mind. "Listen," she said, "the reason I came over was to tell you what's going to be happening at the firehouse. You know when there's a fire you'll get a call on your carry-phone; then you drop everything and go."

"Go to do what? Wasn't I supposed to be having some training first?"

"Well, that's the thing I wanted to tell you. The chief just decided we're going to have a wetdown today. It's like a practice run, you know? So you'll just get your first lessons on the job. So when we get the signal don't get too shaken up. It won't be a real fire, this time, but we have to show up anyway."

"I thought Matya didn't want you doing that."

"I got an extension, just until the Taste of Tupelo's over; they'll need everybody for that . . . Ah, there's the call now. Let's go."

And Rina, composedly ladling something into a container, said: "Stew's ready, so take some with you. You can eat it on the way."

When Lupe and Giyt got to the firehouse all five of the gleaming fire trucks were pulled out onto the apron of the garage, motors going, firemen and women from all over the town clambering aboard. "Here," said one of them, handing something to Giyt. "Put this on."

It was a genuine fireman's hat, like the one he'd owned when he was five years old. Although the shape was the same, this one was bigger and heavier. Also there was an inset square of fabric on the front for Giyt to pin his chrome badge, as soon as they finished making him one. As he clung to the outside of Pumper 3, careening through the streets of the town, the driver—it was that Colly Detslider man from the Energy Island—stole a look over his shoulder and frowned at Giyt. He shouted something Giyt couldn't make out, but Lupe, clinging to the other side of the truck, apparently did. She pulled a slicker from a locker in the side of the truck and passed it to Giyt. "Don't try to put it on now," she bawled, "but you'll need it later—why do you think it's called a wetdown?"

Giyt found himself grinning. This was something like! For the first time, he understood why people volunteered for the fire company. Pedestrians were waving to them as they passed, sirens wheeping, all the other traffic scattering out of their way. It wasn't just humans doing the waving. A flock of Petty-Prime young ones, kits no bigger than mice, chased after the procession on their little roller-skate-sized carts, cheeping and cavorting in excitement, until they reached the electronic limits of their freedom and had to turn back. Even a Slug raised itself out of its moist cart to wave a pseudopod. Then they were out of the town, climbing a trail between a human cornfield and rows of Delt fruit-bearing shrubs. They were heading up the flank of the central mountains, where Giyt had never been before. Off to one side of the road was a pretty little waterfall, to the other a deep gorge. And then the trucks crossed an irrigation ditch, pulled up in a semicircle, and stopped.

They were at the edge of a small coffee finca, with nothing but uncleared native vegetation beyond. These weren't the big trees Giyt had seen below the Slug dam; they were a mass of tangled shrubs, few of them more than waist high, a dozen different species. "Go!" Chief Tschopp shouted. Everyone piled out, uncoiling hoses, hooking pumpers to the giant tanker trucks, revving up the engines. A minute later Giyt found himself part of a three-man team holding the bucking nozzle of a hose that was tearing holes through the patch of native Tupelo crabbushes uphill. He was getting drenched because he'd left the slicker on the truck, but he was impressed with the force of the stream; the sturdy bushes were simply smashed out of the way. Then, a moment later, the fixed water cannon on each truck began to fire, throwing high-velocity streams to the far edge of the patch, and even the few trees on the site were simply exploding as the water struck.

It took the fire company hardly a minute to get fully deployed, and then it was over. Chief Tschopp bawled, "That's it! Everybody secure!"

But it wasn't really the end of the exercise, because then everybody began laying out hoses to drain, winding them back onto their reels at one end as the trapped water flowed out of the other, and they were moving faster than ever. It was only when everything was back in its place that the chief, standing precariously atop one of the tankers, announced: "Fair. Fourteen minutes twenty-two seconds to arrival on scene, fifty-eight seconds to deployment, eight minutes eleven seconds to retrieval. We've done better. Officers? Any comments?"

Lieutenant Silva Cristl raised her hand. "I have one. Giyt, you have to control your hose better. You got me pretty damn wet."

She was, at that. As a lieutenant of fire police Cristl was exempt from the more physical work of a wetdown, but she was soaked anyway. "Sorry," Giyt offered, resolutely not grinning at her.

The chief gave him a suspicious look. "So watch it next time," he ordered. "And get your damn slicker on. Now let's parade."

So Giyt, soaked and uncomfortable under the hastily donned slicker, learned that they weren't quite through for the day, after all. He clung to the pumper's rail as they retraced their path toward the town, now more sedately.

Back in the town they didn't head for the firehouse; they made a ceremonial tour, stopping to wheep their sirens in brief greeting before the firehouses of each of the other species. Giyt was interested to see that each of the other races evidently expected them. All the doors were open. All the fire-fighting equipment of the other companies was on display—green metal tractors for the Kalkaboos, a fleet of smaller, faster trucks for the Delts, an extension ladder for the Centaurians. From his position high on the truck he could see nothing of the equipment of the Petty-Primes, though the doors of their dollhouse-sized firehouse were open. Only the Slugs were missing. Their own firehouse, if they needed one at all in their dank surroundings, was no doubt down in their community. But in each of the others at least three or four members of their own fire companies were standing by, listening to the few words—squeals, gargles, grunts—that came out of the PA system as Chief Tschopp spoke to them through the translator microphone, inviting them all to the upcoming fair.

Then the tankers detached to refill at the lakeshore and the pumpers rolled back to their own firehouse; the chief reminded everybody that they would soon be receiving assignments for their duties at the upcoming fair, and it was over.

In the cart they shared to take them home, Lupe was all smiles. "So how did you like the wetdown, Evesham?" she asked, confident of the answer.

"Actually," he admitted, "I did. One thing, though. I noticed we seemed to have a lot more equipment than the other guys. Do we really need all that firepower?"

"Oh, hell, Evesham, you just wait and see. When we start getting brush fires in the dry season we'll be pumping the tankers dry every time we go out."

"Oh," he said, thinking. Dry season. He would have to do a little digging about Tupelo's seasons, too. He turned and peered up at the mountain, where a large cloud was hanging over the peak. He commented, "Looks like we're going to get rain today, though."

Lupe looked at him peculiarly. "Not from that, Evesham," she said. "That cloud's just orographic uplift. I guess the trade winds are starting early this time."

So there was another key term for Giyt to try to learn something about. But every time he thought he'd have a few moments to put in on a literature search, something stopped him. He had another report to read. Or he had to show up at the gateway to welcome the next arriving batch of colonists. Or Rina disappeared into the sanitary room for longer than usual, and he couldn't think of anything but the chance of miscarriage, hemorrhage, *some* damn pregnancy-related thing . . . until she at last came tranquilly out, smiling fondly at her husband's unnecessary concern.

After dinner that night Rina said, "Hon, let's let the dishes wait. I've got a better idea."

It was a clear invitation; but when they had finished doing what the invitation had intended, Rina propped herself up on one elbow to look at him quizzically. "Is something wrong?" he asked.

"That's what I was going to ask you, Shammy dear."

"Didn't you—"

"Sure I did, hon, but, I don't know, you seemed a little—well, I guess the word is restrained."

He made a joke of it. "Maybe it's time to get the whips and chains out."

"I could if you wanted me to," she said, startling him, but smiling to show she didn't mean it. "But I don't think that's the problem here, sport. I think you've got the baby on your mind."

"Well—"

"Sure you do, Shammy. Listen. You really don't have to treat me as though I were made out of spun glass. It'll be six or seven months, anyway, before we have to start being careful."

"I was just thinking," he began apologetically.

"I know what you were thinking, but you'd be surprised how hard it is to get rid of a baby." She gave him a considering look, then added, "I don't know if I ever told you, but I was pregnant once before."

"You had a baby?" He was suddenly wondering if there was some part of Rina left behind on Earth.

"Not quite. What I had was an abortion. I was fourteen. And my father found out about it." She was silent for a moment, then said, "I did kind of like the idea of having a baby of my own, but I didn't see how I could manage it. Dad sure wasn't going to raise a bastard for me in his house, and what else could I do? I didn't like the idea of being a welfare mother, didn't have any skills to earn a living. So I stuck it out for a while after the abortion, and then I ran away."

It seemed to Giyt that his wife was telling him this story for a reason. The way she was looking at him she seemed to want some reaction from him, but what that reaction should be, he could not guess. Awkwardly he took her free hand and placed it against his cheek.

Apparently it was the right response. She gave him a sudden grin. "You always thought I was pretty dim to give money to every panhandler who came by, didn't you, Shammy?"

"Dim? No, nothing like that!" he protested. "You're just a generous person."

"Not just generous. I owe the street people. They took me in, fed me, showed me places where I could sleep, away from the cops and the weather. If they had anything to eat, so did I. They didn't expect anything back, either. They even put up with the way I was, and I was a lot to put up with—a dumb, weepy teenager. I was a mess, Shammy, and they treated me as though I were a human being. But I didn't want to go on sponging off them."

She leaned over and kissed him. "You know something I've always appreciated about you, Shammy? You never once asked me why I became a whore."

"None of my business," he said gruffly, surprised to find himself touched.

"No," she agreed, "it wasn't, but I guess maybe it is now . . . Daddy. Anyway, that's how. Fifteen years old, how else could I make a living? And here I am." She hesitated. "But, Shammy, there's one thing I would like you to know. I screwed a lot of guys at one time or another. Mostly it was business, but sometimes not. But I never loved anyone else before you."

XII

The Centaurian colony had settled itself on Tupelo for only a few years when they had an unpleasant surprise. An exploring party of another species arrived. They were not welcome. In fact, they were the very people the Centaurians had been fighting their interminable war with, the sluglike inhabitants of Alpha Centauri's fourth planet.

Although the fighting in their home system had temporarily subsided, it very nearly began again on Tupelo. It was touch-and-go for a while, but the sides paused long enough to talk a bit before opening hostilities. They discovered they had much in common. The Slugs in the exploration party were as tired of war as the Centaurians. Cautiously, both sides agreed to try the experiment of peaceful coexistence. They even agreed to share the same island, though at some remove from each other, a decision made easier by the fact that the Slugs preferred the damper, danker climate of the jungle to the plains that had attracted the Centaurians. The two sides signed a solemn compact, undertaking to together occupy what they called the Planet of Peace without fighting, and they created a Joint Governance Commission to mediate any conflicts that might arise.

—BRITANNICA ONLINE, "TUPELO"

The Taste of Tupelo started a couple of days early for Giyt, when the hypermarket called to say his dress uniform for the fire company had arrived. "Fine," said Giyt, who had pretty much forgotten he'd ever ordered the thing. "I'll come right over to pick it up."

"We'll both come, Shammy," Rina told him when he'd hung up, "because I surely want to see what you're going to look like."

At the store Rina sat, peaceably chatting with another shopper, as Giyt pulled the drapes of the store's changing room behind him. It didn't take him long to get into the fire company's dress whites, with their silver buttons and silver-trimmed dress cap. He had never had any kind of uniform on before. And was startled to see how—appropriate?—it looked on him in the changing room's mirror.

Rina thought so, too. "Ah, Shammy," she whispered, tugging his collar straight when he came out, "you do clean up nice, you know?" But standing unexpectedly behind her was Chief Wili Tschopp.

"Very nice," he said. "Keep it on, Giyt. Listen, I heard you were here, so I came over. We need you to make a commercial for the fair. Why you? What do you mean, why you? Because you're the mayor, of course. Don't worry, it won't take long. The cameras are all set up right outside, and I've got your script right here."

So Evesham Giyt had another first for that day, because he'd never recorded a commercial before, either. It wasn't much trouble. All he had to do was read the script, which promised great food, wonderful rides, and such splendid entertainment as Olse Hagbarth playing authentic American jazz on her own piano and the six-year-olds from Ms. Hilda's dance class doing authentic American line dancing. It took three tries before Wili Tschopp was satisfied, but the real drain on Giyt's time didn't come until Rina discovered the commercial was going to be broadcast on the systems of all six of Tupelo's races, with the appropriate language dubbed in. Then Rina was so tickled by the idea of hearing her husband talk Delt or Slug that Giyt decided to give her a treat.

Trying to convert alien TV protocols to anything he had ever seen before took more time than Giyt had expected. But he had his own original recording to match against the ones the others used, and it was, after all, the kind of thing Evesham Giyt was inordinately good at. He took it for granted that the other races would have been eavesdropping on each other's newscasts all along. His guess was right, and after some hard digging he succeeded in unearthing their conversion programs.

The rest was easy. All he had to do was adapt their procedures to the Earth protocols. It was tedious work, but nothing he couldn't handle.

Pleased with himself, he displayed for Rina his own image barking, squealing, moaning in all five of the other languages. She was pleased, too. "Save them, hon," she instructed. When he asked what for she said, "Don't you think our child will want to see them someday?" And then Giyt had something else to ponder over.

The actual day of the Taste of Tupelo dawned to the usual artillery barrage from the expiation of Kalkaboo sins. The day was hot, dry, and, as it turned out, extremely long. Right after first light Giyt reported for duty. He got lucky. To reinforce the recorded messages that invited all the eeties to the fair Chief Tschopp ordered him onto a sound truck. So in the early morning Giyt bumped downhill over that horrible forest road to cruise the Slug settlement under the dam, wheeping the siren and reminding the Slugs over the translator loudspeakers that they, like everybody else on Tupelo, were really welcome to come to the Earther fair.

Apart from moments of terror that the fire engine would turn over as it pitched and jerked down the trail, the job could have been worse. Giyt could have been put to setting up the fair's booths and rides. Besides, it was a chance to take a good look at Slugtown. He would have been more comfortable if he hadn't been sweating in his full dress uniform. But it was bearable, and at least he wasn't the one who was faced with trying to drive the damn thing through the least watery sections of mud between the Slug huts.

By the time he was back at the fairground (which was the broad space of Sommermen Square before the portal, which Tschopp had commandeered for the occasion) he was convinced that every possible Slug had been well and truly told about the fair.

Giyt had seen fund-raising fairs before—barely. Sometimes he had caught a glimpse of them on TV, for that fraction of a second that it took him to realize that this was not a subject that interested him and to move on, sometimes from the window of an autocab that was passing one by and certainly didn't stop. That was as far as it went. At least since childhood he had never been disposed to attend one. Definitely he had never, ever, been one of the sweating crew that worked behind the game counters and in the refreshment stands and operated the children's rides.

In spite of all their efforts at drawing in the eetie colonists, most of the crowd was human. (If *crowd* wasn't too strong a term for the fifteen or twenty people wandering among the two dozen booths; but, as Matya de Mir pointed out when she relieved him for a ten-minute pee break, it was early yet and a lot of people were still at work.) Just after the opening there had been a considerable but brief invasion of Petty-Primes, four or five of their Designated Mothers shepherding what Giyt supposed to be every young one in the Petty-Prime colony. (Which was a lot. Petty-Primes had a very long childhood, which meant that by the time they reached sexual maturity they were fully educated and ready to be adult citizens.) But the Petty-Prime kits hadn't stayed long. They weren't allowed to eat anything the Taste of Tupelo offered. Worse, all the rides were too big, and all the games of chance too hard, for Petty-Prime children. The other eetie communities were represented mostly by two or three pairs of Slugs that were cruising silently around in their damp-conditioned carts, never stopping at any of the booths, but not leaving, either.

Giyt's own job was running what they called the coconut shy. It had hard rubber balls instead of coconuts, with an inviting pyramid of dolls and gadgets at the back of the booth for anyone who could knock one down. That did not often happen. The game was fixed. Each ball had a tiny cupro-nickel core, and Chief Tschopp had privately showed Giyt the button under the counter that would activate a continuously varying magnetic field between the contestant and the prizes. Not even the inhumanly skilled Delts could win unless Giyt let them. He didn't. As a result he had few customers at his booth, next to the wheel of fortune, across the way from the kitchen where Lupe and Rina, among others, were frying potatoes and chicken parts in a huge caldron of fat. Giyt kept looking across at them with concern. It was hot enough where he was; it had to be a lot worse next to the fryer, especially for two pregnant women.

A female voice interrupted his dark thoughts. It turned out to belong to Mariam Vardersehn, his predecessor as mayor of the human colony. "Morning, Giyt," she said, not sounding particularly friendly. "You want to turn off the magnet so I can try to get that Kewpie doll?"

He looked cautiously around, then did as she asked. All the same, she missed with the first three balls, fared even worse with the next three. That was enough. "The twins aren't big enough for dolls yet anyway," she said. "How are you liking being mayor?"

"So far, so good. I guess you don't miss it, though."

She gave him a look, then sighed. "Actually," she said, "it was better than changing diapers in this heat."

Her tone made Giyt give her a closer look. "You almost sound as though you'd like to have the job back."

"What does it matter what I'd like?" she asked moodily. "Only, if you ever make up your mind to quit, be sure to let me know."

So Giyt had something else to think about. As far as he could see, there was no way for Mariam Vardersehn to undo the election that had given him the mayoralty. Unless, of course, he were to resign, but he had no intention of that, if only because he didn't particularly like the woman. For that matter, in some moods he didn't even particularly like the job. But the fact that she seemed to want it back made it just that little bit more attractive to him.

Which, Giyt told himself with amusement, was pretty stupid, and when Hoak Hagbarth came by he was smiling at himself.

Hagbarth winked at Giyt, paid for three balls, missed with each of them, and grinned back at him. "You look happy. Business that good?" he asked.

Giyt, who had no way of knowing how business was supposed to be, shrugged. "I thought there'd be more people, after all the publicity we did. Did you see me on the other-race news broadcasts?"

Hagbarth looked startled. "How can you see the other-race broadcasts? They use their own systems." Then Giyt had to explain that, out of curiosity—he didn't say for the sake of giving his wife pleasure—he had spent some hard hours figuring out how to convert their standards to the ones the human colonists used. "Hey," Hagbarth said admiringly, "that's great. Show me how you did it sometime, will you?"

"Sure."

"I mean really," Hagbarth persisted. "You know you've got a lot of tricks up your sleeve that you say you're going to show me, but I'm still waiting."

"I'm sorry."

"Sorry don't cut it, Evesham. You know what we've got here, don't you? Just a handful of human beings among"—he looked around and lowered his voice—"all these freaks. We have to stick together. So any way we can help each other out, we have to do it, right? Or the freaks will win. Do you understand what I'm saying?"

Giyt nodded.

"I knew I could count on you," Hagbarth said, reaching across the counter to pat Giyt's arm. "We're all patriots here, aren't we? We just have to work at it a little harder than we would back home, that's all."

XIII

The provenance of the extraterrestrial race called "Kalkaboos" is unknown. From other evidence certain facts about it can be deduced. Their native planet's atmosphere appears to have been richer in oxygen than either Earth's or Tupelo's, though the difference is not normally enough to handicap the Kalkaboos in their life on Tupelo. Their planet's sun is almost certainly brighter than Earth's, particularly in the extreme ultraviolet frequencies, but it has never been identified.

The Kalkaboos were the third sentient race to arrive on Tupelo, considerably later than the Centaurians and the Slugs. When the Kalkaboos appeared, they presented a problem for the prior colonists. They had only two options: to resist the new arrivals or to permit them to join. Since resistance would almost certainly involve combat—and since both the Centaurians and the Slugs feared that such a conflict might easily escalate to involve themselves—they decided the lesser evil was to let the Kalkaboos remain, subject to their adhering to the terms of the Treaty of Perpetual Peace. After a short transition period the Kalkaboos, too, were granted a seat on the planet's Joint Governance Commission.

—Britannica online, "Tupelo"

When Tupelo's long, long evening began, the crowds at the fair picked up. Most of the human population put in an appearance for at least a half an hour or so—had little enough choice about it, really, because nearly all of them were relatives or neighbors of a fireman. A scattering of the other races appeared too. Giyt kept feeding balls to a whole Delt family—Papa, Mama, four half-grown young—as they doggedly did their best to knock off a cuckoo clock or a stuffed panda. Even with the magnets working against them they came close—came closer still when Giyt belatedly realized who the male was. "You haven't recognize?" the Delt asked aggrievedly. "I am he who have been you pilot voyaging to Energy Island, God's sake; we have good talk about you famous Earth-human liar Kepigay. How can you have forget?"

"Sorry," Giyt said. He started to reach out to shake hands with the Delt, then thought better of it; he didn't want any of that fetid Delt aroma coming off on him. Instead he surreptitiously switched off the magnetic field. After that it required only four shots from the female to collect three prizes.

Hastily Giyt turned the field back on. When he looked up one of the Delt's eyes was on his face, the other on the hand just emerging from under the counter.

"Thus I had thought," the Delt said amiably. His mate, burdened with her prizes, whispered something warningly in his ear, but the Delt waved her away. "Do not be lacking in intelligence, I not the sort of crude person to make impolite argument with Earth-human friend. You go on where you wish, co-parent. Take self and young to next such deceitful event. I remain a short space of time to ask something of Earth-human friend."

Giyt braced himself for the question as the Delt leaned forward on the counter, both eyes on Giyt and the slaughterhouse smell intense. There was no point in denying the game was fixed. The Delt was quite capable of leaping over the counter to find the switch for himself.

But that wasn't what was on the Delt's mind. "This 'president' person you possess on native planet home, who tell all other persons they not privileged to share in possession of certain secret information considered valuable. What this Earth-human president person being president of, exactly?"

It wasn't hard to explain what a sovereign country was to the Delt—once the Delt was willing to accept the explanation as fact, anyway; his first reaction was unbelieving laughter. But when Giyt finally convinced him that the statement that Earth possessed nearly two hundred quite independent nations wasn't some sort of ludicrous joke Giyt was trying to play on him, the Delt went away, chuckling to himself.

At least Giyt hadn't had to defend the fire company's slippery means of enhancing profits on the coconut shy. He took note of the fact that, in order to know what the American president had said, at least some of the eeties had to listen in on the news broadcasts from Earth. He wondered if Hagbarth knew that, and considered mentioning it to him. But business was picking up, and he put the thought away for later consideration.

The eetie leaders had begun to appear. Giyt caught a glimpse of the Divinely Elected Savior of the Centaurians, Mrs. Brownbenttalon, interestedly sampling the fried potatoes from Rina's booth across the way. It looked to Giyt as though her entire family was with her. Her principal husband was visible as he perched over her nose, nibbling a french fry and tenderly sticking bits of it in Mrs. Brownbenttalon's mouth. There was a younger female with her whom Giyt hadn't seen before, plus a retinue of subadult offspring and a clutch of helper-husbands to keep them in line.

When she spied Giyt she crossed over with her train to greet him. "Hope you stick it well, Mayor Large Male Giyt," she said cordially. "Now look." She pointed her snout at the young female. "This is my daughter, Miss Whitenose, very pretty, right?" Giyt agreed that Miss Whitenose was pretty—for a half-grown anteater, at least. "You give Miss Whitenose three balls," she requested, and the daughter of the house took them without enthusiasm. Without results, either; Centaurian anatomy was not built for throwing. Though Miss Whitenose elevated the first half of her body as much as physiology would allow for the purpose, her best toss barely made it to the base of the prize pyramid. Mrs. Brownbenttalon didn't seem perturbed; probably she had discovered at many a previous firemen's fair that there was no hope of winning at the coconut shy. "Miss Whitenose almost old enough to be fucked," her mother said with pride. "Soon we buy her some husbands from Mrs. Ruddyblaze family and have big party, you bet."

Giyt, unsure of how many intimate revelations of Centaurian sexual customs he wanted to hear, observed tactfully, "She seems to like french fries. I guess Centaurians can eat human food?"

"You bet." It was quite apparent that this was so. Even the smallest of her children were determinedly nibbling away at a french fry apiece. "Centaurians, humans, very similar metabolism; we eat anything you do except meat."

"No bubbly drinks, too," Miss Whitenose put in.

"Right. Bubbly drinks make us fart. Hey, I have question for you. Who have idea to bring kill-persons weaponry here, you or ugly Large Male Hagbarth?"

"Well, actually, yes, it was Hagbarth's suggestion in the first place," Giyt admitted.

"I think so. Very bad proposal. Took persons by surprise, so maybe got wrong idea, blamed you, mistake. No matter. You don't do it again, all right? So I have got idea. You come to Miss Whitenose First Fuck party, okay? We show you good Centaurian food—like this," she added, pointing to one of the smallest of her offspring. The tiny thing had finished its french fry and was now thrusting its nose into what looked like a segment of a bamboo stalk, held for it by one of the helper-husbands. "Bring female mate with you, she welcome. You will have grand enjoyment, don't worry. Now must take kids on dumb high circular ride."

As soon as she was gone in the direction of the Ferris wheel the Principal Slug arrived, purchased three balls, extruded a peduncle at its bottom to raise it to counter level, produced a skinny arm from the side of its body to throw the balls, missed by a meter or more three times, and left without a word. It was evidently time for all the mayors to put in their appearances. Even the Responsible One of the Petty-Primes gave the coconut shy a whirl—pretty hopelessly; he just didn't have the size to knock anything down, although in charity Giyt had turned off the magnetic field. The Responsible One moved on to the Ferris wheel in his turn without comment, just as the High Champion of the Kalkaboos arrived with a party of six.

Once they'd been sold three balls apiece they huddled for a long, low-voiced session of cheeping and screeching that Giyt's translator couldn't quite sort out. What it looked like to him was some Earthly gathering of good old boys organizing some sort of friendly competition—well, some sort of competition, anyway; the voices didn't sound all that friendly—but what they were mostly doing was keeping anyone else from getting to his booth. His attention wandered. He gazed around the fairgrounds, getting a glimpse of a pair of Slugs in the whirl-about ride, their gelatinous bodies plastered around the seats of the car, even their eyestalks retracted. The crowd was really becoming a crowd, he thought, and waved to catch his wife's eye as she doled out her portions of food across the way.

He didn't notice that the Kalkaboos had finished their conversation until one of them stepped rapidly up to the counter, fired a ball at the central stack of prizes, and knocked off a tempered-glass piggy bank. "Congratulations," Giyt said jovially, realizing he had forgotten to turn the magnetic field back on. But while he was picking up the piggy bank for the winner the second one was already there, knocking down a Kewpie doll. The third got another doll, the fourth a key chain in a large plastic box, the fifth a pocketknife. They were getting to the expensive stuff now, Giyt realized, and managed to switch the field back on just as the sixth Kalkaboo, their High Champion, fired his first ball.

He missed. It wasn't even close.

His retinue cackled jovial condolences at him. Or maybe not so jovial. The High Champion seemed to take his failure hard, and he turned and doggedly fired his second ball—equally far off the mark—and his third.

Breathing hard, he turned to glare at his companions, who were raucously taunting him on his failure to score. And then, without warning, the High Champion moaned and clutched his head and fell to the ground.

That stopped the chorus of friendly bickering. All five of the other Kalkaboos immediately surrounded their fallen High Champion, muttering inaudibly to each other, and then picked him up and carried him away.

XIV

Little is known of the religious observances practiced by most of the extraterrestrials with whom the human race shares the planet Tupelo. The Delts and the Petty-Primes don't seem to have any. Nor do the Centaurians, although their leader, puzzlingly, is referred to as their Divinely Elected Savior. The Slugs are said to be intensely religious, expressing their fervor in song. Unfortunately, all their hymns are sung in a special "divine" language, which the machine translators are not equipped to handle.

It is the Kalkaboos whose religious rituals are most public and thus best known. The most conspicuous of their customs is the one which requires them to "explode" and thus destroy each day's burden of sins by setting off small charges at the dawn of the next day. This has struck some observers as grotesque, but not nearly as grotesque as some other customs of the Kalkaboos.

—BRITANNICA ONLINE, "TUPELO"

The good thing about the High Champion's accident was that it happened so fast most of the fairgoers didn't even know what was going on. Chief Tschopp did, though, and descended on Giyt like a thundercloud. "Damn fool," he said. "You should've been watching what you were doing. Now we're going to have the goddamn High Champion sick in bed with a major oxygen-deficiency headache, and I'll be screwed if they don't make some sort of formal complaint before dark. How could you do this to the fire company, Giyt?"

Giyt had no answer, though the accusation was unjust . . . but, well, not entirely unjust, Giyt thought. He should have had the magnets back on before the Delts got there. And he had trouble getting to sleep, weary as he was, when at last the Taste of Tupelo was over and the firemen were allowed to go home and to bed.

When he woke up his first action was to call the High Champion's mates and ask the one who answered how he was doing. "The beloved person is resting," she said without further comment, and cut the connection before Giyt had a chance to apologize.

He sat down at his workstation and stared into space awhile, sipping coffee and brooding over the accident. It wasn't his fault, he told himself again. That raised the question of whose fault it was, but he figured that out quickly enough. The fault belonged to the fire company for secretly running crooked games at the fair. That wasn't honest. More to the point, the fact that the games were fixed probably wasn't a secret to at least some of the eeties. The Delt, for one, had been clearly aware he was being taken. And how did that look for Earth humans as a race? And all for the sake of making a few dishonest cues!

Did the fire company need money that badly? Just for curiosity's sake, he accessed the stats for the Taste of Tupelo in previous years. When he saw what they were, he stared into space a while longer. All bills paid, all receipts recorded, the Taste of Tupelo had never made a net profit of as much as six thousand cues—or, Giyt calculated, just about enough to pay for a new set of tires on a few, but not all, of the company's fire engines.

It wasn't worth it. He was still puzzling over it when Rina

called him to breakfast. Of course she picked up on his mood at once. The morning chorus of Kalkaboo firecrackers to announce the dawn—louder than usual, Giyt thought—made conversation difficult. But as soon as it was over, she asked, "Hon, are you worrying about that Kalkaboo?"

He blinked at her. He had almost forgotten the High Champion's mishap. "Oh, sure," he said. "Sort of. But mostly I was thinking about money."

"Money? Really? Is there something real expensive you want to buy?"

"No, that's not it. Not *our* money. The fire company's." But while he was trying to explain his carryphone rang with the fire company signal. It was an all-hands summons. "We'll talk about it later," he said, reluctantly getting ready to go over to the fairground to help break down the concessions.

This time the work was pure manual labor, not made easier by the way the other firemen joshed him about the Kalkaboo High Champion. Even Lupe gave him a couple of friendly jabs until she saw that he was really unhappy. Then she said, "Well, forget it, Evesham. Kalkaboos are always passing out for some reason or another; the atmosphere's too dense for them here or something. He'll be fine."

It was hot work, but not particularly hard work. It went quickly enough. What eased the labor was Ex-Earth's generosity with handling machines. Once the smaller pieces were crated and the booth walls were flat on the ground, three forklifts trundled up. They lifted the material onto a flatbed trailer, which carted them off for storage. Giyt went back to the firehouse with the last load, while others remained to tidy up the space the fair had occupied.

He had never been in the storage warehouse before. From the outside it looked like a low-roofed shed behind the firehouse. Inside it was dug deep into the ground, and a lot bigger than he had expected. All that space was needed, too, because it was crammed full of equipment: spare parts for the fire engines, extra hoses, even an entire additional pumper truck. One bin contained six additional water cannon, far bigger and more powerful than the ones mounted on the trucks. He gazed at them for a moment, puzzled, then turned to Lupe. "What are these things?"

She glanced at them and shrugged. "They're just extras. We don't use them. They're too powerful for the kind of work we do—I think back on Earth they demolish burning buildings with them. Hoak probably knows, if you want to ask him."

Giyt did, but not as much as he wanted to ask him about finances. But Hagbarth didn't show up at the firehouse, and when Giyt found a chance to call him the man announced he was really in a hurry. "Finances? Why are you worried about that kind of thing, Giyt? Well, tell you what I'll do, why don't I come over to your place after siesta, that okay?"

"That would be fine."

"Fine. And, oh, by the way. The High Champion's still in a coma."

"Coma?" Giyt was startled. "Nobody said anything about a coma!" But Hagbarth had already cut off.

Giyt slept poorly during the siesta. Long before it was time he slipped out of the bed, leaving Rina gently breathing behind, and placed another call to the mates of the High Champion. "In present condition of beloved High Champion is no change," the female Kalkaboo said, and cut off. The translation programs weren't adequate to let Giyt tell anything useful from her tone.

To take his mind off it, he went back to thinking about the community's finances. The wealth of material in the fire company's warehouse had been a total surprise to him, far more than a thousand Taste of Tupelos could ever hope to pay for.

He decided to dig a little deeper. It turned out that most of the data he wanted was in a secure file, though naturally not secure from Evesham Giyt. He accessed the community's whole balance sheet without difficulty.

What he found made him very thoughtful. Tupelo was a gilt-edged proposition, but basically a charity operation. They were living on handouts from Ex-Earth. Very generous ones. Somebody was investing a great deal of money in a venture that was providing next to no cash returns at all.

But *why?* Tupelo was a whole planet, undoubtedly packed with riches. In the days of Earth's conquerors they had gained more than military victories, they had gained sources of gold, spices, rare woods, treasures of many kinds. Why couldn't Tupelo pay its own way in the same fashion? Charity was all very well, but what if the philanthropists ever got tired of giving?

When Hagbarth arrived, looking mildly resentful at Giyt's imposition on his time, the first question Giyt had for him was: "What happens if Ex-Earth runs out of money?"

Hagbarth gave him a suspicious look, then relaxed. "Don't worry yourself about that. Never happen, Giyt. Ex-Earth is *loaded."*

"It looks that way, all right. But where does the money come from?"

Hagbarth shrugged. "Public-spirited citizens. People concerned about the future of the human race—hell, Giyt, all that should have been in your briefing materials. You didn't get any?" He rolled his eyes. "What can I tell you? Ex-Earth pays the recruiters so much a head for volunteers, so once they've got you to sign up, what do they care? Anyway, the money's there. We have pledges from some of the richest people in America, and some of the biggest corporations, too. And I'm not talking about just one-time donations. They've all made fifty-year pledges, and they'll keep their words."

Giyt nodded. "And what happens when the fifty years run out? There's what left, thirty-five years or so?"

"Long enough not to worry," Hagbarth said, smiling.

"For you and me, maybe. But I do worry. I've got a child coming."

Hagbarth said sympathetically, "Yeah, I see what you mean. Olse and I haven't been that lucky, so maybe I haven't really thought much about that kind of thing. I guess we figured if Ex-Earth pulled the plug we could just go back to Earth and retire."

"But what if we don't want to do that?" Giyt persisted. "If we have a kid that grows up here, what's he going to do back on Earth? Besides, my wife likes it here."

"That doesn't surprise me," Hagbarth said shortly.

His tone made Giyt look at him in surprise, but Hagbarth's face wasn't giving anything away. "Well, what I've been thinking," Giyt said, "it doesn't have to be that way. Couldn't we pay for ourselves?"

"Pay how?"

"Ship stuff back to Earth. Earn money."

"Well, we do the best we can that way, Giyt. You know that. We send back all that souvenir stuff to Earth that we make here—"

"That's not money, Hoak. The amounts involved are pitiful. We should try to earn real money. The other races do, don't they? I mean, they're always sending local stuff home through the terminal. I presume it earns money for them. We could do the same."

Hagbarth was looking wary but no longer suspicious. "What kind of local stuff?"

"Organic materials, for a start. The Petty-Primes ship

whole saplings and bushes back, roots and all; I think it's so they can be checked for possible pharmaceuticals or new food crops, that sort of thing. Why don't we? And the Delts do a lot of manufacturing. We could do much more of that, too. Not just gadgets—real goods. We've got metals and stuff from the polar mines. We could build things—some to ship home for credit, a lot for ourselves right here."

Hagbarth pursed his lips. "You've never been to the polar mines yet, have you? Sure, they've got processing stuff up there, but most of it isn't ours. We just have a little corner of the works. What you call boutique factories, you know? Anything big, they don't do much more than forty or fifty copies in a run."

"So we can build some new factories, can't we? So there will be something the Tupelo humans can do to earn money instead of living on handouts?"

Hagbarth looked as though he was tiring of the subject. "Well," he said, "maybe you've got something there and maybe you don't, but I guess it could be looked into. Tell you what. When the Earth commissioners come for the six-race meeting I'll see if I can get them to send some specialists along, check over what the possibilities are here. How would that be?"

"Fine," said Giyt, making a mental note to remind Hagbarth of his promise.

"Then that's settled. I'd better be getting along—and listen, you won't forget about those programs for me, will you? Because—oh, wait a minute."

He paused, listening to a message from his carryphone. Then he looked angrily at Hagbarth. "Shit," he said.

"What's the matter?"

"It's the goddamn Kalkaboo High Champion. He just died."

"Died? But I thought . . . Oh, hell, that's too bad."

"Yeah, well, they'll be boiling him all night—"

"Boiling?"

"It's what they do, Giyt. So the funeral will be at dawn tomorrow, and you'd better be there. See, basically they figure you killed him."

XV

Well, what do you say, folks and folkesses? Did we have one grand time at the Taste of Tupelo yesterday or did we not? The beer was cold, the rides were fun, and weren't those little kids just adorable? Even the eeties. Sure, if you're the picky kind of person that's always looking for the worm in the mango you can say a few things went kind of wrong. I'm sorry I had to arrest two of our citizens—I'm not going to say their names over the air, but you all know who they are—but, hey, a night in the cooler straightened them right up, and they'll be home with their loved ones this morning. And it's too bad what happened to the Kalk High Muckamuck, but if the Kalks can't play a friendly game of chance without throwing some kind of a tizzy fit when they lose, whose fault is that? Anyway, I'm sure we all join in offering our sincere sympathy to his spousal units and all the other Kalkaboos for his funeral services this morning.

But what's the use of looking at the dark side? Put it all together, it was a great Taste, and I want to be the first one to rise and move that we pass a real vote of gratitude to Chief Wili Tschopp and his hard-working, fun-loving men and women of the volunteer fire company, even if, heh-heh, I happen to be one of them myself.

—Silva Cristl's early morning chat

The funeral of the High Champion, like all major Kalkaboo events, took place at dawn. So an hour before daybreak Giyt had to visit the Kalkaboo general store in order to buy a firecracker for the ceremonies.

Giyt had never been in the Kalkaboo store before. It was crowded. Nearly everyone else present, naturally enough, was a Kalkaboo. None of them spoke to him, and they looked at him, if at all, only out of the corners of their eyes, but he recognized that they were all on the same errand as himself.

What puzzled him was what size firecracker to buy. The Kalkaboos themselves were buying all sizes, from tiny beads to things the size of a baseball. He looked around for a friendly face but found none. He did, however, see the Petty-Prime Responsible One picking up something about as big as a thumbnail, which emboldened him to reach for another of the same size from the bin.

It was the wrong choice. A feathery hand snaked past him to clasp his own, and the voice of the translator in his ear snapped, "No. Not adequate. Come with." And a Kalkaboo Giyt did not recognize led him to the back of the store. There was a muttered exchange with a clerk, who retired to the storeroom for a moment and emerged with what looked like a bright blue grapefruit. "Pay now," Giyt was ordered. "This little other thing is detonator for making bomb bang. Don't push till it's time. Now go."

The object weighed twenty kilograms at least. By the time he got it to the cart, where Rina was waiting, he was panting.

For the ceremonial the Kalkaboos had preempted the square in front of the transporter, the same space that had held the Taste of Tupelo just a day earlier. As Giyt and Rina got out of their cart they found they could smell the late High Champion even before they saw the pot he had cooked in. Actually he smelled rather appetizing, a bit like a lamb stew. Rina had hurried next door for advice and so had been able to explain to her husband that, yes, Hagbarth hadn't lied. Kalkaboos simmered their dead overnight. Lupe didn't think you could call it a religious thing, exactly, but it was certainly a pretty much inviolable custom, like the human habit of embalming. What they did with the corpse afterward was unclear, because Rina hadn't had time to get more details from the de Mirs. As they sniffed the odor of cooking High Champion Giyt and Rina stared at each other with a wild surmise. "You don't suppose—" Rina began.

"Jesus, I hope not," said Giyt. But as they got out of their cart, Giyt gingerly holding his penance under one arm and the detonator in the other hand, they saw that there was food, all right, but of a more conventional sort. Most of the crowd was milling around a dozen huge and fully laden banquet tables.

"What do we do, Shammy?" Rina whispered. "We can't eat Kalkaboo food."

Giyt shrugged, grateful that at least they were apparently not expected to eat Kalkaboos. Where the crowd of mourners was thickest, Giyt could see the intact body of the late High Champion, removed from its cooking pot and slowly cooling inside a glass-sided sort of coffin. Or fish tank, because it seemed to be filled with water. The High Champion floated submerged inside, eyes closed, arms folded over his chest, the great floppy ears stirring slowly in the water. He was nude. Apart from that, simmering in a stewpot all through the long Tupelovian night didn't seem to have changed his looks much. Next to the High Champion's tank were three large covered pots, each with a Kalkaboo standing beside it as though guarding its contents.

The big question on Giyt's mind was what to do with his huge firework. Nearly every person present, at least a thousand Kalkaboos and a representative or two of each of the other races, had a firecracker of his or her own, though he didn't see any that approached the mass of his own monster.

He wondered what they were planning to do with the things. It didn't seem sensible to set them off at random in this crowd, especially his own mammoth one. And the question was becoming urgent, because he could see the sky already graying around the island's central mountain.

An elderly female Kalkaboo solved the problem for him. She came hurrying through the mob, made an expression of astonishment when she saw the size of what he carried, then beckoned him to follow her to a roped-off enclosure strewn with what looked like egg cups, in varying sizes, made of solid metal. Mourners were putting the larger firecrackers into the cups, and the largest cup of all, a hundred-kilo giant of fire-stained steel, appeared to be reserved for Giyt. When his burden was emplaced, the female hurried him out of the enclosure and bade him stand just outside the rope. He looked around for Rina, but she was lost in the crowd.

Then a drumbeat sounded. The crowd became silent, all turned toward the east, and just as the first edge of the sun popped over the mountaintop, the salvos began. Each Kalkaboo with a small firecracker tossed it into the enclosure. They exploded on impact. At first it was only sharp rifle cracks as the smaller ones went off; then one of the Kalkaboos holding a detonator like Giyt's own pressed it. Then there was a larger blast, then a series of them, and then Giyt sighed and pushed the button for his own giant charge. Orange flame leaped up toward the sky. The concussion almost knocked him over, and the immense explosion nearly deafened him; and then it was over.

All the Kalkaboos around Giyt were looking at him with expressions that might have been respect, or equally well could have been loathing. He glanced uneasily toward their waiting cart, but Rina firmly shook her head; it wasn't time to leave yet. After a moment the mourners began chattering among themselves, turning toward the tank that held the late High Champion.

The Kalkaboos standing by the pots had the covers off now, and one by one they raised their pots and dumped the contents into the tank. Giyt had a confused impression of something moving about in the fall of water from the pots, and then he saw what it was. Each pot had been filled with a dozen or more eel-like things, each a few centimeters long, and as soon as they were in the tank they went about the business of feeding on the stewed carcass of the recent High Champion.

Someone tapped him on the shoulder. He turned to see the female who was his guide, and she was speaking to him. He had to turn up his earpiece to hear her say, "They eat. We eat. You eat," demonstrating the translation program's skill at declining at least the simplest verb forms, as she urged him toward the buffet tables.

Well, Rina and Giyt didn't eat there, exactly, although they did nibble. The Kalkaboos were knowledgeable enough to have provided some human-edible cheeseburgers, bought frozen from the human store; not quite knowledgeable enough to have defrosted them. The Giyts gnawed politely around the edges as best they could, but not for long. As soon as Giyt saw a chance they stole away, found their cart, and headed for home, where they dumped the remains of the cheeseburgers into the disposer.

By then Giyt's ears had stopped ringing, and enough of his hearing had returned to let him put in a little preparatory work at his station before heading for the weekly commission meeting. All the same, he resolved to do his best to avoid running up any more Kalkaboo expiation bills, however unfairly accrued. One of those monster firecrackers had been enough to last him. It was the sort of thing, he thought, that was better employed in blowing up tree stumps, or maybe demolishing small houses.

But all in all, Giyt was fairly well pleased with himself. He had met the obligations of the situation with reasonable credit, and when he arrived at the Hexagon he was prepared to present his very first original proposal to the group.

He was early, but not as early as the Responsible One of the Petty-Primes or the Principal Slug, who were whispering to each other at the Slug podium. Mrs. Brownbenttalon arrived a moment later and greeted Giyt. "Hey, Large Male Giyt, you make good bang, eh?"

"Oh, were you there? I didn't see you."

"No," she agreed good-naturedly, "you much too occupied with hellish big bang. How you like dopey Kalkaboo funeral? After disgusting little snakes eat meat they burn decedent's bones, you know? And then lucky Kalkaboos each get one disgusting snake to keep for pet." She paused to listen as her husband muttered in her ear. "Oh, right. Listen. Tonight we do Miss Whitenose First Fuck party. You need to cheering up now, so you and mate come, okay? Now got to chair dumb meeting. Not to take long because we probably got to have dumb Kalkaboo ritual real fast."

"What ritual?" Giyt asked, staring after her, but she had already scuttled to her post at the Centaurian point of the Hexagon as the Delt General Manager arrived.

That was, evidently, as full a quorum as they were going to get. There was no one at the Kalkaboo podium, only a glass fishbowl that, Giyt saw incredulously, contained one of the eel-like things, torpidly swimming as befit a creature with a very full belly. Mrs. Brownbenttalon clicked one of her claws against the lectern and said, "Okay, meeting called to order. You all got all reports, read when you feel like, nothing special, so move to accept, okay? Good. Now, since there no other business—"

Giyt hadn't expected her to move so fast, but he was

ready. "Madam Divinely Elected Savior Brownbenttalon," he called, "I do have some other business."

That stopped her for a moment. She peered silently at him over the fur on her long nose, beady little eyes blinking. "Mayor Large Male Giyt, have not available time at present time for necessary time for unknown other business."

"I'll just be a moment," he reassured her, and went right on. "What I want to talk about is a proposal for a joint six-peoples effort to make better use of the resources of Tu—of our planet. We could start with the possibility of finding useful new pharmaceuticals to return to our home planets. I am sure most of you have already surveyed the, ah, biota of this island and the ones nearby, and no doubt you've long since found many valuable substances. Unfortunately, my own planet has not been so enterprising, and we have a lot to do to catch up. But, unless I am mistaken—and I've discussed this with Mr. Hoak Hagbarth—none of you have actually conducted a similar investigation of the biota of the other island chains on this planet. Yet they may have things of great value. I understand that, because of the great distances, there has been little or no contact between the different island arcs since the time of the planet's K-T incident, and so their biota may be quite different from our own here." He glanced at his notes, taken from his time with the data file earlier. When he looked up they were all staring at him. "It is a matter of relict populations and mutations," he explained. "The relict populations may be quite similar to our own—though there might be considerable differences because of differences in climate—but the mutations, which are quite random, will surely have produced many new species and varieties, perhaps even quite new genera." He paused, gazing at Mrs. Brownbenttalon uncertainly. "Am I going too fast for you?"

She made a noise that might have been a snicker. "Actually too slow, Mayor Large Male Giyt. Making great demands on patience of new Kalkaboo High Champion, who waiting for meeting end. Look, he entering now for ritual combat."

It was the first Giyt had heard of the ritual combat. He didn't know what she was talking about, but as the new High Champion came grimly in, followed by a dozen sullen-looking dignitaries of his community, it was all quickly explained. "Earth Human Mayor Giyt," the Kalkaboo announced, "you have caused the death of our beloved former High Champion, and as successor of same I must wipe out unendurable stain on Kalkaboo honor. Prepare self for combat!"

And he sprang at Giyt over the audience seats, floppy ears flopping, scrawny arms outstretched to claw at him.

Giyt had never thought of himself as a warrior, didn't like fighting at all, and had done very little of it in his life. Nevertheless, in high school he and every other student had had to take the compulsory martial-arts courses just to give them a fighting chance of making it home after class.

In any case, the Kalkaboos were not a large race; Giyt was twice the size of the new High Champion–elect. He ducked those grasping arms, bent, caught the eetie around the waist—his scrawny body was much hotter than Giyt's—and threw him two meters across the room.

The Kalkaboo yelped in astonishment, tried to get up, yelped again, and lay there, clutching one shoulder and glaring up at Giyt. "Are Earth humans insane?" he whimpered. "What you did that for?"

"Jesus, Giyt," Hagbarth complained, "what did you do that for?"

Giyt protested, "He jumped me. Anyway, it was a fair fight."

"Asshole! It wasn't any kind of fight at all. It was just one of those damn Kalkaboo customs, for God's sake. All you were supposed to do was take a fall and let him claim victory—you know, to avenge what you did to the guy before him, so he could confirm his claim to the job—and then everything would've been fine."

Giyt blinked at him. "Take a fall?"

"Quit. Bare your throat. Tell him he won," Hagbarth explained. "Are you having trouble understanding me? That's what you should have done. But no, you had to make a real fight out of it. Jesus, man! I guess I'm lucky you didn't just kill him, too, and I don't think they've got a firecracker big enough for that."

XVI

Funeral services for Dr. Fitzhugh J. Sommermen were held today at Washington National Cathedral, after which his ashes were placed in the Great Columbarium in Arlington Cemetery. At the interment the president gave a short commemorative address, calling Dr. Sommermen "a true American hero, modest, dedicated, and strong." The president added, "What this great man did for his country will live forever in the memories of all Americans, for it was he who opened America's pathway to the stars." Interestingly, almost none of the foreign dignitaries who had been invited for the ceremony attended.

—EARTH NEWS BROADCAST

A few months of being a public figure had done one thing for Evesham Giyt. It had taught him all the ways in which private was better. A public person had no hidden humiliations. They were all right out in the open and, in a community as small as Tupelo's, there seemed to be no person of any age, gender, or species who didn't know all about Giyt's. Not that most people were hostile—that is, not counting the Kalkaboos, who unanimously froze him with silent glares of loathing at every chance. But most of the rest of the population, human and eetie, seemed to think the whole situation was just a pretty good joke.

It was a joke Giyt tired of pretty quickly. So although Mrs. Brownbenttalon's party was within reasonable walking distance, Giyt called a cart to take them there. Walking would mean that passersby could say things to him along the way that Giyt didn't want to hear. He wondered briefly if they were still welcome at the Centaurians'. Rina, thrilled at the idea of a party, did her best to reassure him. "Don't sweat it, hon," she coaxed. "You made a mistake, but nobody warned you, did they?"

Nobody had. Least of all the one person who should have, Hoak Hagbarth; and one of these days, Giyt thought as they got out of the cart, he ought to talk to the man about that.

Mrs. Brownbenttalon's home was a lot more lavish than anything else Giyt had seen on Tupelo. As the official residence of the Centaurians' Divinely Elected Savior it was built on the grand scale. It consisted of four or five smallish but brightly colored one-story structures, connected by breezeways. Like an ancient Roman villa, the whole thing surrounded a pretty garden with a reflecting pool and a stand of bamboo-like trees rustling against each other in the breeze. The whole thing looked more California than Tupelo to Evesham Giyt, and he was surprised to see how many guests were present. Ten or twelve of them were Centaurian matriarchs like Mrs. Brownbenttalon herself: another several dozen were their most favored husbands along with a fair number of young ones; but the mayor equivalents of most—though, conspicuously, not quite all—of the other races were also on hand. The only Tupelovian race wholly absent was the Kalkaboos, and Giyt had a good idea of why.

Miss Whitenose came to greet Rina and Giyt as they got out of their cart. It was her party, and she was enjoying being the center of attraction. "Most excellently nice you come," she said. "You eat something? Good Centaurian edibles here, all checked by Ex-Earth chemists many long times since, quite okay for your species to process and excrete." She clicked her front talons together without looking over her shoulder. Immediately two or three males leaped forward bearing the sort of bamboo joints, sealed at both ends, that Giyt had seen at the firemen's fair. Miss Whitenose took the two largest, held them to her ears for a moment, then expertly opened one end of each and offered them to the Giyts. "Dopey Earth-human meal-handling utensils," she said to the air, and two more males eagerly proffered tapered ceramic spoons. "You eat this excellent provision," she ordered.

The joint was warm, and when Giyt sniffed at its contents they smelled faintly Italian—some kind of Parmesan-like cheese, he guessed, though as far as he knew Centaurians kept no dairy animals. He glanced at Rina, who smiled at him, dipped her spoon into the open top of the joint, and tried it out. "Oh, nice," she said appreciatively. "Give it a try, Shammy. You'll like it."

As a matter of fact he did. What was inside the bamboo joint was a sort of pudding, the texture of an avocado but with crunchy little sticklike things in it. It tasted, as much as anything, like a well-prepared risotto, with a few spices he could not identify.

"Delicious," he said. Miss Whitenose nodded graciously.

"I tell you this already," she said, and clicked her talons again. Whereupon the hovering males dashed away to a row of cooking pots, returning to their task of helping other males boil up additional segments. Miss Whitenose didn't look after them but made a soft, snickering noise. "They new husbands just purchased for me," she explained proudly. "Work asses off, hope to be picked for great honor of to be first to do me. Now come meet other guests."

She led the way to where Mrs. Brownbenttalon was holding court, reclining on an elevated cushion and chatting with five or six other beings at once—a pair of other Centaurian matriarchs, plus two half-grown females younger than Miss Whitenose, and several members of other races. Giyt recognized the Principal Slug, the Delt General Manager, and the Petty-Prime Responsible One and his wife—well, one of his wives, anyway; Giyt was not very clear on Petty-Prime mating customs.

To his surprise, the tiny Responsible One climbed up on one of the seats and thrust his paw toward him for a handshake. "Excellent see you, Earth Mayor," he piped. "Interesting combat this day at meeting."

Giyt swallowed a spoonful of the pudding. "I can explain—" he began.

"What explain? You bitch damn Kalkaboo up, about time. Make too goddamn much noise every dawning, get sick and tired of it."

"Have awful bad breath, too," the Principal Slug said—or slurped; Giyt could hear the slushy, wheezy sound of his voice even above the translation in his ear. And Mrs. Brownbenttalon said, "Kalkaboos pissed off in major way now, you know. Won't come Miss Whitenose First Fuck party because you here. Who care? Of course," she added casually, "now they tell everyperson you trying steal everyperson private secrets, take good stuff, send home to Earth-human planet."

That made Giyt blink. "Are you talking about the proposals I made at the commission meeting? But that's not what I was suggesting at all. I simply proposed that everybody get together, all six races, and make a systematic survey of what this planet has to offer. I'm sure we'd find resources that could be exploited for everybody's benefit."

"Yes, idea is quite preposterous, have understood completely," Mrs. Brownbenttalon agreed, and the Petty-Prime said, "Preposterous, naturally, but also very sweet. Obviously you are being quite kindly person, Earth Mayor Giyt. Too bad so ignorant."

* * *

It was Rina who rescued Giyt from that conversation; they had to circulate, she said, and they circulated. A couple of subadult Centaurian males were beating softly on sacks of something or other that gave off a muffled sound—not a very pleasing sound to Giyt's ears, but at least Centaurian music wasn't loud. The Giyts paused by the refreshment tables, studying the contents. Rina ventured to try what appeared to be a canapé—a sort of pale lavender rosebud capped with a dab of what looked like brown sugar—but grimaced at the first bite and looked for a place to put it down. Giyt accepted a bamboo tube of something to drink from an eager male servant; it was more like prune juice than anything else, but mildly alcoholic and not too awful to drink. He was still brooding over the conversation with the others. "But I was only suggesting mutual cooperation," he muttered in Rina's ear, and she shook her head.

"We'll talk about it later, Shammy, okay? This is a *party*. And, look, I think the bride is about to make a choice."

At the center of the atrium Mrs. Brownbenttalon had moved over on her dais and her daughter had joined her. The two females whispered to each other, glancing and pointing at one or another of the prospective bridegrooms, all of them belly-down on the ground before the dais, their eyes closed and their whole bodies quivering.

There was a ritual to the selection process. Miss Whitenose was juggling a mittful of objects, some ordinary pebbles along with one of those lavender rosebuds. After a considerable amount of whispering with her mother she abruptly tossed one of the pebbles at a male, who turned and crept mournfully away. Another pebble; another disappointed suitor. Then when only one was left, she threw the rosebud hard and clean at the remaining one, who yelped in joy, leaped up onto the dais and burrowed into the curls of her fur.

Giyt glanced wonderingly at Rina, who returned his look; but after a moment of applause from the audience Miss Whitenose gracefully came down from the dais and headed for one of the smaller buildings. Mrs. Brownbenttalon turned to Giyt, cackling. "I know what you think," she said. "You think she going do it right in front of us, correct? But no, not at all, young couple don't need bunch people hanging around staring at them when they do all-important first fuck. Take mind off serious business they busy at, you see? But we naturally got cameras in private doing-it room, keep record in family database so children can someday see actual impregnation which produced selves. You Earth humans do similar ritual, wedding album thing, right? So everybody come along, we observe performing on the TV!"

When the party seemed to be ending the guests lined up to take their leave of Miss Whitenose—no, Giyt realized, she was Mrs. Whitenose now, a full matriarch in the Centaurian community. Giyt absently joined the end of the line, Rina's hand in his. At least one question had been settled. He had wondered how somebody the size of Mr. Brownbenttalon was able to stick it to somebody the size of Mrs. Brownbenttalon, but the TV screen had given him the answer. It turned out that the biggest part of a Centaurian male was his sexual organ. Like a whale's, it was invisible in normal life, because he kept it rolled up inside him until needed, but then—

He stole a glance at Rina, and was not surprised to see that she was wearing a faint, contemplative smile. "Jealous?" he murmured.

She blinked and looked up at him, but before she could respond, Giyt became aware that something was tugging at his trouser leg. It was Mr. Brownbenttalon. "You don't go yet," he whispered. "Honored wife say please you stick around, we talk on assorted subjects, get to know each other better, okay? Just have patience few ten minutes while junior males and kids clean up."

So the Giyts dropped out of the line and sat quietly, watching the cleaning-up procedure. One of Mrs. Whitenose's lesser husbands brought them stalks of the pruney beverage and offered more of the foods. Rina declined hers. "Shammy, hon? Mr. Brownbenttalon invited me to look at their kitchens," she said. "All right if I snoop around a bit?"

"Snoop away." Giyt comfortably sipped from his bamboo tube—yes, the liquid definitely was alcoholic—as he watched her chatting with the males and subadult females as they bustled around cleaning up. The whole household was busy. One group of males was burning the debris, another thriftily carrying away the uneaten food, a third sawing sections from the stacked bamboo stalks. Giyt wondered absently if their own child would be as helpful around the house. Then he wondered what it was going to be like to have a child in the house in the first place. He hoped the de Mirs would stay on as neighbors. That way their own child would have playmates right next door, and teenage babysitters handy when they reached that point. . . .

A voice piped in his ear: "Are you being done okay, Large Male Giyt? Plenty food, plenty beverage? You want more, easily got." Giyt turned to see Mr. Brownbenttalon gazing up at him, his little claws poised to click for service. Giyt forestalled him.

"No, I'm fine." He thought for a moment, then decided it was a good time to apologize. "Listen, I'm sorry if my being here kept the Kalkaboos away."

Mr. Brownbenttalon reared back on his hind legs, snout elevated toward Giyt. He was hissing faintly in embarrassment. "Please!" he begged. "Extreme discourtesy to revered wife if have substantive talking in absence of her beloved presence, okay?"

"Well, of course, but I only meant—"

"Please! All right discuss weather, extreme handsomeness of Mrs. Whitenose new husbands, unpleasant odor of Delts, sports events. Things that nature. Not thing of significance."

Giyt sighed. "Sure," he said. And when all the things of no significance had been used up, Mr. Brownbenttalon was satisfied. He went away, furiously clicking at the way the lesser males were doing their housekeeping.

Giyt was content to be left alone. He found talking about nothing hard work. Being abandoned in solitude wasn't all that much better, though. It gave him time to reflect on his numerous blunders, and about what sort of unforeseen unpleasantness was likely to strike next, and most of all about the—not exactly unpleasant, but certainly *worrying*—fact of Rina's pregnancy. He wondered if the excitement of the party was really good for her. There was no point in asking Rina about it, of course. She would just laugh at him. Fondly, to be sure, but still—

He heard her call his name and saw her threading her way among the busy male Centaurians toward him. She had a bamboo segment in her hand and a faintly startled, mostly amused expression on her face. One of the younger Centaurian males was tagging patiently after her. "Look at this, Shammy," she ordered.

He took the piece of bamboo in his hand, turning it over. It seemed to be filled with some green, pith-like plant substance, but—

He yelped and almost dropped the segment. The Centaurian male darted quickly in to catch it and scuttle away. "Did you see?" Rina asked. "That little thing like a lizard in it? The cook just took it out of a cage and put it in there; now he's going to cap it off with the lizard thing inside. And then, when it's eaten everything, they boil up everything that's left in the tube."

Giyt felt his stomach go queasy. "And that's what we've been eating? Lizard shit?"

"Well, that's one way to put it," she admitted. "Tasted good, though, didn't it?"

Giyt was spared answering because Mrs. Whitenose appeared. You could not say she was sprightly—that sort of step did not go with the low-slung Centaurian anatomy—but there was something self-satisfied about the way she moved.

"Thank you to wait so long," she said. Giyt caught a glimpse of two little eyes peeping out of the fur on her back: her new husband, silent, perhaps exhausted from his recent efforts. Mrs. Whitenose added: "My mother asks you come talk a bit now. Present moment is time of feeling-good relaxation. You know saying about parties? Extraordinarily delighted see guests come, even more extraordinarily delighted see them go away again—but listen, not meaning present company, of course."

Mrs. Brownbenttalon was lying comfortably on a mossy mound of earth, with her main husband now affectionately grooming the fur above her eyes and a lesser husband pouring little glass cups of a beverage for the guests. When Giyt took a sip he almost choked; this wasn't the juice he'd had before. It was distilled, had to be close to a hundred proof, and not bad.

Mrs. Brownbenttalon was solicitous. "You like? This good stuff. Don't serve at party, guests get too rotten drunk, make fights, especially stinky Slugs."

"Also Earth-human Large Male Hagbarth," Mrs. Whitenose put in.

"Oh, yes, bad guy, Hagbarth. When he here he awful, you know? He act like he think he hot waste product. Very contemptuous of races wiser far than, excuse me, Earth humans.

We do not do that way. Our practice is always judging individuals, not races, even stinky Kalkaboos," she said grandly. "You okay Earth human, Large Male Giyt. We think."

"Well, thank you," Giyt said, looking around. More Centaurians were showing up as their chores were finished, lesser males and subadults, silently congregating at a respectful distance around the matriarchs to listen.

"You are welcomed. Well, what about party? Have good time? You like food?" When both the Giyts expressed admiration for the food, she bobbed her long nose in agreement. "Always good have plenty fine food. When Pentagon is full, bellies fill themselves."

"Pentagon?"

"Sure, Pentagon. That what you Earth humans call building with five sides," she instructed him. "Is place where us five Divinely Elected Saviors on Joint Governance Commission congregated before large-male Earth humans arrived. Much debate about what do with you guys when you dumb little machine ship arrive, you bet!" she said, cackling. All the males and children cackled too; only Mrs. Whitenose, seemingly lost in a dreamy reverie, was silent. "Then decided purpose of peace-treaty planet was to learn peace, right? Needed for survival of rest of us? Probably needed for survival with you large-male persons, too, so voted in, no dissent."

The male on her back giggled and squealed, "*Much* dissent, actually." But Mrs. Brownbenttalon reached up with her hind leg and swatted him amiably.

"Not dissent," she corrected. "Discussion, of course. For many days—Slugs objected at first, too many vertebrates—but finally unanimous. So sent you guys portal thing so you come here."

Giyt frowned in surprise. "You *sent* the portal?"

"Of course sent portal. What else?"

"But . . . Professor Sommermen . . . "

"Ah," she said, her snout wrinkling in comprehension. "That large-male Earth-human guy—what he just do, Mrs. Whitenose?"

Addressed, her daughter roused from her fond daydream. "He die."

"Sure, he die. Remember myth now. Like Santa Claus, you know? Like myth of non-Earth-people persons coming to Earth planet in crockery dishes, abducting Earth humans for sexual games."

"Yuck," said Mrs. Whitenose.

"Yes, typical Earth-human myth," her mother said. "Bizarre but very sweet. You didn't know?"

Giyt glanced at his wife to see how she was taking all this. Better than he was, he thought. She looked interested and amused. Doing his best to control himself, he said, "I'm sorry, but I don't know what you're talking about. Didn't Dr. Sommermen invent the portal?"

"Him? Large-male Earth human? Invent portal?" She was giggling at the idea, and so were her husband and daughter. "No way! Take damn good wizardly science knowledge for building portal, you don't have. Can't get, either," she added complacently, "because portal constructed so you guys can't open up, else biggest damn bang ever. Of course, now all are most glad your people are here," she added hospitably. "Most your people, anyway."

"Not counting Large Male Hagbarth, we mean," Mrs. Whitenose put in.

Giyt didn't know what sort of expression his own face was displaying until he saw the way Rina was looking at him. She patted his shoulder. "Don't take it so hard, hon," she said.

It was certainly good advice. The trouble with taking it was that he was indeed hard hit. Giyt did not think of himself as a naive person. He was not startled to learn that people in power told lies.

But this lie? What was the point of it? Only out of some kind of Earthie vanity, some refusal to admit to the rest of the human race that somebody was smarter than they?

Mrs. Brownbenttalon was still talking. "You come to all-six-race confabulation talk in Hexagon when it begin," she advised. "When people from all home planets meet here, you know? Good thing. You learn much. Also big pain, because they scoot us mayoring persons all the hell out of said place, but this cannot be helped. No Joint Governance Commission meeting possible then because place full of peace treaty people. You know Treaty of Perpetual Peace document yourself?"

"I'm afraid not," Giyt admitted. "There's been so much I had to catch up on."

"You do such! Most important. Peace treaty is reason Peace Planet exists. Very tedious document, sure, but very important. Is in database and very valuable for survival. With treaty now, persons, husbands, and young on home planets live in security, no more wars."

"Old times of war *horrible,*" Mrs. Whitenose squeaked. "Much destruction, cities in ruin."

"But long, long ago, even before us great ancestors born. And all repaired now," said Mrs. Brownbenttalon. "Home planet completely restored to state of great beauty and prospering, not counting radioactive waste areas."

"It must be a wonderful place," Rina said politely. "I'd love to see it."

"Never happen," Mrs. Whitenose said positively, and her mother gave her a reprimanding look.

"What Mrs. Whitenose mean," she said, "is of course humans don't come to Centauri planet, Centaurians don't come to human Earth planet, not ever. Meet only here. Much better that way."

"Had experience of other races visiting our planet," Miss Whitenose said, shaking her pointy nose. "Other races come first in dumb little fire-squirting rocket ship thing. I am talking Slug here, you understand? Long, long, long ago. At first all friendliness, talk trade, talk friendship, talk all kinds animal excrement stuff but don't mean; come next time in battle fleets, you know? Bang-bang-bang bombing, shooting, killing. Very much killing in which many, many persons die, also males. No good. Know better now. You stay your place, we stay our place, everybody happy."

"And no shooting," added Mr. Brownbenttalon.

XVII

The armistice treaty agreed to by the Centaurians and the Slugs (who, of course, were also Centaurians, which somewhat confused earlier researchers) was so complete in spelling out the conditions of peace between the two extraterrestrial races that, as the so-called Treaty of Perpetual Peace, it became the document which all subsequent species signed.

Under the peace treaty all signatory species agree, in painstaking detail, to refrain from attacking each other and to eliminate all weaponry on any spacecraft approaching within 356,803 kilometers (so the translation reckons the units of the original draft) of any signatory's planet. The signatories further agree that the Peace Planet (known on Earth as Tupelo, the name given to it by the original exploring team at Huntsville) was to be perpetually disarmed, with no weapons of any kind except the equivalent of bug sprays and mechanical flyswatters. That was all the significant parts. The rest was codicils, four of them, of which the one for Earth was most recent, admitting the other arrivals to the original compact subject to the same provisions as for Centaurians and Slugs.

—BRITANNICA ONLINE, "TUPELO"

The morning after the Centaurian party Giyt took Mrs. Brownbenttalon's advice. As the translated text of the treaty scrolled through his screen he whistled to himself. "No weapons of any kind" obviously meant no weapons at all. What had Hagbarth been thinking of with his nonsensical application to bring in guns? And for that matter, why hadn't Hagbarth warned him about Kalkaboo customs? Or that his proposal for jointly exploiting Tupelo's resources with the eeties would be laughed down?

Obviously Hagbarth was deliberately withholding information that Giyt needed to do his job properly. Why? Was he just intent on making Giyt look bad? And if so, what was the reason for that?

And, thinking of information withheld, what about Mrs. Brownbenttalon's little bombshell concerning Professor Sommermen and the portal?

He attacked the system again, but there was nothing new about the portal to be found on a quick search. He sighed and prepared to dig deeper. He created a scout program to dig through the whole huge database for conjunctions of key terms, wherever they might be found. But by the time the Kalkaboo morning barrage told him it was sunrise, nothing useful had turned up.

He showered and dressed abstractedly, sat abstractedly down to the breakfast Rina had made for him. She looked at him quizzically. "Are you all right, Shammy? Not hung over from last night?"

He blinked at her, mildly indignant. "I didn't have that much to drink, did I?"

"Of course not, hon. You just seem a little down. It isn't still that business with the Kalkaboos?" When he shook his head she changed the subject. "Shammy? Do you mind if I leave you alone for a while today? It's Lupe and Matya. Today's their anniversary, and they've got this kind of romantic idea, they want to go off for a picnic in the woods without all the kids around. So I promised I'd babysit."

"Sure. I'll be fine."

"You're positive? Because I could bring the little kids over here after I get the others off to school—"

That got his full attention. "No, no, that's all right. Should you be doing all that in your condition, though?"

She beamed fondly at him. "You're sweet, Shammy, but I'll be fine. I love my condition, and you know what? I love you, too."

Giyt was just sitting down to his terminal again when he heard someone at the door. It turned out to be one of Mrs. Brownbenttalon's lesser husbands. He was carrying a package as big as himself, that was wrapped in a shimmering silk-like fabric, decorated with flowers. Giyt scrambled to find his translator button and put it in his ear, just in time to hear the little creature say, "Object is freely given gift for enjoyment of you from honored wife and also from highly esteemed principal daughter. You observe have cart vehicle waiting? Reason for waiting of cart vehicle is must return quickly to home for urgent household duties." He expertly detached a tiny record plate from the package and held it out for Giyt. "Sign signature for gift, please?"

Giyt pressed his thumb on the glassy section of the plate and scrawled his name over it, surprised and pleased. But as the Centaurian was getting into his cart another cart was pulling up behind it, and the good feelings evaporated as Hoak Hagbarth got out.

Hagbarth scowled curiously after the departing cart, but, if he had something to say about it, Giyt didn't give him the chance to get it out. "Hagbarth, why is everybody lying about the portal?" he demanded without preface.

The expression on Hagbarth's face changed in a way Giyt had never seen before. The scowl didn't go away. If anything, it deepened, but at the same time Hagbarth's pale eyebrows went up in incredulous shock. "Oh, God," he moaned, "what is it with you now, Giyt?"

"You know what I'm talking about. The portal. Sommermen didn't invent it. It was given to us by the eeties. I want to know why that's been lied about."

The frown and shock melted away from Hagbarth's face, leaving only polite incredulity. "It was?"

"Of course it was. Mrs. Brownbenttalon told me about it herself."

"Oh, right. You were at her place last night, weren't you? How'd you like it?"

"Look," Giyt said. "We're not talking about the party. We're talking about why Ex-Earth tells everybody the portal was Dr. Sommermen's invention when it wasn't."

"Well now, how would I know that? Be reasonable, Giyt. I just work for Ex-Earth, they don't tell me any secrets."

"But you must know *something*."

"No I mustn't. I don't, and that's all there is to it. Aren't you going to open your present?"

It was a standoff. Clearly if Hagbarth did have any information he wasn't going to share it with Giyt, who surrendered and began to unwrap the package. It turned out to be half a dozen of the bamboo segments Mrs. Brownbenttalon had served, and Hagbarth's scowl was replaced with a look of revulsion. "Oh, Christ, look what they're giving you! It's some of that damn lizard shit."

Whether Giyt agreed with the sentiment or not, he felt obliged to defend his hostess. "It's not so bad. We had some last night."

"Oh, yeah. You were going to tell me what went on there."

Actually, Giyt hadn't intended to tell the man anything at all, but there was always the chance that if he kept on listening to Hagbarth the man might involuntarily tell him something useful. He said, "I guess you'd call it a kind of coming-out party for her daughter."

Hagbarth nodded wisely. "Yeah, I know those Centaurian parties. Pretty damn boring and lousy food, right? Mrs. B. used to invite me and Olse now and then, but, you know, they're eeties, aren't they? They have their ways, we have our ways. I'm not saying our ways are *better* necessarily, but still. Anyway, we really couldn't stand being around that kind of company. Did anything interesting happen while you were there?"

"Well, the Kalkaboos didn't show up—because I was there, I think." He waited to see if Hagbarth would take the opportunity to remind him what an idiot he was for injuring the new High Champion, but all the man said impatiently was, "Sure, sure, but what did you talk about?"

The trouble with asking questions of Hoak Hagbarth was that it always wound up with Hagbarth asking all the questions. Giyt was getting tired of the one-way conversation. He said vaguely, "Oh, different things. Look, I think I ought to put this stuff in the fridge."

What he was hoping was that Hagbarth would take the hint and leave, but the man only followed him into the kitchen, laughing. "Why bother? What could happen to it to make it any worse? Anyway, you were telling me about what you talked about at the party."

Giyt cast about for subjects he might want to let Hagbarth know about. The way the other races had seemed to despise the Kalkaboos? But he didn't really want to mention Kalkaboos to Hagbarth. What Mrs. Whitenose had said about Hagbarth himself? That was almost tempting, but Giyt decided on a neutral subject. "They were telling me about the war they had with the Slugs, long ago. Did you know about it?"

"Well, sure. Must've been a real donnybrook—nuked

each other's planets, killed off millions of people on both sides. Did they say anything about the kinds of weapons they used?"

Giyt searched his memory. "Nothing specific, no."

"Well, they started out with old-fashioned rocket ships—the Slugs and the Centaurians are in the same solar system, you know. Then they got high-tech, but they don't talk much about that. You know," Hagbarth said, sounding indignant, "it wouldn't hurt them to be a little more open with us. We haven't hidden anything. Anything they want to know about Earth, we tell them—well, mostly we do, anyway. And there are a lot of people back on Earth who think we haven't been getting a fair shake from them, that way."

Giyt nodded and shrugged at the same time—the nod to indicate comprehension; the shrug for well, what can you do about it? Hagbarth was silent for a moment. Then he said abruptly, "Oh, listen, I almost forgot. I came here to talk to you about something."

Giyt gave him a suspicious look. "The portal codes?"

"Well, that, too, but I guess you would've told me if you had them for me? Yes, that's what I thought. No, what I wanted to tell you was Lieutenant Dern wants you at the firehouse today after siesta."

Lieutenant Dern was the operations officer for the fire company, so Giyt was pretty sure he knew why. He asked the question anyway. "What for?"

"Training, and I think she's going to pull a quiz on you, too. Have you been studying?"

"Well, not really."

Hagbarth grinned at him. "So then it's a good thing you've got a couple of hours, right? And listen, if I was you I'd just pitch that bamboo crap in the garbage. Mrs. B. will never find out."

* * *

So that meant one more burden on Giyt's suddenly insufficient time. There wasn't any help for it. Resigned, he gave up the notion of doing a little more digging into some of the things he really wanted to know and got down to the business of studying.

The list of things a fireman was supposed to know was formidable. There were the schematics of the pumpers and the water cannon to learn, the theory of putting fires out to study (cool them with water, smother them with foam), the proper names of every air pack and peavey hook in the company's arsenal to memorize. It wasn't any more difficult than any of the college assignments Giyt had easily aced long ago. He had educated himself in far more complex subjects many times, for school or just for the pure pleasure of learning. This stuff was child's play compared to, say, identifying Napoleon's order of battle as he marched on Moscow, not to mention some of the more abstruse areas of network theory. If this one was a burden it was primarily because it was compulsory, had been most unjustly dumped on him without warning. And what did it matter whether he passed Lieutenant Dern's quiz or not? What could they do to him?

So, having established that there was no good reason for him to cram for the test, Giyt did what he always did. He began to study, and he made good progress by the time he had to leave the house.

On the way to the firehouse Giyt stopped in at the house next door to tell Rina about Mrs. Brownbenttalon's gift. He had to whisper, because one of the littlest kids was asleep in a bassinet by her feet, while Rina was trying to feed another in a high chair. Out in the yard, where Rina could keep a watchful eye on them through the open door, the rest of the de Mir get was playing raucously with a bunch of little pink Petty-Prime kits. "That was nice of the Brownbenttalons," she said absently, aiming a spoonful of mush at the momentarily open mouth and expertly connecting. As he left she added, "Shammy? I'm glad to see you making some friends."

On the way to the firehouse Giyt wondered if that was what he was doing. He hadn't had much practice at making friends. For that matter, he hadn't even had very many acquaintances back in Wichita, because every person who knew who Evesham Giyt was automatically became a potential threat to his carefully secured lifestyle. Well, and because he hadn't much wanted any friends, either, he admitted to himself. The company he liked best was his own.

And of course Rina's.

As he entered the firehouse, the first person he saw was Lieutenant Grazia Dern. She was definitely not a friend. She had already let Giyt know, pointedly, that she was very close with the former mayor, Mariam Vardersehn, and thus not too friendly to her replacement. The only other fireman present at that moment wasn't a good candidate for friendship, either, since he was the man who had been turned down for permanent family relocation to the polar factories, Maury Kettner.

Giyt's training for the day turned out to involve a lot of hands-on practice, some enjoyable, some not much fun at all. After half an hour in the station Giyt thought he would never want to reel up a hose single-handedly again, but then Kettner took him out into the field. It got better then. Kettner let him drive the truck around the fringes of the lake to the foliage on the far side. That was interesting in itself, and then Kettner let him fire the water cannon at the brush along the roadway. That was pretty much pure pleasure: all that power under his hand! They had gone all the way down to the riverside below Slugtown before Giyt realized his "training" had served another purpose: under Kettner's guidance his driving had widened a stretch of that horrible downhill road by a couple of meters on either side.

He didn't mind. He didn't even mind the stowing and draining after twenty minutes of blasting holes in the foliage along the banks of the foul-smelling stream, where one of the great cargo submarines from the Pole floated half submerged, waiting to be unloaded. But then, when they got back to the firehouse, the lieutenant was gone and Chief Tschopp was waiting to give him spot oral quizzes on what he had learned in his screen session.

That wasn't what Giyt wanted at that moment. He was wet and sweaty and his arms were tired from holding back the kick of the water cannon. What he wanted most of all was to go home and take a shower. He didn't do well on the quiz, and when Hoak Hagbarth strolled in in the middle of it, Giyt looked to him for a diversion.

It didn't work that way. "For Christ's sake, Giyt," Tschopp exploded. "Pay attention!"

"He don't catch on real fast, does he?" offered Maury Kettner, watching.

"He does not," Tschopp agreed in disgust. "What's the matter, Giyt? You too busy playing those little bedtime games with your lady to study?"

That was going farther than Giyt was prepared to accept, but as he was tensing to reply Hagbarth cut in. "Now, now," he said mildly, "watch how you talk about somebody that's about to become a mother, Wili. Come on. Tell Evesham here you're sorry." Tschopp looked rebellious, but muttered something that might have been an apology. "Now, that's better. Are you through with the mayor? Because I need to talk to him about something."

He didn't wait for an answer, just jerked his head toward the chief's office. As the two of them entered, Giyt asked, "How did you know Rina was pregnant?"

"Oh, hell, Evesham." Hagbarth smiled. "Everybody knows everything around here, didn't you know that? Except about the freaks. They keep a lot of secrets from us." He closed the door on the man who was the office's rightful occupant. "That's what I wanted to talk to you about." He reached into his pocket and pulled out a ring, set with a topaz—obviously fake—the size of a pigeon's egg. "There's a recorder in the stone, Evesham. What I'd like you to do, I'd like you to just wear it next time you see Mrs. B., and maybe get her to talk a little more about what armaments they've got—"

Giyt stared at him. "You want me to spy on her?"

"I wouldn't call it spying, exactly," Hagbarth protested. "Just for archival purposes, you know? And it's not that we want to know anything they shouldn't be willing to tell us anyway—"

"No."

Hagbarth looked at him incredulously. "You don't mean that," he said.

"Actually I do. No. I won't do it."

"Christ, Giyt, where's your patriotism? You could be doing yourself some good, too. You can bet the eeties know everything there is to know about Earth—who knows what kind of spy stuff they had in the drone they sent the portal in? I mean," he added hastily, "if they did do that, like they say. And we've never gotten a ship near any of their planets. Hell, we don't even know where the Kalks and the Petty-Primes come from! And the scout ships the Huntsville people sent to Alpha Centauri and Delta Pavonis never even reported back—I give you one guess why."

Giyt frowned. Put like that, it sounded damning. But he said firmly, "Mrs. Brownbenttalon's a friend, and I don't do that to my friends. I'm not going to rat her out for you."

Hagbarth looked him over in silence for a moment. Then

he sighed. "So we might as well pack it in," he said. "I guess your principles do you credit."

But Giyt was quite sure he didn't mean it. What Hagbarth meant, what the tone of his voice said for him, was *I'm going to remember this.*

XVIII

The star Delta Pavonis, which at a distance of some eighteen light-years is one of our Sun's nearest neighbors, has long been known to have planets, some of which were suspected of bearing life. That is why the extrasolar exploration team based at Huntsville, Alabama, directed one of its first probes toward that system. That probe was lost. (So was the one directed toward Alpha Centauri.) It wasn't until the first humans arrived on Tupelo that it was confirmed that planets of both stars did in fact possess civilizations.

The Delts—as the species from the Delta Pavonis planet are called—are structurally similar to humans, although their triangular skull and independently operating eyes give them a rather bizarre appearance. Biochemically, however, they are quite different. Sulfur is a major constituent of their chemical makeup and their diet, which has an unfortunate effect. Sulfur compounds are notoriously among the most malodorous of chemicals.

—Britannica online, "Tupelo"

Sure enough, Hagbarth didn't forget. It didn't take him long to show it. He appeared on Giyt's doorstep with a record pad in his hand. He looked both surly and impatient. "Jesus, Giyt," he said, "did you forget the mayor has to sign off on new housing? I've got these places going up to put our people in for the six-planet summit, and I can't let them be occupied until you do your job."

Giyt knew that. What he didn't know was why Hagbarth had come over in person when he could perfectly well have used the net. He signed in silence and handed the plate back to Hagbarth. "Thanks," Hagbarth said, but he didn't leave. He eyed Giyt without speaking for a moment, then said, "I don't guess you've changed your mind."

"About wearing your spy ring? No."

"All right," Hagbarth said, apparently doing his best to sound reasonable. "Then how about this? How about showing me how to listen in on Mrs. B.'s private transmissions? You could do that the way you did with the Petty-Primes, right?"

"I could. I won't, though."

"Come on, Giyt! I'm not asking you to do it for me personally! It's for all of us. The Centaurians and all the other freaks will be sending reports back to their home planets. Who knows what they're really up to? If we could just get a look at what they're saying to the people back home—"

Giyt shook his head firmly. "No."

"Christ, Giyt!" Hagbarth's tone was both anger and disgust. "Maybe I've misjudged you. You sure don't live up to your stats."

Giyt felt a warning tingle. "When were you looking at my stats?"

"I've been looking at a lot of things, Giyt. It's a funny thing, though. There's not much documentation for you."

And how did you know that? Giyt asked, but not out loud. Anyway, he was pretty sure he knew the answer. From his base on Tupelo, Hagbarth didn't have the facilities to make enough of a search in Earth records to be inconvenient. There was only one other possibility. Someone on Earth had done it for him. Giyt shrugged warily. "There's been some sloppy record-keeping, I guess."

"Sure," Hagbarth said, heavily sarcastic. "Or maybe somebody not so sloppy messing with the records? Somebody who's pretty good at tinkering with the net? It doesn't matter, though. There wasn't much on you, but there was a pretty complete data file on your wife. The lady's had a really unusual career, hasn't she?"

Evesham Giyt did not have much experience of anger; he had arranged his life so that there weren't many occasions for it. Now he felt it, and felt it more strongly than he ever had. He kept his voice controlled. "What are you trying to tell me, Hagbarth?"

"I'm telling you that I'd like the two of you to be a little more cooperative, that's all." Hagbarth's expression was now smug; the son of a bitch was beginning to enjoy himself.

Giyt chose his words with care. "The thing is, Hagbarth, we just don't like cooperating with scum. Do you understand me? The answer is still no."

The smugness disappeared from Hagbarth's face; they locked eyes. Hagbarth was the first to break away.

"Ah, Giyt," he sighed, "What's the use? Just remember, I tried to warn you."

As Rina had reminded him, Evesham Giyt had never had many friends in his days on Earth. But there was another side to that coin. He hadn't had any enemies either, or at least he hadn't had any who knew where to find him. While here on Tupelo he definitely had acquired at least one certifiable enemy, and one, moreover, who was prepared to work at it.

Giyt got confirmation of that when Rina came storming back from the neighbors', her face dark with unexpected anger. "Have you been watching that bitch Cristl's show on the net? Well, you better take a look. Go back to about twenty minutes ago." And when he had backtracked to the beginning of the woman's call-in show there she was, Silva

Cristl, wearing her fire lieutenant's uniform with the jacket unbuttoned enough to show her cleavage, smiling into the camera. Her caller's face was pic-in-pic below her, and Giyt recognized him at once: Maury Kettner, the man who had wanted to move his family to the Pole and had been turned down.

Only, according to what the two of them were saying on the screen, he hadn't been: "We'll certainly miss you around the firehouse, Maury."

"I'll miss you guys, too," Kettner said, flushed with the importance of being on the net, "so I just wanted to say good-bye for a while to all my friends. And to say thanks to Mr. Hagbarth, while I'm at it. He really came through for me, so I and the family are on our way to the Pole. No thanks to the mayor, you know. I must've asked him a dozen times, and he just wouldn't do a thing."

"I know what you mean." Cristl was grinning, too. "I hope he's a better fireman than he is a mayor."

"Well, you'd lose that one," said Kettner, chuckling as he was replaced by the next caller. The little picture showed a middle-aged woman, faintly familiar; Giyt thought maybe she was one of the ones he'd seen on Energy Island. She had criticisms of her own:

"Listen, I heard what Maury was saying about the mayor, and he's damn right. You know what this Giyt did to the boss Kalkaboo, don't you? How's that going to look when all the big shots come here for their meeting? I have to say, I really miss Mariam Vardersehn."

"There'll be another election one of these days," Cristl said consolingly.

"Yeah, and the dumb voters just might put Giyt right back in."

"Well," said Lieutenant Cristl, pursing her lips in a knowledgeable expression, "I don't know if you have to worry much about that, sweetie. There's a lot that hasn't come out yet, take my word for it, and not just about Giyt himself, either. Now let's go to the next caller."

That was enough for Giyt. He clicked it off while Rina protested, "They're being so *unfair!*"

"It's not a fair world," Giyt said absently, thinking about something he didn't want to say out loud in Rina's presence. And of course, Rina's next remark was right on that subject. "What do you suppose Cristl was talking about—stuff that hasn't come out yet?"

Giyt didn't answer her for a moment. He was wondering just what Hagbarth might have found out—and even more, how Hagbarth had known where to look. He said, "I suppose we'll find out sooner or later."

It wasn't later. In fact it was a good deal sooner than Giyt had expected. Rina had hardly returned next door to practice parenting on the de Mir kids when she came flying back. Both Matya and Lupe were with her, carrying the smaller children; Matya looked indignant, Rina wore anger and unhappiness, and Lupe seemed to have been crying. "Shammy," Rina said, "I don't know how to tell you this, but somebody's been telling around that I used to be a whore."

Giyt froze. He hardly heard Lupe sobbing, "I told you, Matya! You shouldn't have said anything!"

And Matya, half defensive, half repentant: "I thought she ought to know what those bastards at the firehouse were saying about her. They're all Hagbarth's buddies, I hated Lupe going there."

"They're not all like that," Lupe protested.

"No, but the ones in charge are. Evesham? I'm sorry as hell about this, but really you did have to know. Hagbarth's got all these regulations that he pulls out when he wants to. He might even be able to get you kicked off Tupelo, like Shura Kenk."

"She's the one who used to live here in your house," Lupe supplied.

"I remember," Giyt said. "But I thought she just got tired of living on Tupelo and went home."

"Went home! Hagbarth had her thrown out. They said she'd molested one of the Grayhorn kids—the twelve-year-old, a born liar if I ever saw one. But they believed what he said. So they sent a special rocket up to the pole and flew her back in the middle of her shift to face the charges."

"She didn't do it, of course," Lupe put in. "She said so, and we believed her. She said Hagbarth was just ticked off at her for something that happened at the factory."

"But the mayor deported her. Well, it wasn't just the mayor. It was Hagbarth, of course. And he could do that to you, too."

Rina looked questioningly at Giyt. "Maybe that's not such a bad thing, Shammy? Maybe we ought to go back home anyway."

"Oh, please no, Rina!" Lupe begged. "Everybody knows what a turd Hagbarth is. It'll all blow over. We don't want you to leave!"

"Do you really want a whore living next door to your children?"

"We want *you*, Rina!"

And Matya chimed in: "What does it matter what you did a long time ago? I mean, do I care? Back home, I used to work for the IRS."

The good thing about being on Hoak Hagbarth's enemies list was that it sure did cut down on the number of people who came to ask Giyt for favors. The bad part—

Well, there were more bad parts than Giyt could count. Never mind the crazy, silly problem with the Kalkaboos; never mind the possibility that Hagbarth might kick them right back to Earth. What troubled him most was what all this was doing to Rina. She had just barely got used to her status as the pregnant wife of a well-respected man when she had to shift gears and get used to his new status as a semi-pariah and, worst of all, to her own. It wasn't just the embarrassment. It was a situation that Giyt was certain couldn't be good for the baby. For that he intended never, ever to forgive Hoak Hagbarth.

Then there were the second-order derivatives of that bit of nastiness. One big question, for instance: How had Hagbarth found out about Rina's past? There was nothing about that in the open records even back on Earth. Giyt had made sure that was so long ago, as a minor and unmentioned courtesy to a friend. Had someone back home done some serious digging? And if so, were they likely to do the same sort of digging in Giyt's own records? They would certainly have a tough time, because he had erected some pretty solid blocks over everything that related to his own history. But would the blocks withstand a really serious attack by a really high-powered investigation?

If Giyt were still back on Earth himself he could certainly handle that problem. He had included plenty of fire alarms and snooper-detection systems, so that he would be warned of what was happening in plenty of time to derail any imaginable inquiry. But he wasn't on Earth.

The best he could do here on Tupelo was to create a scout of his own and task it with roaming through the files back on Earth and reporting back to him. Creating it was no particular problem, either, but the scout couldn't be transmitted until the next time the portal was open. Then Giyt couldn't hope for a response until the time after that.

He did it anyway. When he had finished he noticed an unusual food aroma, and when he went into the kitchen he found Rina cooking up a huge batch of french fries. "Oh, they aren't for us, Shammy," she said, decanting them onto paper to drain. "Remember, we got that nice present from Mrs. Brownbenttalon? Well, we never gave her anything in return—like, you know, a thank-you present for having us over? And I remember her whole family was crazy about french fries at the fair. Do you think she'd like that?"

"I guess so. Well, sure she would," he said, less interested in the gift than in the fact that Rina seemed to have put Hagbarth and his gossip about her out of her mind.

"So when they're ready, would you like to take them over to her place for me? I'd do it myself, but I promised Lupe I'd help her take the little ones to the clinic for their checkups."

He would. He did; and so an hour later he got out of the cart at the gate of the Brownbenttalon residence with a thermally wrapped kilo of french-fried potatoes in his hand.

The whole Centaurian compound was fenced in, and the entrance gate was not exactly a gate; it was more like a cattle-crossing guard for some ranch on Earth, metal plates carrying a small electrical charge to discourage the smaller children from wandering away. They were no barrier to Evesham Giyt, but he waited politely until an immature female bustled up. "Oh, it is Large Male Giyt," she said, clearly surprised, apparently pleased. "Wait kindly." And a moment later Mrs. Brownbenttalon herself appeared, followed by a gaggle of subadults and children.

She raised her foreparts to give her little paws room to work, looking like a thoroughly bowed frankfurter as she rested her weight on her belly to rip the package open. "Ah, tubers in fat!" she exclaimed, giving every appearance of delight. She sampled a couple for herself, then indulgently handed the rest out, one fry apiece, to the children. "Is notably kind of you and same-size wife, yes. Look how they gobble! Now you come in, have small beverage, okay?" And then, when they were settled in the little garden with two males hastening to bring them the beery drinks, she inquired sociably, "You tell how are things progress with you? Is all completely well?"

"Just fine," he said automatically, but the question hadn't been entirely sociable. Mr. Brownbenttalon raised his nose out of his wife's back fur and clucked reproachfully at him, while his wife simply gazed in silence at Giyt.

"Well," Giyt confessed, "maybe not *absolutely* fine." He hesitated. She didn't seem to know about the rumors floating around the Earth community, and he didn't want to discuss the troubles among Earth humans with a Centaurian, anyway. But Hagbarth wasn't his only problem. "It's the Kalkaboos. I don't know what to do about them."

"I conjectured this." She sighed. "You don't know what to do, no one else do either. Stinky, noisy people, Kalkaboos, always getting feelings damaged. You want me helping for this situation?"

"Helping?"

"Can do so," she said modestly. "I have personally among them some certain less unreasonable acquaintances. Could negotiate on behalf of you if you wish, perhaps arrange some arrangement to reduce tensions maybe, what do you say?"

"Well . . ." he began, but she raised one paw to stop him, its single twisted talon gleaming.

"It is not necessary to express copious thank-yous," she said benevolently. "You know next commission meeting? You don't go there by yourself. You wait. At proper time I come by your dwelling, pick you up, take you to meeting so you can expiate offense given to new noisy Kalkaboo High Champion. Have no further fears, Large Male Giyt. It is all to be okay."

When he got home Rina was just taking her leave of Lupe and the children. She hurried to join him, putting up her face to be kissed. "So did Mrs. Brownbenttalon like the fries?"

"Oh, sure," Giyt said absently, sniffing. "She said to thank you very much. What's that smell?"

"We've been wondering about that. Lupe said she thought maybe some Delts had been around, but it doesn't smell Delt to me. Anyway, would you like a cup of coffee?"

She started the coffeemaker, but left to take a message on her screen. She was gone long enough for the coffee to be ready, and Giyt was just pouring out two cups when she came back, broadly grinning. "Guess what, hon? I heard from my sister again. They *loved* the clock, Shammy! They say all the neighbors are green with envy because—Shammy? Is something the matter?"

He hadn't been able to keep from changing expression. "Nothing," he said. "I just remembered . . . No, nothing."

"You sure? Well, anyway," she said doubtfully, but picking up speed, "they're really impressed by what I told them about life here on Tupelo. Salen says she'd cut out of Des Moines and emigrate in a hot minute, it sounds so good, but her husband's a real stick-in-the-mud—"

By then Giyt had his expression under control. He nodded and smiled while he considered the sudden enlightenment that had just come to him.

Rina's call to her sister! That had to be how Hagbarth had tracked her record down. Once somebody who was looking for dirt on the Giyts knew that the sister existed it wouldn't take a major expert to find out everything there was to find out about Rina.

When Rina set down her coffee cup and excused herself for a moment Giyt pondered the consequences. That answered a question for him, but like many answers, it was of no practical help. There was nothing for him to do about it, least of all reproach Rina for giving Hagbarth's gang the chance to dig up old dirt. The damage was done.

"Hon?" Rina said, frowning as she came back. "I'm afraid the toilet won't flush. What do you suppose is wrong?"

Giyt was no plumber, but it didn't take long to find out the answer. When inspection of the bathroom showed nothing obvious, he looked out at the back of the house.

There was an excavation that hadn't been there before, and a rank smell of sewage. While they were out of the house somebody had dug up their drains. And it seemed that Hagbarth's harassment was not going to stop with gossip.

XIX

Good morning, guys and guyinas, it's me again, your Voice of Tupelo, Silva Cristl, with a weather report that'll cheer you up. The bad news is that Hurricane Sam has intensified overnight; now it's Class Five, with winds over three hundred kilometers an hour. The good news is that it's going to miss us. We'll get some rain out of it, sure, but we'll miss the big winds. Speaking of big winds, did you hear there's a movement to rename the hurricane? People don't want to call it Hurricane Sam anymore. They want to call it Hurricane Evesham, because it's a lot of hot air that misses the mark.

—Silva Cristl's morning broadcast

Giyt didn't want to talk to Hoak Hagbarth. Given a choice, he would have cut the man out of his life entirely, but the mess in his backyard left him little choice. Something had to be done.

When he tried to call Hagbarth about getting it fixed, the man didn't answer his personal communicator; when he called the Hagbarth house, only Olse Hagbarth was there. "You say they dug up your backyard? Really? Well, I did hear something or other about a complaint of stopped-up drains a while back, but I'm afraid I wasn't paying much attention."

When Giyt asked who had made the complaint she only shrugged. "I guess you'd have to ask Hoak about that. Well, no, he isn't here right now. He's in a major meeting—you know, getting ready for the six-planet congress—and I can't interrupt him. Anyway, the sewers are Slug business, you know. Why don't you file a requisition? Although they're so backed up with the congress coming heaven knows when they'd be able to get around to it."

She was right about that. The Slugs were so busy getting ready for their VIPs to visit that there wasn't a single Slug in the waterworks office. In fact, there was only one person there, and that person—oh, when your luck was bad, it was bad all the way—was a female Kalkaboo.

When she saw Giyt coming, she raced him to the door, but he got inside the office before she could lock him out. Sulkily she retired to her desk.

At first Giyt thought she wasn't going to talk to him at all, but evidently her sense of duty overcame her revulsion. "Have no authority accept requisition," she told the air, unwilling to look Giyt in the face. "Slugs all in Slugtown, performing extremely great group sing for safety of soon-arriving leaders. Go away."

"But it's an emergency," Giyt protested.

"Yes, of course emergency, what difference? This work you are complaining not done by Slugs anyway. No work order in file. No progress report. So not Slug, so Slugs probably not going fix anyway. You don't like? You ask head Slug about same at commission meeting of joint governance, see how much good that do you. Go away."

The visit to the waterworks office wasn't quite a total loss. At least he had found out that the ruin in his backyard wasn't part of some official maintenance program. Which left only one possibility: it was more of Hoak Hagbarth's teaching Giyt a lesson.

The ameliorating fact was that the lack of waste-water disposal wasn't a *desperate* emergency. The de Mirs had offered them the use of their own facilities at any hour of the day or night. Then when Giyt got back from the waterworks office, he inexpertly managed to hook up a hose drain to the kitchen sink. It took an hour of swearing and getting wet, but when he was finished, Rina could at least cook, the waste spilling out onto what passed for their lawn.

None of that helped to alleviate the smell from the backyard.

Smoldering, Giyt snapped on the human-language broadcast to take his mind off Hagbarth's malice. What was on was a delayed broadcast of an Earthly hockey game. He watched it unseeingly until Rina called to him. "Hon? You haven't forgotten you've got a commission meeting coming up?"

He had. What's more, he had also completely forgotten about Mrs. Brownbenttalon's promise to mend matters with the Kalkaboos.

Mrs. Brownbenttalon hadn't, though. By the time Giyt got more or less cleaned up from his exploits with the kitchen drain, there the Centaurian was, leaning out of a cart before his door and calling to him. "What you do," she instructed as soon as he was inside, "is totally prepared by me. You perform return bout with new High Champion, okay? Nothing serious, you understand. No maiming. But element of paramount importance you must remember is you positively must not this time win." She bobbed her long nose at him for emphasis. "No more discuss this, please. What is terrible smell?"

And when Giyt told her about his troubles with the Slug repair crews she sighed. "Slugs," she said mournfully. "Who can do anything with Slugs? Perhaps you do like Kalkaboo lady say and ask head Slug at commission meeting, maybe he in good mood. Usually not. Now we have conversation of trivial matters so you compose yourself. You like this fine weather we having now, temporarily?"

There were a dozen or more persons milling around outside the door of the Hexagon, humans and eeties mixed. Giyt eyed them warily, but there did not seem to be any Kalkaboos among them. As Giyt entered, one of the men caught his arm. "Where the hell are we supposed to sit, Giyt?" he demanded.

Actually it was a fair question. Inside the building Delt and human crews were ripping out most of the seats usually supplied for the audience. New and obviously a good deal more comfortable chair equivalents were stacked along the wall, ready to be installed for the comfort of the delegations. Giyt gave the man a helpless shrug and entered cautiously.

All the other members were already in their places, even the Kalkaboo High Champion, who did not even look at Giyt. Mrs. Brownbenttalon piped to the room in general, "Sorrow for lateness. I and Earth human had business of nonpublic nature. Please begin."

And the Principal Slug, acting as chair for the day, slapped the desktop with one extruded member for order, commanded the work crews to stop their noisy activities, and began the meeting.

It was not a peaceful one. It seemed that every member of the commission had a complaint to make or a demand to register. The Principal Slug was first, usurping the privilege of the chair to point out that there were not enough damp-conditioned carts available in working order for the use of their delegation from the Slug home planet. Then the Petty-Primes' Responsible One protested that the traffic involved in preparing for the meeting was so heavy that their small carts were at risk of being run over in the streets, and then the Delts weighed in by announcing that the other members of the commission were taking up time on frivolous matters when they should have ratified the seat assignments on the suborbital polar rocket and, really, they should move along so the work crews could finish preparing the hall for the six-planet meeting. Even Mrs. Brownbenttalon indignantly proclaimed that all that work should have been completed long ago, because more staff members for the six-planet meeting would be arriving very soon, and the accommodations for the Centaurians were not ready.

It did not take Giyt long to figure out what was motivating them all. The audience was much larger than usual, uncomfortably perched on whatever surfaces were left for them. Most of them were eeties—Giyt even saw the female Kalkaboo from the waterworks office—and among them were a number he had never seen before.

Those newcomers, he realized, had to be advance staff members for the delegations from the home planets. What the mayors were doing was showing off for the high brass. Only the new Kalkaboo High Champion was silent. He did not speak, did not look at Giyt, hardly moved at all except for the flapping of his huge ears. The only time he paid any attention at all was when Giyt found an opening to bring up his own business with the Principal Slug. Then the Kalkaboo conspicuously turned his back, while the Slug in the chair slobbered reprovingly, "These smelly drains leak purely unofficial personal matter, Mayor Giyt. Not to come before this body never. No other proper business? Good. Meeting I now adjourn."

Well, Giyt thought, he hadn't really expected any more. Meanwhile, what about this other matter? He started over to ask Mrs. Brownbenttalon what had gone wrong with her arrangements with the Kalkaboos.

That was when he found out that nothing had gone wrong at all.

He had incautiously turned his back on the High Champion. Before Giyt knew what was happening, the Kalkaboo leaped off his platform and bore him to the ground. "Die in wretched agony, vicious murdering person!" he shrieked, pounding Giyt's head against the floor. But not really very hard, and not for more than a moment. Then the Kalkaboo rose and said politely, "Thank you. Vengeance is now complete. Expect you recover from this beating soon."

When vengeance was complete, it seemed, it was complete, and it produced some unexpected dividends. The High Champion of the Kalkaboos did not become friendly, exactly—friendliness did not seem to be among the behaviors in the Kalkaboo repertory—but he did something better than that. He beckoned to the female Kalkaboo from the Slug office and whispered into her great ear. She in turn spoke to the Principal Slug, who listened for a moment, then called to Giyt. "Am informed repair requisition of you on file, so work will be done. Is quite irregular. Slugs, however, always cooperate reliably, this our nature."

And then the next morning, as he was breakfasting with Rina at daybreak, they heard the pop of an explosion outside their own door. When they peered out they found it was pouring, but they caught a glimpse of a Kalkaboo running away in the rain. "I guess they didn't trust you to set off your own firecracker, Shammy," Rina said. "Anyway, it's all straightened out now, right?"

"Looks that way," he said, and returned to his pancakes, more cheerful than he had been in days. At least the problems with the extraterrestrials on Tupelo seemed to be healing themselves.

The humans, however, were a different matter. The stresses there were not healing themselves. They were getting worse.

XX

The last species to reach Tupelo before the arrival of the Huntsville probe were the Petty-Primates. Once again, the identity of the solar system they come from has never been established, although it seems clear that, in regard to the conditions that affect life, their planet was quite like Tupelo, and thus no doubt a good deal like Earth itself.

Physically, the Petty-Primes are tiny. More than any other terrestrial creature they resemble tailless, hairless monkeys. Yet with a brain less than a tenth the size of a human's, they have demonstrated enough intelligence to develop a highly sophisticated technological culture. That is surprising in itself, but the Petty-Primes have another quality that is still more unlikely.

That is their life span. Earthly ethologists have drawn a sort of curve, plotting mass against longevity for mammalian species, and it demonstrates that the smaller the creature, in general, the shorter its life expectancy. Not the Petty-Primes. They are completely off the curve. Their childhood extends for nearly thirty years, so that by the time a Petty-Prime is sexually mature it has gone through decades of learning and experience. The length of their lives as adults is equally astonishing. When the first humans reached Tupelo some of the original Petty-Prime colonists were still alive and well, though since then most have either died or returned to their home planet.

—BRITANNICA ONLINE, "TUPELO"

The more Evesham Giyt thought about it, the more he was convinced that this world would be a better place if Hoak Hagbarth weren't in it, either back on Earth or, preferably, dead.

That was a conclusion that startled him. Giyt had never before in his life wished for any other person's death. It wasn't that he planned to do anything about it. He had no intention of getting into a shoot-out with Hagbarth, even if either of them had had weapons to shoot each other out with. But to punch the man stupid, yes, that was a tempting possibility. Bash him bloody and then kick his ugly face in—yes, definitely that scenario had real attractions for Giyt. . . . Or would have had, if Rina hadn't begged him to let the matter pass; "All he did was tell the truth, Shammy," she said, dry-eyed and somber. "The whole thing is my fault."

"*Nothing* about this is your fault!"

She gave him the pursed-lips look that meant, *You're entirely wrong and I'm certainly right, but I don't choose to debate it any further.* All she said was, "Please, Shammy. I'm asking you to let it go. For me."

Well, he couldn't let it go. But he couldn't go against the wishes of the mother of his unborn child, either. And while he was considering just what he *could* do, Rina cleared her throat. "You know, Shammy," she said, "if we had to go back—well, what I mean is, if we *wanted* to go back—it wouldn't be all that bad, would it?"

It took a moment for Giyt to understand what she was saying. Then he was firm. "Not a chance. We're not going to bring up our son in—"

"Or daughter," she said. "I haven't checked."

"Whichever. Anyway, we're not going to raise our family in some damn slide-room in Bal Harbor."

She looked at him, considering. "It wouldn't have to be in Bal Harbor, Shammy. I've been thinking. My sister and her husband have a three-roomer. I'm sure they'd be glad to have us, just till we got settled."

"No!" he said. "No way!" He looked at her accusingly. "I thought you liked living here in this house!"

"Actually, I love living here, Shammy, and I love our house. I never had a home of my own before, just places where I worked. I slept there after my clients had gone away, but they weren't homes. All the same, we have to face the simple facts."

Giyt put his arm around her, touched. The simplest fact of all, of course, was that back on Earth there were his stashes of mad money, plenty to buy any kind of house Rina wished, and if there wasn't enough there it would be easy enough to make more in the same way . . . assuming he was willing to go back to stealing for a living. And assuming he was prepared to do it on grimy, worn-out Earth.

He shook his head. "We're not leaving," he said. "I give you my word, Rina. We're going to bring up our kid right here on Tupelo."

So Giyt had made his wife a promise.

Evesham Giyt didn't have a lot of experience in keeping promises. He hadn't had to. He hadn't been in the habit of making promises to anyone. But this promise he was determined to keep. He was not going to allow Hoak Hagbarth to kick them off the planet of Tupelo for any reason at all.

But then, when Giyt had begun to search the files for those regulations that Hagbarth could invoke when he chose, it began to look as though there was a real problem there. There was in fact an Ex-Earth statute that said any colonist could be deported for what was called "aggravated antisocial behavior." The language was opaquely legal, but when Giyt read it over, he saw that it could have been that sort of charge that had terminated Shura Kenk's residence. Could have, at least, if she was actually guilty, whatever the de Mirs chose to believe. What was less clear was whether the regulation could be used against Rina. Could it, for instance, be made retroactive to cover acts committed light-years away and long in the past?

After the third or fourth re-reading Giyt still couldn't tell, and when he showed it to Rina, neither could she. "See, hon," she said, "you're really smart about some things, and I'm not so dumb, either, but that's lawyer talk. People like us aren't supposed to understand it. You need somebody to tell you what it means. You need a lawyer."

"I don't know if there are any lawyers here on Tupelo," he said, studying her. Rina seemed subdued, naturally enough, but as far as Giyt could tell she hadn't been crying. But then Rina wasn't ever a crier.

"Neither do I, but the way to look for one . . ." she began, and then stopped as a message override flashed on his screen. They both looked at it. It was for Giyt, and what it said was that the first official party of delegates for the six-planet conference was about to arrive, and his presence was required to greet them.

Giyt groaned. Rina shook her head. "You'd better go," she said. "What I was about to say was that the way to find out if anybody here is a lawyer is to check the personnel files. You go change your clothes. I'll do it for you."

"But they're all classified," he protested. "You'd have to bypass the blocks, dig into the protected files—"

"Sure," she said cheerfully. "I can handle that, remember? The trouble with you, hon, is you think you have to do everything yourself. You have to leave some things to your partner."

Pulling on his clean pants, Giyt pondered that thought. He had never had a partner before. And, as a matter of fact, it didn't take Rina long to get through Hagbarth's pretty primitive security blocks. While he was brushing his hair she came in and leaned on the doorway, watching him. "There isn't anybody who calls himself a lawyer," she reported, "but I did a deeper search and I found two people who had a little legal experience, anyway. One worked as a paralegal, and the other dropped out of law school in her first year."

"Good work," he said, to cheer her up.

"Well, maybe so," she conceded, "but I don't think it helps us much. The paralegal's Olse Hagbarth. And the other one is Silva Cristl."

When Giyt arrived at the square in front of the portal the rain had nearly stopped, which was a good thing, but there was something less good going on. He had expected to find at least a couple of dozen people there, waiting to greet the incoming VIPs. He didn't. There was no one there at all except for a pair of Delt workmen, tinkering with a cart at the edge of the square in spite of the continuing drizzle. When he asked them what was going on, one of the Delts turned a single eye on him, the other still gazing at the exposed mechanisms of the cart. "You don't hear?" the Delt said. "New word recently coming. Slug bosses being delayed, don't say how long. Maybe twenty minutes, maybe who knows?"

"Never say how long," the other one put in. "Slugs, you know? But maybe give us time to get this busted old junk pile juicy enough for delicate Slug persons before getting here, that assuming you let us go on with repairing task."

The delay was news to Giyt. He wondered whether the fact that he hadn't received the amended message was more of Hagbarth's petty harassment or just simple inefficiency. It didn't matter; either way he had time to kill.

He considered going back home to wait. It didn't seem like a good idea. He might not be there long enough for any real purpose. He also might not get the word again in time to get back for the actual arrival, and why give Silva Cristl something new to gossip about on her broadcasts?

He moved away restlessly. He had a lot on his mind, but it didn't seem to want to concentrate on any one subject. As he wandered, he was thinking about the turgid wording of the Ex-Earth regulations and wondering whether the Slug workers had started to fix his drains yet and noticing the fact that he was getting wet. Was the rain going to get harder again? Giyt had had little experience of hurricanes. He had checked out the weather reports and understood that the hurricane itself had missed their islands by a couple hundred kilometers; all they were getting was the arc of storms that spiraled around its trailing edge. He saw a few people moving around in the street, mostly eeties; they seemed to assume the worst of the rain was over, at least. . . .

Then he saw a pair of humans, and one of them was Hoak Hagbarth.

They seemed to be discussing something Hagbarth was displaying to the other man on his portable. When they looked up, Giyt looked away; he didn't want to talk to Hagbarth. Evidently the feeling was mutual. Hagbarth gave him only a glance, then turned to the other man with a hand on his shoulder and led him toward the portal. Giyt stared after them, trying to identify the other man. Was it one of the people from the hypermarket? He wasn't sure, and probably, he told himself, that was one more sign of his failings as mayor of the Earth community. A good politician would know all his constituents by now. Giyt admitted to himself that, whatever his other virtues, he wasn't a very good politician.

A whirring behind him made him turn to see a doll-sized Petty-Prime cart drawing up. The Responsible One leaned out. "Apologies for not offering ride to portal," he squeaked, "but you observe inadequate space in passenger side this my vehicle." He seemed to be making a pleasantry, so Giyt tried one in response.

"It's my fault for having too much growth hormone in my system," he said.

The Petty-Prime gazed at him blankly for a moment, then exhaled in a soft, uncomprehending sigh. "Anyway," he said, "express regret for potential for no longer sharing Joint Governance Commission duties, perhaps." He waved a small paw and accelerated his cart away.

Whatever he meant by that. Giyt really *had* to get at those translation programs one day soon, he told himself, and then remembered that maybe he wouldn't be present to have to worry about such things very much longer. Meanwhile, he had VIPs to greet.

When he got back to the square the keepers of the security switches were lounging by their posts, Hagbarth included, and a large group of Slugs were hooting one of their mournful hymns nearby. Other mayors were arriving, too. Mrs. Brownbenttalon poked her snout out of her cart and beckoned to him. "My husband here say to tell you congratulations on excellent fall you took for new Kalkaboo stinky High Champion," she said. "I share sentiment. Extremely well done, I say!"

"Thanks," he said, nodding at the tiny male in his wife's neck fur. "I hope I'm not late."

"Be commoded, Large Male Giyt. Is last-minute decision of Slugs to arrive early, laster-minute to be somewhat later, typical Slug thing." She paused to listen as her husband chittered in her ear. "Oh, yes," she said. "Have sorrow about unfortunate forthcoming event—no, waiting a bit now, no time for discussing bad news. Hear warning dingle."

The chime had sounded to announce the imminent arrival of the leaders. As Mrs. Brownbenttalon flopped out of her cart the waiting Slug delegation redoubled their hooting, the people at the security switches came to attention, and the golden glow began to surround the portal as the field built up.

Then it was all very quick. The chamber door opened. There was the pop of expelled air from inside, the glow cleared, and two large Slugs appeared, eye stalks waving. They were immediately surrounded by Tupelo's own Slug delegation, escorted to the waiting damp-controlled carts, and borne away.

Giyt blinked after them. "That's it?" he asked.

"That is the all of the it," Mrs. Brownbenttalon confirmed, already getting back into the cart that had brought her. "No orations. No shaking of hands, no sniffing of noses, nothing like that. Only all us dignitaries required properly physically present here at time of peace treaty delegation arriving or will take offense. Is a Slug thing," she added, looking around and lowering her voice. "Delts are even worse and, hey, you know all about Kalkaboos from own self's experience already, right? Esteemed Giyt wife possess wisdom creating associations only with Petty-Primes and Centaurians such as self. Presume former-mentioned esteemed wife presently condoling."

"Condoling?"

He heard a tiny chittering as Mr. Brownbenttalon poked his nose out of his wife's neck fur and spoke confidentially into her ear. "Oh, is understood," she said to Giyt. "You don't know yet. Well, you hearing soon enough, only not from us. Centaurians don't like telling bad news. We hope for seeing you in more happy time. Good-bye."

On the way home Giyt reflected on yet another cryptic utterance. He couldn't tell how much of the mystery was due to deficiencies in the translation programs and how much to simple eetie weirdness; but as the cart approached his house he got a hint of what Mrs. Brownbenttalon had been talking about. There were Petty-Prime kits playing happily in the mud of the de Mir yard with the younger de Mir children, and on the de Mir porch was their mother, with both of the de Mirs and his own wife, talking earnestly to each other while the children played. As Rina caught sight of Giyt she excused herself and came toward him, looking worried.

He was peering over her shoulder at the Petty-Prime female. "Isn't that the wife of your farming friend?"

"Ex-wife, actually; they change partners a lot, I understand. But they're friendly, and he told her something she came hurrying over to tell me. It's Hoak Hagbarth, Shammy. He's circulating a recall petition for you. He doesn't want you to be mayor anymore."

XXI

It's official, all you misters and mizzes, they're getting ready to jump! Our official delegation to the six-power meeting is getting final instructions from their governments, and they'll be arriving here on Tupelo in three days. Let's all be there to give them a good old Tupelo welcome when they come! Because, remember, these aren't Ex-Earth people, these are the official representatives of the old United Nations, and that means they're speaking for the head honchos of our whole damn home planet! So we want to look our best for them. Too bad there's one little piece of housekeeping that we probably can't have finished cleaning up by then—you all know what I mean! But there'll be plenty of time to take care of that later on.

—Silva Cristl's broadcast

If there was one experience that Evesham Giyt definitely did not want to have as mayor, it was being fired. If his term of office had come to its scheduled end, he could have walked away happily. He might even be willing to peacefully resign; in fact, that thought had crossed his mind more than once. But to be kicked out? No, that was something else entirely. It was unacceptable.

It didn't take Giyt long to find out why they hadn't seen

the recall petition on the net. Someone had, not very expertly, cut the Giyts and the de Mirs out of the basic loop, so that all that came to their personal screens was a censored version of what went to the whole community. Once Giyt had an idea of what to look for, he located it in less than half an hour and created a detour around the block.

Then he studied the petition with growing distaste. It wasn't very specific. There wasn't anything that actually said that Rina had once been a prostitute or that accused Giyt himself of any serious misdeeds. But in and among all the whereases—presumably Olse Hagbarth's work, or Lieutenant Cristl's—there were a lot of words and phrases like *malfeasance* and *prejudicial conduct*, and what they all added up to was that the people who signed the petition were asking for a special election to be held to kick Evesham Giyt out of his job as mayor.

Rina came in, and peered over his shoulder. "Lunch is ready," she announced, counting the names. "Seventy-six signatures," she said thoughtfully. "They need twenty-four more to make it count."

He turned to gaze at her. "How do you know that?"

"I looked it up, of course. It's what the regulations say: a recall petition must be signed by at least ten percent of the voting citizens, and that's a hundred. You know what I think, Shammy? I think they're having trouble getting the hundred. There are a lot of people who like you."

But there were a lot who didn't, too. While he was eating his lunch Giyt studied the signatures on the hard copy, trying to fit a face to each name. More than half the members of the fire company had signed. So had, he estimated, a majority of the various people who had asked him for favors at one time or another and been turned down. So had the former mayor and her husband, and all those were easy enough, if not pleasant, to understand. But there were at least a dozen signatures that Giyt hardly recognized. Certainly he could not remember ever having done anything to offend them.

When he said as much to Rina, sitting pensively across from him and nibbling a stalk of celery while he ate, she shrugged. "Hagbarth's had plenty of time to hand out favors. I guess they owe him, don't you think? That's how politics works."

"I suppose." Then he looked at her more closely. "You're not eating," he accused. She shrugged again, and he remembered some of the things he'd learned about pregnancy. "Hey! What is it, is it this morning-sickness business?"

"It turns out it isn't just in the morning," she admitted ruefully. "Now, Shammy, don't get all worried about it. It's just something that pregnant women do. I'm going to go to the clinic this afternoon for a checkup anyway, and they'll give me something for it."

"I'm going with you," he announced. "I—wait a minute." There was an action message coming in on his screen, and when he looked at it what it said was that the Delt delegation would be arriving in ninety Tupelovian minutes. "Damn," he said. "Well, I'm going to go with you anyway."

"Oh, hon. That's sweet of you, but what's the point? I can handle it by myself; you stay home and work until it's time to meet the Delts."

But Giyt didn't stay home, he went right along with her, as much to be ready to glare down any citizen who chose to give his wife any dirty looks as because he thought she needed company.

There wasn't any of that. Business was slack at the little hospital building, and the couple of people sitting in the waiting room seemed more concerned with their own problems than with whatever was happening with the Giyts. The doctor on duty took Rina into the examination room without comment, except to firmly veto Giyt's notion of coming with them, leaving Giyt with nothing to do but wait.

The proper place for that was the waiting room, but Giyt was too restless for that. He roamed around the little building, pausing in front of the window that looked on the cribs for newborns. There was only one baby there, with a medic who looked faintly familiar bending over her. Giyt wondered what it would be like to see his own child in that place, perhaps exchanging with other new fathers the ritual cigars that nobody was ever going to smoke . . . if anybody was going to be friendly enough with Giyt for that sort of sociability. If, for that matter, they were still going to be on Tupelo when the baby got around to being born.

The medic had finished what he was doing with his charge, saw Giyt outside, and came out to speak to him. "Remember me?" he asked. "I was the one who helped you with the kid that was choking? Anyway, I just wanted to tell you that I'm on your side. So's Cheryl here," he added, nodding to the woman who had come out of the pharmacy across the hall.

"So are most of us," she said, shaking Giyt's hand. "I don't go much for politicians, but I can stand you a lot better than that damn Vardersehn woman. She was always coming around and telling us what to do. At least you don't interfere."

So Giyt was in a much better mood when Rina came out of the examining room. "She gave me a patch," she said, showing it. "She says that'll control the nausea—and listen, hon, you don't have to come home with me. Go welcome the damn Delts. You're a sweet man, but you worry too much."

But actually, he told himself on the way over to the portal, he couldn't help worrying about her. Maybe *worrying* wasn't exactly the right word. He was sensible enough to know that morning sickness wasn't a life-threatening kind of thing. What was on his mind was that he wanted to protect her. Evesham Giyt, who had never concerned himself with covering any ass but his own, had now assumed total responsibility for the well-being of the woman he had married. It wasn't a rational thing; it was the old story of the caveman guarding his mate.

And when he got to the square and saw Hagbarth preparing to take his place at the switches, he gave the man a belligerent look, but succeeded in not going over to him and punching him in the nose. Hagbarth looked startled and turned hastily away. Which gave Giyt some minor satisfaction.

All the other mayors were there, with a large company of Delts waiting to greet their dignitaries. Giyt nodded to Mrs. Brownbenttalon, returned the gesture when the Petty-Prime Responsible One waved a paw at him, even got a greeting from the new Kalkaboo High Champion. One of the Delts broke ranks to come over to him; Giyt recognized him as the pilot from their trip to Energy Island. "Hey, you Earth Person Giyt," he said affably, both eyes on Giyt. "Greetings. Regrettings, too, because hear stinky Hagbarth person trying screw you. Pity. All us Delts think you not quite so bad. Comparing to other Earth persons, I mean. Sorry we can't vote, this matter none of our business, you know."

"Well, thanks," Giyt said, somewhat touched.

"Anyway," the Delt went on, one eye wandering toward the portal, where the golden glow was just beginning to develop, "what I wanted asking you, what do you think? How long you guess it take them for bouncing you out? Reason want to know, can then get bets down in the pool."

By the time Giyt got home again he felt reasonably sure that if the recall vote included all the eeties on Tupelo, he would probably win in a landslide. It didn't, of course. But, all the same, it was a cheering thought, at a time when such thoughts were scarce.

Rina greeted him at the door, looking flushed and pleased with herself. "I've got something to show you, Shammy. Come in here a minute."

What she had to show him was her screen, which was displaying a freeze frame of eight or nine human beings, all looking either solemn or angry or just dejected. "It's that Shura Kenk's deportation hearing, hon. It took a little hunting, but I found it. Only I don't think it's much use for what we want, because there aren't any lawyers there, either."

She touched a key and the picture began to move, Giyt gazing wonderingly at it. It wasn't much of a trial, if that was what it was supposed to be. Not only weren't there any lawyers, there didn't seem to be any witnesses, either. Former Mayor Mariam Vardersehn was sitting in what appeared to be the chair, while Hoak Hagbarth was reading a list of accusations concerning Shura Kenk. Who sat in a straight-back chair, listening but hardly speaking; she was the one who looked dejected, and had reason enough.

There did not seem to be a lot of justice being dispensed at this hearing. Even the complainant, the twelve-year-old Grayhorn boy, wasn't present. When Hoak Hagbarth had finished, the half a dozen others in the room—Silva Cristl and three or four others Giyt recognized to be from the firehouse prominent among them—whispered among themselves for a moment or two. Then Cristl nodded to the mayor. "Looks like she's probably guilty, Mariam," she said, "and anyway what can we do? The eeties wouldn't have any respect for us if we let somebody like that stay here. So she has to go."

That was it. All that was left was for Mayor Vardersehn to pronounce the sentence. "Since a jury of your peers has found you an undesirable presence on this planet," she lectured, "you are hereby given forty-eight hours to collect—

what?" As Hagbarth was whispering to her. "Oh, sorry, I was thinking of something else. You're given sixty-seven Earth hours—two Tupelo days, that is—to collect your belongings and report to the portal for return to Earth. The session is concluded."

"What do you think, Shammy?" Rina asked anxiously as the screen went black.

He said, "I think it's a classical frame-up."

"Well, yes, but did you notice something else? Do you remember what Lupe said, that Kenk claimed the real reason they were out to get her was something about the Pole?"

Puzzled, Giyt looked at her. "But she didn't say anything about the Pole."

"Right, hon. Like that old Sherlock Holmes story, you know? Dr. Watson asks him what was interesting about the dog barking. And Holmes says, why, just the fact that it didn't bark at all. Do you see what I mean? Shura Kenk didn't mention the Pole at her hearing."

XXII

The physical plant on Tupelo's polar continent comprises fourteen main manufacturing domes scattered over nearly four hundred square kilometers. These are in general linked by covered passages, supplemented by robot ground-effect vehicles to transport materials back and forth. In addition to the main complex there are eleven additional sourcing sites. These are mineral mines, where robot moles sniff through reefs of ore and extract it for processing, and refineries, where the ore is cooked into pure metals, then batch-processed into whatever alloys are required for scheduled production runs in the factories. In addition there are six relatively small oil and natural-gas wells, providing fuel for the polar continent's dedicated power plant as well as feedstock for its chemical factories.

The autofactories themselves receive these raw materials and fabricate them into whatever is required for the use of the inhabitants of Tupelo, or for export to their home planets.

—Britannica online, "Tupelo"

Shura Kenk not only hadn't said anything about the Pole at her hearing, she hadn't said anything at all. Nevertheless Giyt took his wife's words seriously. He had decided long since that although Rina's reasoning was sometimes a little hard to follow, she was usually right.

So he sat himself down to recheck everything there was in the databank about the polar factories. A lot of the information was in what Hoak Hagbarth had presumably thought to be secure files. That wasn't much of a problem to Giyt. What was a problem was what he had discovered on his first look at Ex-Earth's business correspondence. A lot of the most potentially interesting material employed code words for whatever it was talking about.

What was even more of a problem was that he didn't know what he was looking for.

At the end of two hours of digging he had found out more than he ever wanted to know about the products of the Earth factory at the Pole. In recent months the machines had turned out a bewildering variety of cookware and clocks, underwear and utensils, dolls and toys in a dozen varieties, construction materials, personal hygiene products, bed linen, cutlery—all routine stuff, as far as Giyt could see. It all appeared to be properly accounted for, too. Bills of lading showed that the goods had gone into the robot subs that carried them to the island and then either to the hypermarket or, as export goods, to the portal for shipment to Earth. Almost all the runs were small. That wasn't surprising; that was the special virtue of an autofactory. At need you could produce, say, six gross of carpenter's nails if you wanted them, and you could make them in a dozen different sizes. For that matter, you could make a single nail if you happened to want just one. You could make just about anything at all, as long as the manufacturing specifications were in the factory's memory and the raw materials were at hand. And all the specifications were there. There was file after file of manufacturing protocols for endless lists of components for endless items—most of them incomprehensible to Giyt. What, for instance, was the purpose of one file, apparently unerased because forgotten, which contained a complete set of stats for eetie body odors?

That one Giyt could not figure out. Were the colonists perhaps planning to create a line of dolls to export to the eetie planets—because they were programmed to odor-respond only to eeties? It seemed like a dumb idea to Giyt. If the Centaurians or the Kalkaboos wanted anything like that they were perfectly capable of manufacturing the things themselves. Or—he thought ruefully—maybe it wasn't all that dumb. If someone as resourceful as himself couldn't figure out what they were doing with the data, maybe leaving it unerased was quite smart.

When he checked on what the factory was currently making, he got another surprise. All the screen had to say on the subject was a legend: *Currently under manual control.*

That didn't make any sense at all. Autofactories weren't ever run by manual control, except maybe in the brief periods when someone like Giyt's father was teaching the machines how to assemble a particular device. Assuming the polar factory was that quaintly old-fashioned. Which Giyt couldn't really believe it was.

Then he discovered another curious thing. Checking the production runs of the last month's output he noticed that the factories seemed to have been idle for quite a lot of the time.

That was, at the least, an inefficient use of facilities. If nothing else, the factory might as well have been churning out more clocks and toy airplanes to go back to Earth. But there it was. Production was apparently halted for days on end, more than once, though raw materials seemed to have continued to flow in.

He leaned back, taking a sip from a cup of cold coffee, regarding the screen. Maybe Shura Kenk had been on to something. Was something odd really happening at the Pole? And whatever it was, who was doing it? Hagbarth was the leading candidate, of course; but what was the man up to?

Just for curiosity's sake—and because he was stabbing into the files at random, anyway—he spent a quarter of an hour trying to find out what some of the eeties might be doing with their own factories at that moment. He chose the Petty-Primes, because he had already broken their basic protocols, but all he found out was that they were making 512 of one listed item and 4,096 of another, but what those items actually were he had no idea.

Still . . .

The numbers made him think of those other cryptic inventory numbers he had observed long ago. He searched for that file again, and when he found it he glumly regarded the lists of TARBABIES and GRABBAGS and RUTABAGAS and COPTS. They meant no more to him than they had the first time he saw them. But numbers were numbers, so Giyt did what he had done successfully so many times before. He set up a program to look for coincidences anywhere in the files of Ex-Earth, in the stats from the factories themselves, in the personnel files of Hagbarth and his wife—anagrams, birthdays, anniversaries—anything that might match the numbers.

When fatigue finally drove him to lie down for a little rest he let the program run. He had trouble getting to sleep. He didn't seem to be getting anywhere. But he had no place else to go.

When Rina woke him to tell him that his presence was requested to greet the incoming Kalkaboo delegation, she had two other items of news. The Slugs had finished repairing their drains, and now they could use their own toilet again. And Hagbarth's petition seemed to have plateaued out: "He's stuck at eighty-nine signatures," she said with satisfaction. "He needs eleven more, and I don't think he's getting them."

It didn't take long to see that the Kalkaboos were officially greeted—only a small ceremony, with minimal fireworks—and then, almost immediately, the next delegation was due.

They were the Petty-Primes. There were a lot of them—eighty or more, Giyt guessed, so that it took three portals full to get them all to Tupelo. The Responsible One and his entire family were joyously bustling around, affectionately greeting every one of the scores of arrivals by name. It took forever. Mrs. Brownbenttalon seemed amused. The Delt General Manager and the Kalkaboo High Champion were stolidly patient and the Principal Slug, of course, was a Slug. It was only Giyt who fretted over the length of the proceedings; and then, when all three batches of VIPs had arrived, the Responsible One had something else to keep everyone there. There was a meter-high platform, more like a picnic bench than a stage, and the Responsible One lined up fourteen of the most important members of the delegation on it as a sort of receiving line. One by one, every non-Petty-Prime in the crowd was walked past. There wasn't any hand-shaking, exactly—too much danger of crippling a tiny Petty-Prime paw in a huge human fist or sharp Centaurian claw. So they merely touched digits and exchanged greetings.

It was the kind of meaningless event that Giyt would have done his best to avoid. He didn't want to hurt the Responsible One's feelings, though. The little creature had been kind. Besides, exchanging a few meaningless courtesies took very little conscious thought. Giyt went right on thinking about the polar factories as he patiently plodded along the line. For a moment he considered taking the Responsible One aside—or Mrs. Brownbenttalon or one of the other mayors—and asking if they had heard anything, well, *peculiar* about human goings-on in the polar complex. But it might be an embarrassing question for them. Anyway, what could they know?

As he left the line he saw Hoak Hagbarth and his wife just entering it, between a Centaurian female and a pair of Delts.

That gave Giyt a new thought. The trouble with the Pole, with all its mines and autofactories, was that it was nearly nine thousand kilometers away. He thought of Hagbarth's amiable offer, made back in those long-ago days when Hagbarth was still being amiable, to fly him up there on the suborbital rocket for a sightseeing trip. He wondered if he could find anything useful if he went there in person. Then he wondered if that offer was still open. Probably not. Besides, it would mean leaving Rina alone to face whatever nastinesses the Hagbarths might think up next.

He nodded his farewells to the eeties he knew and went home, his mind still turning over all the questions and worries that did not seem to find any solution. And when he sat down at his screen he found that at last he had been given a break.

Something had turned up in the program he had left to run. When all the numbers had been crunched, it turned out that the number of the things code-named COPTS was precisely the difference between the number of chiplets reported on hand at the beginning of the month and the number reported as used in the manufacture of all the items the factory produced that month.

There was no doubt about it. Far more chiplets were being imported than ever went back into the dolls and gadgets the Earth human polar factory ever shipped out, and the numbers were not small.

Someone was stealing. And that someone could only be Hoak Hagbarth.

Giyt sat back, considering what to do next.

If this had been one of the great corporations he had occasionally worked for on Earth, his job would have ended right at that point. All that would have been left for him to do was to turn the information over to the head of security. Chiplets were smaller than sequins, but they cost money. Big money; some formerly trusted employee would soon be facing a spell in jail.

The trouble was that it didn't add up.

True, the fiscal systems for the human colony had been pretty badly designed and worse run. That was why Giyt had had to fix them, and ultimately why he became mayor. But what was Hagbarth going to do with a couple thousand stolen chiplets?

He could re-export them to Earth and sell them there, sure. They would be worth quite a lot. But that meant having confederates in the Ex-Earth organization on Earth. And anyway the sloppiness in the fiscal systems that let him cover up that theft could just as easily have been subverted in some simpler way—say, to divert credit balances to a dummy account like Giyt's own.

Rina came in, yawning, to bid him good night, and then got a good look at him. She came alert. "Shammy, what is it?"

"Minute," he said, double-checking, just to make sure. The machines were surpassingly good at arithmetic, but you never knew.

He did know. There were no mistakes. "Look at this," he commanded, and when Rina had taken in what was being displayed on the screen she looked less triumphant than puzzled.

"Why, Shammy? Why would he go to all that trouble when he could just steal the money the same way you—well, you know what I mean."

"I do. I thought the same thing myself, but there it is. What I don't know is what to do about it."

"Why," she said, stooping to kiss him good night, "sure you do, hon. You're the mayor. Mayors are supposed to uphold the law. So do it."

Do it.

She was right. Apart from any personal satisfaction he might get out of it, Hoak Hagbarth was a criminal and he ought to be brought to justice.

But brought to justice how?

That was a harder question. He could report the matter to Ex-Earth. But who would he be reporting to? Almost certainly Hagbarth had confederates back there on Earth, probably in Ex-Earth itself, and wasn't it likely they would be the ones to receive the report? Perhaps he could spread the word to the American law-enforcement agencies. But what would they care about something that happened on Tupelo?

So he had some very valuable information, but who could he tell it to?

Just as he was puzzling over this, another message appeared on his screen. The Earth delegates were arriving. There would be six of them, the notice informed him, and when he checked the names he saw that only one of them was an American. That, of course, was because this time it was the old United Nations, not Ex-Earth, who had supplied these ambassadors.

But that one American was Dr. Emilia Patroosh, the woman who had gone with him to Energy Island; and so Giyt had his answer to at least one question.

He got to the portal just as its golden glow collapsed. Besides the obligatory eetie mayors, twenty or thirty Earth humans were waiting to greet them. Most of them, he saw with some surprise, seemed to come from the fire company, both

Hagbarths among them. Olse glanced at Giyt as he arrived and gave him a small, reproving shake of the head.

But she didn't speak, because both the Hagbarths had more important things on their minds. As soon as the transmission was complete, Hagbarth leaped down from his post in the control loop and advanced on the six Earth delegates, all smiles, hand outstretched to reach any other hand it could reach. He wasn't the only one. A dozen of the other Earth humans, Olse included, were moving purposefully to greet the newcomers.

The plenipotentiaries were an oddly assorted lot for Tupelo. One was a tall, mournful-looking woman with purple-black skin and a bright bandanna over her head—a Maasai from Kenya, according to what the roster had said. There was an elderly Swiss man and an even older Korean one; one Egyptian, one New Zealander . . . and Dr. Patroosh.

She was the one who counted. Giyt tried to push his way toward her . . .

And got nowhere. A large hand gripped his arm and a voice from behind said, "Want to do something useful for a change, Giyt? Give us a hand with the goddamn baggage."

It was Wili Tschopp, looking unfriendly. Giyt tried to pull his arm free, without success, as Tschopp was tugging him toward the stack of bags and cases. "Let go," Giyt said. "I want to talk to Dr. Patroosh."

"But she don't want to talk to you, Giyt," Tschopp said reasonably. "Look, she's gone already."

And she just about was; Hagbarth was deferentially helping her into one of the waiting carts and getting in beside her. Most of the other ambassadors were boarding carts as well, except for the tall Maasai woman, searching through the baggage for something of her own, pausing to look at them curiously. "What's the trouble?" she asked, her voice surprisingly deep.

"Nothing," Tschopp said while Giyt simultaneously said:

"I'm the mayor here. I've got something important to say to Dr. Patroosh."

"Oh," said the woman, peering down at his face. "Yes, I've heard of you."

"Then help me—"

But she was shaking her head. "I do not think I can," she said. "We're here to represent our whole planet, Mr. Giyt; we can't get involved in local disputes like this recall question. Dr. Patroosh shouldn't talk to you at all, and neither should I."

XXIII

This is your overnight weather report. Farm areas west of the central massif will experience occasional showers, growing heavier by daybreak. East of the massif, upper levels, possible showers and windy; at town level, partly cloudy with a high of twenty-four degrees; near shore, warmer but dry. The polar station has a 90 percent probability of a major snow event, as the hurricane which narrowly missed the islands has moved north by northeast and appears to be joining a circumpolar low, possibly creating near-blizzard conditions.

—TUPELO WEATHER SERVICE

Evesham Giyt wasn't in the habit of taking no for an answer, especially when the no came from someone other than the person he wanted to ask. Although it was the middle of the night, as soon as he got home he tried calling Dr. Patroosh. She didn't answer, neither on her personal access code nor the one for the house she had been assigned. When the fourth or fifth call wasn't answered he put his clothes back on, called for a cart, and had himself driven over to the house. It was as dark as all the others around it, both human and eetie, and no one responded to his knock.

Frowning, Giyt went home again. There had to be a way to reach the Earth delegate, but what was it? With Rina softly snuffling—you couldn't call it snoring—in the next room, he sat down at the screen again.

There wasn't much for him there, either. When Giyt tried to access the polar manufacturing program again, he once again got the *manual control* legend.

That was highly improbable. It was also what he had more or less expected. Something was definitely fishy at the polar factories, and try as he would he could not find a way into the mystery.

The answers were either on Earth or at the Pole itself. Going to Earth wasn't an option, if only because his departure would be a victory for Hoak Hagbarth. Should he go to the Pole, then? When he checked the schedules he found the suborbital rocket was on the island, due to return to the Pole the next day. He could bully his way onto it as mayor, he thought.

But he wanted to know what was happening on Earth, too.

It didn't take Evesham Giyt long to find an answer to that. He set about creating a super-scout, the most complicated of his career, to sniff through the entire net until it found just what Hagbarth and his gang were up to.

It took time. It would take more time than that to produce any data that would be any use to him; he encoded it to go to Earth in the next transmission, but then, even after it had found out what he wanted to know—if it did—it would have to wait for another transmission to report back to him.

At least it was a tangible step. When weariness finally drove Giyt to bed he felt he had accomplished something.

Dawn was lightening in the east when the din of Kalkaboo fireworks woke him. They seemed louder than usual; some of them must be expiating particularly nasty sins, Giyt thought, maybe to impress the delegates from their home planets. By the time he was dressing after his shower the noise had stopped, the sun was well and truly up, and Rina stuck her head in their bedroom to remind him that there was a note on his screen. The Centaurians were arriving.

Giyt had more or less got used to the arrival of these foreign dignitaries without quite knowing what was going to happen at any of them. Each was different. This time, although it was hardly more than dawn, what looked like every Centaurian on Tupelo was there before him. In the first rank he recognized Mrs. Brownbenttalon and her newly elevated daughter, Mrs. Whitenose. There might have been others he knew, but he couldn't pick them out in the mass of several hundred of the great females, with their smaller males and young romping around among them. When they saw Giyt they made way for him to join the other mayors in the front row, but he detoured as he caught sight of Hoak Hagbarth lurking by the portal.

"Hagbarth!" he called. "Wait a minute."

The Ex-Earth man had already hastily turned to take his place at the control switch, but he was blocked by a dozen Centaurian females crowding toward the portal. "Listen," Giyt panted, catching up to him. "I really need to talk to Dr. Patroosh."

"But she doesn't want to talk to you, Giyt."

"I'll believe that when I hear it from herself. Mind telling me where she is?"

"I do mind, and, listen, Giyt, even if I didn't, don't you think the lady would like to be left alone? Considering what time those poor people finally got to bed? Considering they got a full day's work ahead of them? Now would you please let me get this bunch in?"

There was no arguing with that. The Delt in the control

group was already screeching furiously at Hagbarth to join them. Disgruntled, Giyt took his place in the rank of mayors. He hardly noticed when the chime sounded, the portal began to glow, the door opened, and the four Centaurian VIP females, their husbands peering excitedly out of their fur, emerged. He was considering his next action. Perhaps Patroosh was staying at the Hagbarth house; he could go there and demand entrance—preferably before Hagbarth himself got there.

He didn't linger any longer than protocol absolutely demanded, but as he was heading for a cart a tiny Centaurian male scuttled through the crowd, calling his name. "Large Male Giyt! This is I here, principal husband of Mrs. Brownbenttalon, you recall me? Be waiting briefly, please!"

"I'm in kind of a hurry—"

"Yes, surely. Deeply regret interrupting, but esteemed wife ask me to inform you. You wish find Earth female Patroosh, she say, having overhear you talk with Large Male Hagbarth person, correct? She say good idea go see New Zealand Large Male. Thank you. Now must return instantly for completing of welcoming high-ranking co-species persons."

It took a lot of knocking and ringing to get anyone to answer the New Zealander's door, and when the man showed up, half dressed, he looked seriously annoyed. Even more so when Giyt announced that he wanted to see Dr. Patroosh. "Who the hell are you?" he demanded. "The mayor? Oh, right, the bloke that wanted to bring weapons into Tupelo. What the hell did you want weapons for?"

"It wasn't my idea. Can we talk about it some other time? I just need to see Dr. Patroosh."

The New Zealander looked suddenly suspicious. "What've you been hearing about her and me?"

"Nothing. I just need to talk to her."

The New Zealander studied him for a moment, then

shrugged. "Well, why don't you come on in? I think she's probably out of bed by now."

So she was, but she was still wearing a wrapper over a frilly nightgown. It suited her, with her hair down; in fact, she looked quite pretty, and Giyt could see why doubling up was not a hardship for the New Zealander.

She did not, however, seem pleased to see Giyt. "Yes?" she said frostily. And she remained frosty while Giyt told her his shadowy suspicions about Hoak Hagbarth.

The New Zealander was listening intently. When Giyt finished he said, "What've I always told you, Emelia? It was a mistake to let Tupelo be an all-American project."

Patroosh gave him a tolerant look. "But that's only temporary, Jemmy. America's where Ex-Earth has been getting all its funding, so naturally America has a special interest. But they say they're definitely going to open it up to the rest of the world real soon now."

The New Zealander gave her a skeptical look. "I think we ought to listen to what this man has to say."

"Ah, Jemmy," she said crossly, "don't you think we've got enough on our plate? We've got to bring up the question of exchanging ambassadors again, and that's going to be a long, hard fight."

"But it's important," Giyt put in.

She shook her head. "Listen, Giyt," she began, and then hesitated. "Well," she said at last, "I guess you ought to know. Hagbarth's pretty down on you. Says he misjudged you. Doesn't think you're the right kind of person for the colony. And he has some stories about your wife—"

Giyt's expression hardened. "I know what he says about my wife."

"I don't really *care* what he says about your wife. But it makes a problem. If the Ex-Earth rep and the mayor are feuding, it complicates things here."

"But if the Ex-Earth rep is committing a crime—"

"Depends on what kind of crime it is, Giyt," she said kindly. "The UN can't do anything about embezzlement out here, can it?"

"I don't know that's what it is," he said obstinately. "It could be anything. It could be something that damages relations with the other planets."

"Yes, it could," she agreed, "but we don't know that, do we? As far as I can see, we don't know anything at all." She meditated for a moment, then sighed. "Giyt, I'll tell you what I'll do. When I'm back on Earth I'll ask Interpol a few discreet questions. If they know anything, I'll try to follow up."

Giyt, torn between knowing he ought to thank her, wanting more action: "When will that be?"

"A while. The ambassador-exchange thing is going to take time. Maybe a couple of weeks, even. But that's the best I can do. If you wanted me to do anything here, you'd have to have more evidence. Now will you please leave us alone so I can get dressed?"

More evidence? All right, Giyt thought, I'll give her more evidence. And when he got back to his home he asked Rina, "Do you think you'd be all right by yourself if I went to the Pole for a day or two?"

XXIV

Welcome, welcome, and welcome to our wonderful visitors from good old Mother Earth! And a special welcome to our dear old friend, Dr. Emilia Patroosh, who we all fondly remember from her visit here just a few months ago when she came to investigate the problems with the new generator system planned for Energy Island. And I've got some really good news for everybody, because tonight's the night! Our own dear Hoak and Olse Hagbarth are having a cookout at their home and all six of our honored guests have graciously consented to be present to meet you. Everyone's invited! And I don't have to tell you that a grand time will be had by all when we partake of that famous Olse Hagbarth hospitality! See you there!

—Silva Cristl's broadcast

The decision to go to the Pole was made. Implementing the decision was harder. The first thing Giyt tried was polling the other mayors about revising the passenger list for the polar rocket.

He didn't get very far. The mayors weren't hostile, exactly, but they were clearly unwilling to get into a dispute between Earth humans. Even Mrs. Brownbenttalon was no help. "Could gladly give to you Centaurian seats if available, Large Male Giyt," she said, "but fact is, got no Centaurians going this trip or not next trip either, too. Wait. I maybe try Kalkaboos."

What she tried was to call the Kalkaboo High Champion on her own to see if he could be got to turn a seat loose. That didn't work, either. Downcast, she reported: "New Kalkaboo High Champion no better than old Kalkaboo High Champion. Talk much, do little. Say always permanently willing helping out good friend and assassin of predecessor who has made amends therefore, Earth-human Giyt, but not in this particular case. Say friend Giyt surely aware delegation of high persons from home planet presently present here and maybe would not be approving."

"Well, he could ask them," Giyt said.

"Certainly could. I spoke so also. He say not advisable, could cause problem. What sort problem he mean," she added, "is maybe home planet bosses might be annoy, could think stinky new Kalkaboo High Champion not as good as stinky old one. Stupid, you think? Sure. But what you going do? Is how Kalkaboos are, mostly. Now let me try Delts."

The Delts weren't helpful, either. When Giyt had to report failure to his wife she was warmly sympathetic. "Look on the bright side, hon. Here are all these people that aren't even human, and they do their best to help you—some of them, anyway."

"A very few of them," he grumbled. "And what the Delt said was that he'd do it in a minute, but the Slugs would have a fit because they're naturally scum. I hate the way these people talk about each other."

"Why? It's just talk, Shammy."

"It's not the kind of talk I'm used to," he insisted.

She sighed. "You've led a sheltered life, hon. When I was a kid in Newark, Mom was always making little jokes about the drunken Irish and the dumb Poles, and we all talked mean about the Protestants, and we and the Protestants never had a good word to say about the Afros or the Asians.

Didn't mean much. We kids all played together, and our parents all got together for the Fourth of July parade and the Christmas baskets for the poor. The eeties just talk that way, hon. They get along. They've been doing it for hundreds of years, you know, and never any big fights. Which is a lot more," she added ruefully, "than you can say about any of our countries back on Earth."

Giyt considered trying to stow away on the rocket—impossible—or just showing up at the launch pad and trying to bully his way aboard—just as impossible. Then he faced up to reality. He only had one alternative left. He had to swallow his pride and ask Hagbarth for help.

That wasn't easy, and what made it harder still was that he couldn't get Hagbarth on the screen; his personal access didn't respond, and when Giyt tried the one for the Hagbarth house, it was jammed up. He would have to do it in person.

When he got to Hagbarth's house he saw what the problem was. The cookout reception for the delegates was in full swing. He had to abandon his cart half a block away, because hundreds of people were swarming around the house. As he tried to pick his way through the crowd he got surprised looks from nearly everyone, some uneasily reluctant to meet his eyes, some staring at him with frank loathing. He was still a dozen meters from the front door when Hagbarth himself came steaming up. "What are you doing here, Giyt?" he demanded.

"I want to go to the Pole," Giyt said.

Hagbarth didn't laugh. He barely smiled—well, "sneered" might have been a better word, though he spoke mildly enough. "Can't be done. Don't you follow the weather reports? They had this big blizzard at the Pole. They're still digging out. No time to have tourists."

"I'll take my chance."

"Well, Giyt, you won't. Not this time. There's no room on the rocket. Don't you pay any attention at the commission meetings? You guys allocated us two seats, and they have to go to highly qualified technicians just waiting for a ride; we need them on duty there, Giyt. The factory might break down without them. Maybe next time."

"Which is when?"

"Well," Hagbarth said reasonably, "how can I tell? You never know when some of these home-planet people might take it into their heads to bump everybody and go up and take a look for themselves. Maybe next week, maybe not. Now I've got guests to attend to."

In the end, it wasn't Hagbarth or any of the eeties he'd asked who gave Giyt help. It was Rina.

"Hon?" she said, coming into where he was bent over his screen again, sounding doubtful. "I don't know if it's such a good idea. It wouldn't be comfortable, that's for sure—"

"What wouldn't?"

"Well, my friend—you know, the Petty-Prime female, the one that's married to the horticulturist? You've seen her over here. Anyway, she says they've got space reserved for their whole family on the rocket. They're willing to wait. So if you're sure you really want to go there . . ."

XXV

The polar power plant was primarily Delt, in both construction and operation. The mines were largely Kalkaboo, though the Centaurians and the Slugs had combined on the lab work that made possible the processing of the ores. The factories were everybody's.

In its original form, the polar complex began with three structures set at the vertices of an equilateral triangle. One of the structures is for the Centaurians, one is for the Slugs and the Kalkaboos combined, and the third common to all three for shipping and warehousing; it is near this third building that the landing and launch pad for the suborbital rocket is located. Two kilometers away is the dock for the robot submarines, which carry heavy cargo to the island settlement. This is kept ice-free by waste heat from the power plant, though the structures themselves are often banked high with drifts.

Earth's single structure is one of four hived off from the original Centaurian structure, the other three being an additional dome for the Centaurians and two that are the property of the Petty-Primes.

—BRITANNICA ONLINE, "TUPELO"

The opening session of the six-planet meeting wasn't scheduled to begin for nearly three hours, but a lot of the delegates and their staffs were roaming the town. In the cart to the lakefront Giyt saw clumps of them wandering around like any tourists anywhere, taking pictures, getting souvenirs. Giyt wasn't paying much attention to them. He was preoccupied with the prospect of making a polar flight under the conditions the Petty-Primes' generosity made possible, while Rina wasn't looking at the visitors at all. She was withdrawn and worried. It wasn't until they were getting into the boat for the ride across to the launchpad on the far side of the lake that she glanced at the other passengers and said in consternation, "They've all got heavy coats, Shammy! You don't even have boots. It's winter up there!"

Giyt had noticed the same thing, but tried to reassure her. He wouldn't be out-of-doors at all, he promised. It didn't satisfy Rina. "No, Shammy," she announced, "you need somebody to take care of you. I'm going to come along."

She very nearly did board the ship at the last minute, as a matter of fact. Very likely would have done it, too, in spite of everything, if there had happened to be an available unoccupied seat in the Pole rocket.

But there wasn't. "No more seats, certainly none at all, definitely not any, no," the Delt at the door announced morosely. "Two seats remain open now for Earth-human persons, yes, but taken. Persons are late, too! Persons better damn come soon so captain get this vehicle back in time for watching of opening ceremonials, otherwise captain be damn mad!"

"I'll be taking the Petty-Prime space," Giyt informed him.

The Delt gave him the benefit of a concentrated stare from both eyes. "You say what?"

"It's all right. The Responsible One gave his permission for the switch."

"Ho!" the Delt snarled. "Responsible One? Gave permission? That very sweet, but, tell me, is Responsible One perhaps person who must now have task of to remove

Petty-Prime seating structures from vehicle, so as to make physically feasible space for person your volume and mass to occupy? Still more not to be forgiven injustice!" As he turned to enter to do the job he flung over his shoulder, "For female Earth-human person, still no. Not possible at all."

Giyt turned to Rina. "So you see there's no room. But I'll be all right."

"Maybe so," she granted dubiously, "but also maybe not. What if these other people don't show? Then there'll be room, won't there?"

But that was a faint hope, quickly dispelled; the sound of a motor from across the lake was what dispelled it. A boat was speeding toward them, and as it was slowing down to touch shore Giyt saw who was in it. There was a driver, and two men huddled in parkas behind him. *"Damn!"* Giyt muttered. The men were Wili Tschopp and Hoak Hagbarth.

When the driver got out it turned out to be Olse Hagbarth, unctuously friendly. "Came along to see your hubby off?" she asked, chummy enough to make a cow puke. "Me too. Isn't that always the way for us wives? We stay home with the housework while our men go off—what? You go along with him? Oh, no, hon, you mustn't think about going along. Even if there was space for you. The acceleration in that rocket is *fierce!* Not so bad for a healthy man, maybe, but do you have any idea what it might do to that precious little baby inside you?"

Giyt's big fear was that his wife would punch Olse Hagbarth in the face, but she didn't. Rina allowed herself to be led morosely away across the charred surface around the pad, and Giyt hoisted himself into the entry door as the Delt mechanic brushed past him. He paused to speak to Giyt, half apologetic, half aggrieved. "Is now as good as can make it, which not in fact specially good, you know? You having nasty ride. Do not later speak didn't tell you so."

When Giyt tried to strap himself in he had to agree. The

space intended for eight Petty-Primes was, in fact, large enough to hold an adult human male, but only if the human squeezed himself into the fetal position, knees almost touching his chin. As the Slug pilot came by, checking everyone's fastenings, he made a sound of reproach at Giyt. "Not proper stowage!" he slurped. "Can cause most grave discomfort in delta-vee conditions. Urgently you lie quite still in both ac- and deceleration modes, otherwise potential for snapping of structural members. Not ship's, yours."

Giyt prepared himself for the worst, his thoughts on this new development. What was he to do about the presence of Hagbarth and Tschopp on the suborbiter? They could have only one reason for this last-minute decision to come along. That was to keep an eye on him, and that he could not allow. He would have to lose them somehow.

Then there was no more time to think. The Slug pilot extruded himself to the front of the vessel—actually, in its erected takeoff position, to its top. In the surveillance mirror over the pilot station, Giyt could see the Slug taking his place at the controls. He didn't have a seat, exactly. All the other passengers, except Giyt, had custom-tailored sitting (or perching) places. All the pilot had was a sort of rubbery bowl.

As it turned out, that made good sense. The pilot didn't bother to warn the passengers when he started the engines. He didn't have to. Giyt heard the rolling thunder of the rockets beneath him. The craft began to shake. The noise grew louder until it was all but unbearable, and then the ship slowly began to lift. Then it picked up speed. . . .

That was when Giyt saw the wisdom of the form-fitting chairs. He knew perfectly well what G-forces were supposed to be like, because everybody did. At least he had thought he did, but he had not anticipated how hard the platform he was resting on would become, or that his chest would be compressed until it was hard to breathe, or that the keycard in his hip pocket and the clasp of suspenders at the small of his back would suddenly feel like knives thrusting into his flesh. He could not see how the other passengers were faring, but in the overhead surveillance mirror he could catch glimpses of the Slug, now compressed into a sort of thick pudding in the bowl, his eye stalks pulled back into his body, a few tendrils stretched toward, but not quite reaching, the toggle controls.

Then the noise stopped.

The pressure was gone. The rocket was in the ballistic portion of its flight now, with no thrust at all and no weight. Giyt took a deep breath, savoring the pleasure of breathing freely again. He glanced toward the passengers next to him, the pair of male Delts who were already twisting their heads to check the condition of their mates behind a pair of similarly packed Kalkaboos. Everyone was chattering away—incomprehensibly to Giyt, because somewhere along the acceleration the translation button had been pulled out of his ear by the G-forces.

While he was hunting for it he heard peremptory gurgling from the Slug and looked up. The pilot, restored to three dimensions, had hoisted himself out of his cup and was growling at Hoak Hagbarth. Who had unstrapped himself and was floating free, coming toward Giyt. "I know, I know," Hagbarth snapped at the pilot. "I'll get back when I have to." And then to Giyt: "Damn that Tschopp! He always gets airsick, and he never gets to the bag in time. Look at me!"

He was dabbing at his knee, where there was a definite smear of something on his pants that smelled nasty. Giyt could hear the sounds of Wili Tschopp busily vomiting in the seat just above him.

Giyt didn't answer him. He managed to stretch an arm to retrieve the translation button he had just spotted on the floor. He didn't trust himself to speak. Hagbarth hesitated on his way to the toilet. "I guess you're wondering why we're here, with the six-planet meeting going on and all."

"Actually," Giyt said, "I'm not." And replaced the button in his ear as he closed his eyes. And didn't speak to Hagbarth again.

Coming back to the surface wasn't worse than the takeoff, but it wasn't appreciably better, either. If Giyt wasn't having the breath squeezed out of him quite as much, there was instead a whole hell of a lot more shaking and bouncing about as they reentered the atmosphere. Then the ship danced around a bit on its rockets as the pilot finally did in fact do a little piloting, making sure it was centered on the polar factory pad before he let the craft drop onto its massive shock absorbers for the last half meter or two.

Then they were there. They had to wait, strapped in their seats—waiting, Giyt supposed, while people outside foamed the ground the landing rockets had broiled. Then everyone began getting into their cold-weather gear—those that had it, anyway, which is to say everybody but Evesham Giyt. A moment later, responding to some cue from outside, the Slug pilot slithered down past the passengers, bulky in his rubbery cocoon of electrically heated fabric. He wrenched the door open and, without saying a word, left the ship.

Giyt took that to be permission to do the same. So did everyone else, all at once. Even after Giyt got himself free of the restraining gear it took him a while to lever himself down through the tangle of other passengers and out into the shockingly frigid wind. The cold made him catch his breath, which actually hurt as it entered his lungs. It would have been even worse if it hadn't been for the foamed, but still hot, ground underfoot—

No, he discovered. It wasn't ground, and it wasn't foamed, either. What was underfoot was mud, soaked by the melting snow and cooked to a slurry by the landing rockets. It was still steaming, and it was ruining his shoes. They were in a sort of well surrounded by snowbanks, and meltwater was still gurgling away through culverts.

Someone had gouged out a series of planked steps to get them to the top of the snow, where a duckboard path led them to the waiting hovers. Giyt ran toward them, but Hoak Hagbarth ran faster. He was there before Giyt, panting and irritable, no longer bothering to pretend to be friendly. "This one," he ordered, pointing to one of the hovercraft. "Get in."

Giyt did as told; this was not the time to try making a break. A Delt followed him; then Wili Tschopp, morose and shaky from his airsickness. Giyt was shivering too, his teeth chattering, but at least the car was relatively warm. The bad part of the warmth was that both Tschopp and Hagbarth, though swaddled in their bulky parkas, definitely stank. The Delt took one look at them with both his wandering eyes, then conspicuously leaned away from them as the car began to move.

A few hundred meters away, the factory buildings were bathed in light. Giyt squinted at them, trying to reconcile the remembered schematics of the polar complex with what was before his eyes. Most of the buildings were the familiar golden domes of Delt architecture, linked by their mole-run connecting tunnels, but what the car was heading for was a chunky, square-edged block, ten meters high but dark and windowless. That, Giyt realized, would be the central facility, from which all the others branched off. The car didn't stop outside, but went right through an air-curtain door without pausing.

Inside, they were in a bare room, corridors leading away from it in several directions. There was a sort of reception desk, untended except for a Delt technician, who roused himself from sleep to greet the Delt from the rocket. There was a distant thudding of heavy machinery in operation somewhere not too far away. At least in the building it was warm.

The two Delts disappeared in the direction of their dome while Tschopp and Hoak Hagbarth headed for toilet facilities—not the same ones, Giyt noticed—to clean up. "Wait here. Maury'll come and show us around," Hagbarth growled as he left.

That Giyt did not propose to do.

He looked swiftly around to orient himself. He knew that the Earth dome, as the latest built, was part of a necklace of three other domes, the Centaurians' and the Petty-Primes'. Since the factory plenum belonged to everybody, the wall readouts were in a wild variety of notations and languages. Giyt recognized the dancing dots and slashes of Petty-Prime script on one door and ducked into it. He hurried down the broad hall on the other side until he was almost run over by a pair of forklifts, one with a human driver and the other slaved to the first one—on the way, no doubt, to offload cargo from the rocket. "Excuse me," he called over the grinding whine of the forklifts. "I'm Evesham Giyt—the mayor, you know."

The driver was muffled in cold-weather gear, but his face mask was hanging loose from his helmet. "Really?" he said in surprise. "Still?"

Giyt disregarded it. "Am I going right for the human factory dome?"

The driver took his time about answering. "Shouldn't you be with somebody?" he asked.

"Of course not. I'm the *mayor.*"

The driver brooded over that for a moment. "Well," he said, "most of the guys have taken some personal time. To watch the opening ceremonies of the conference, you know." He thought for a moment longer, then added doubtfully that he didn't personally get to the factory very often, but if Giyt wanted to keep going to the Centaurian control room there was a female there, stuck with the duty like himself, who might know the way. And who liked to gab. And since the whole operation was of course automated, didn't have much else to do.

Giyt didn't hesitate. It wouldn't take Hagbarth and Tschopp much longer to make themselves presentable, and he didn't want to waste his best chance to get rid of them.

He found the Centaurian control room easily enough, and at least part of what the forklift driver had said was true. The Centaurian shift manager was curled up on a pad in front of the controls, lying on her side with her paws relaxed and displayed: three of her paws were white, the other the dun color of her fur. A wall screen was displaying the opening ceremonies of the six-planet meeting, but she wasn't attending to it. She was murmuring softly to the husband who was nestled in the soft fur under her chin.

They did not look as though they wanted to be interrupted. But the male was peering at Giyt with bright eyes, and when he whispered something to his mate she turned her snout toward the door. "What person are you?" she demanded.

"I'm Evesham Giyt. I'm looking for the Earth-human factory dome."

"You got visiting permission pass? No? You got no chance going that place alone, Large Male. You go away or I call—wait one." Her husband was whispering to her. Then she looked at Giyt in a different way. "Oh," she said. "You *Mayor* Large Male Evesham Giyt. You guy bitched up stinky Kalkaboo guy, right? Why had not spoken so right away?"

"That was just an accident—" he began instinctively, but she was still talking.

"Mrs. Brownbenttalon litter-sister of my junior husband here," she said with pride. "She say you pretty good guy. I also think it; damn Kalkaboos always getting damn feelings hurt. You want see Earth-human dome, sure, Mr. Threewhiteboots here take you, show you where everything located, no problem. But when you are got there, please, you tell him quickly hurry right back."

The little male took Giyt in a Centaurian cart—no seats, just a sort of pad with grips to hold on to—and when he had delivered Giyt to the human autofactory dome, he didn't wait to be told to hurry back. He was quickly gone, to whatever intimate moments the couple had been heading toward.

There was a screen and a door, but the door wasn't open. The human autofactory, of course, was locked.

Giyt could hear rumblings from inside. That meant nothing about whether anyone was there; the nature of an autofactory was that it was automatic. Likely enough anybody who was supposed to be on shift had taken off to watch the opening ceremonies of the six-planet meeting, like everybody else.

He flexed his fingers and sat down at the screen. There were not many combinations or passwords that could keep Evesham Giyt out, and it took only five minutes to establish that this wasn't one of them.

When he entered the chamber the rumbling sounds were louder. They came from where a cascade of the talking dolls were dropping out of the assembly machine onto a moving belt, to be picked up by the packing members and stowed in shipping cartons. Several dozen filled cartons were already stacked against a wall, waiting for shipment.

And none of that was of any interest to Giyt.

He looked around and found locked storerooms. These looked more promising. Their locks, too, were only a small inconvenience. But while he was working out the combination, his screen buzzed and half a dozen legends appeared on it. The one in English read: *Earth human Evesham Giyt has wandered away from his party. If you see him please inform Central Command of his whereabouts so he can be returned.*

He scowled and picked up his pace; the communications would not remain so polite. One after another the locked doors opened. Behind the nearest one, surprisingly in this warehouse where no one but humans ever went, was a store of Kalkaboo dawn-bangers—big, bomb-shaped firecrackers, of the size that required detonators. Behind the other doors—

Behind the other doors was worse.

There was no reason for any Earth human to possess Kalkaboo firecrackers, even little ones, to say nothing of these monsters. But the other things in the locked storerooms simply had no business existing on Tupelo at all. They were Earthside weapons, and there were hundreds of them. Handguns. Minicarbines. Assault rifles. Grenades. Mortars. Even shoulder-launched missiles, the kind that rocketed to an enemy's position and then exploded with a shower of high-velocity shrapnel. And when he looked more closely at the missiles he saw the answer to two puzzles.

The missiles bore sniffer vents. They would follow the airborne odor of a target and explode over the target's head, and that explained why there had been that almost forgotten data file on the scents of the eetie races on Tupelo.

And to make them work required high-tech computation . . . and that explained something, too. That had to be where the missing chiplets had gone.

XXVI

The story of human warfare can be told as the evolution of handheld weapons. As the English longbow spelled the end of armored knights at Agincourt, the machine gun marked the final defeat of the cavalry charge in World War I. World War II produced a temporary reversal, as the major weapons became the airplane and the tank, while the foot soldier could do little more than exploit the breakthroughs that air and armor made for him. But then came the handheld antitank rifle, the flamethrower, and most deadly of all, the shoulder-launched bus. This was a missile that could carry any sort of weaponry—shrapnel, chemical agents, even mini-nukes. It would be programmed to explode at a given point or on detection of enemy troops, given away by their body heat, their sounds, or even the aroma of their bodies. It could fire around corners and from concealment; it made the foot soldier the equal of a tank.

—Britannica online, "Weapons"

The thought came too late to be useful, but if he had thought of it in time it would have been no trouble at all, Giyt told himself, to have brought a microcam along. He could be photographing the whole thing. That would be enough evidence to convince anybody, and then he could be taking it to the people at the six-species conference, there to blow the whistle on whatever foretaste of hell Hagbarth and his buddies were planning for Tupelo.

But he had no camera. What then?

There was plenty of physical evidence here, and that would do as well as pictures. The trouble was that the physical evidence was all too big to carry. He needed something small enough to hide on his person. There was no way he was going to get onto the return rocket—past Hoak Hagbarth—if he was carrying a shoulder-launcher or a carbine, much less one of the Kalkaboo bombs.

Thoughtfully he pocketed a Kalkaboo detonator, but that wouldn't prove anything; there were multitudes of them on sale in the Kalkaboo store in the town. What else? There was no ammunition visible for the minicarbines, but the assault guns were loaded; he slipped a clip out of one of them and stowed it away.

Then he tackled one of the buses. If he could take one of them apart to get its chiplet out, that would remove all doubt. On Earth there were plenty of experts who would be able to read the programming on the chiplet, and that would show just what the thing had been built to do.

Figuring out what had to be done was easy. The execution was a lot harder. The damn buses weren't meant to be disassembled by amateurs. Worse, he had no tools. There probably were tools somewhere around, maybe in the same place as the ammunition for the minicarbines, but he didn't know where that was. So he had to do it the hard way. It would have to be a simple smash and pry operation—with the added worry at every step that if he hammered a tad too hard he might detonate the explosives and fuel in the bus. Time was a problem that couldn't be ignored, either. Sooner or later Hagbarth and the others would be checking the factory in their search for him. By then he had to be elsewhere, and ready to give them some kind of lying apology for going off on his own . . . and hope they bought it . . . and then—

assuming that somehow, against all the odds, he had been lucky enough to get away with that much—somehow manage to get back on the suborbital rocket's return flight with his booty intact.

He didn't quite see how he was going to manage any of that, but meanwhile he had the present job.

Wonderfully he managed to get two of the buses open enough to fish out the chiplets, all the while rehearsing—and rejecting—the things that he might say to Hagbarth. Not that there was anything he could say that would make a difference if Hagbarth had the animal cunning to check out his secret arms cache for himself, because anyone who looked at the two buses would see they had been tampered with. For what good it might do, he put them at the back of the stack. Then he locked all the storeroom doors, erased his programs from the screen, let himself out, relocked the door, and started back down the hall.

He didn't get far before he heard the whir of an approaching cart, and of course it was Hagbarth.

Hagbarth wasn't alone. Tschopp and that other man from the fire company—Maury Kettner?—jammed the cart beside him. They all leaped out as soon as the cart had stopped, scowling angrily at Evesham Giyt.

It was time for the lying to start. "Jesus," Giyt cried enthusiastically, "am I glad to see you guys! This place is wild. I finally did find the factory, but the damn thing's locked up."

Hagbarth studied him thoughtfully without speaking. He gave Maury Kettner a nod; the man turned and walked away as Hagbarth said, "So you were just wandering around, is that what you're saying?"

"Trying to find the factory," Giyt agreed, doing his best to see where Kettner was going; afraid he knew the answer in advance, but seeing no choice but to tough it out. "This is a very confusing place, Hoak."

"Of course it is. Why didn't you wait for us?"

"Well, you took so long," Giyt improvised, looking over his shoulder. Kettner had opened the factory door and disappeared inside. He was taking a long time in there, though. Had Giyt left some sign of his entrance? "Anyway," he added, "I ran into a couple of eeties, and they gave me directions."

"But when you got there it was locked."

"Locked, right," Giyt agreed.

Hagbarth nodded, poker-faced. "Was there any special part you wanted to see?"

"Oh," Giyt said, shrugging vaguely, "just to get a general idea, you know? So I'll know what I'm talking about when I see Dr. Patroosh."

"She's a busy woman, Giyt. You don't want to bother her with a lot of unimportant stuff."

"No, of course not," Giyt agreed. "It's just that—"

But his voice trailed off. The factory door opened. Maury Kettner came out, and his expression was cold. Worse than that, he was carrying one of the carbines from the store, and Giyt observed unhappily that Kettner, at least, had known just where to go to find its ammunition clip.

He was staring at Giyt, but it was to the others that he spoke. "He was into the stash, all right," he said. "The seals were broken."

Hagbarth exhaled a sigh. "Ah, Giyt," he said reproachfully, "what did you do that for? More important, what are we going to do with you now?"

It was a rhetorical question. If aimed at anybody, it was at Evesham Giyt; but it was Wili Tschopp who answered it. "There's always the Heckslider way," he mentioned.

It took a moment for Giyt to make the connection, and then Tschopp spelled it out for him. "You know about Harry Heckslider, don't you? The one who fell out of the chopper on the way to Energy Island. See, he got curious, and he just wouldn't listen to reason."

"Now, wait a minute," Hagbarth said good-naturedly. "Why do you think Evesham here would be like that? You don't have any special love for our alien brothers, do you, Evesham?"

Hagbarth's tone was friendly enough—no, Giyt decided, a lot too friendly. The man was putting him on. He said, temporizing, "I've got nothing against them."

"Really? Not even the Kalks?"

"Well, I thought they gave me a lot harder time than was called for—"

"Damn right they did! I really hated to see them working you over like that, Evesham. Not that the others are all that much better. Can't ever trust any of the freaks, that's what I say. You know they've all been scouting Earth for years, don't you?"

Giyt was honestly surprised. "Scouting Earth?"

"You bet! They've got their ships orbiting the Sun, watching us, learning everything about our capabilities—how do you think they got that portal to Earth so fast?"

"Why, I guess I never thought—"

"No," Hagbarth agreed bitterly. "You never did. Most people don't, but there they are, and you know what kind of weapons they've got, because your Centaurian friend told you all about their old wars." He was breathing heavily. He collected himself and spoke more reasonably. "Anyway, Evesham, you're a patriotic guy, aren't you?"

I am? Giyt asked, but not out loud. Actually he didn't know the answer. He had never given much thought to patriotism, but now . . .

Hagbarth was going right on: "I mean, you know what the score is. The freaks would do us in in a minute if they had the chance. What do you think the Kalks have all those big explosives for? And the Delts have those harpoons—think they don't think of using them on the rest of us now and then? They've got all the weapons they need to wipe us all out, they just don't call them weapons. And what do we have?"

"Well," Giyt said, pretending to think it over, "I guess we have those water cannons."

Hagbarth grinned at him, then turned to the others. "See? I told you he wasn't so dumb. But that's just piss-ant stuff, the water cannons. They couldn't really save us if the freaks tried a coup. Which they could do at any time. So that's what we need the other stuff for, right?"

Giyt gave another imitation of a man trying to work a hard question out. "Maybe you're right," he admitted. "One thing that kind of puzzles me—"

"Yeah?"

"When you got me to try to get some weapons imported. Was that just so no one would think you already had some here?"

Hagbarth grinned and clapped him on the shoulder. "Smart," he said admiringly. "So how about it, Evesham? You won't say anything to anybody about what you saw, will you?"

"I guess not."

Hagbarth patted his shoulder again approvingly. "That's good, Giyt. Glad to have you aboard. Just to make sure, you won't mind if we search you, will you?"

Giyt let out a long breath. He was not a violent man, and there were three of them. There was no way he could stop them if they wanted to search.

"Oh," he said, reaching inside his tunic. "You mean you'd

be looking for something like this?" And he took out the Kalkaboo detonator and displayed it, wondering if they were too far from the bombs for it to work.

"Hey!" Tschopp yelled. "Careful with that thing!"

Giyt was careful. He pressed the button firmly and with care; and as it turned out, they weren't too far away at all.

XXVII

The segregation of industrial facilities at the polar installations is not only dictated by political considerations—each species has its own private workplaces—but is a safety measure. The passages connecting the domes are secured with blast-proof doors. In addition, the Delt-designed roofs, though massive enough to withstand any snow load likely to occur in this region, are deliberately designed with fault lines so that, in the event of an explosion, most of the force of the blast will be exerted upward. This is deemed necessary in case of accident, but no such accident has ever occurred.

—Britannica online, "Tupelo"

Giyt could see that Hagbarth's mouth was moving. That was how he knew that the man was saying something, or from his expression, most likely furiously bellowing something, but just what Hagbarth was bellowing was drowned out in the thunderous crash and rumble from the doll factory. Giyt saw that the door to the factory was bulging toward them. For a moment he thought it would fly open, but it didn't; it swelled and shuddered, but it held. As the echoes of the explosion died down, Hagbarth gave Giyt a petulant look. "What the hell have you done *now?*" he asked, and didn't wait for an answer. With Kettner he raced to the door and tried to pull it open. It resisted. Kettner set down the minicarbine to get a better grip on the door, while Tschopp was staring after the other two, open-mouthed incredulous and scarlet-faced angry.

Even a nonviolent man can find a little violence in him now and then. Giyt didn't even pause to think. From behind Tschopp he kicked at the back of the man's knees. As Tschopp went sprawling Giyt was already running, as far as he could get from the men with the guns—down the corridor, around a turn, through an open door, down another short hall.

The hall ended in a doorway with a glowing orange sign over it. The sign was in the curlicues of the Delt language, but Giyt knew what it was: That door went to the outside world.

He paused for the fraction of a second to consider. Did he want to go out into the freezing polar night again? Did he have a choice?

Put that way, it was a simple decision. When he grasped the handle it was cold to the touch. When he pushed the heavy door open the blast that came in was colder still. He hesitated, thinking about just what it was going to be like to be out, dressed as he was dressed, in that fierce Arctic gale; but he knew the others were not far behind him. Outside, at least, the dark might hide him.

He stepped through, hugging himself against the freezing blast, and let the door close behind him.

That was the first disappointment.

Outside in the open, it wasn't really that dark. Overhead the colors of the aurora washed across the sky, rust-red and pale blue; they weren't bright, but they were widespread, in places obscuring the icy bright stars. The aurora gave light enough to see by, surely. If Hagbarth and the others followed him out, the one that held the carbine could pick him out in a moment, and then—

Then it would be very bad for Evesham Giyt.

He floundered to where the winds had scoured away most of the snow and began to run, his lightweight shoes crunching against the gritty crust left from some earlier snowfall, his feet already feeling as though they were beginning to freeze. He expected at any moment to hear shouts from behind him, and then, no doubt, the pippity-pop of the minicarbine. Or did you ever hear the shot that got you? Weren't the bullets moving faster than sound? So perhaps he would hear nothing at all, but he would feel something, all right. What he would feel would be the punch-punch-punch of a dozen rounds from the minicarbine stitching themselves across his back . . . and that would be the last thing he ever felt, in the moment when life would come to an end for Evesham Giyt.

The second disappointment was that there was nowhere to hide.

Giyt thought wildly of clawing out a foxhole in the snow, maybe covering himself with the stuff. He didn't think about that for long. Even assuming it was possible, assuming he could do that kind of work with the bare hands that were already stiffening up, he knew what would happen then. Either Hagbarth and the others would find him anyway, or he would simply freeze to death.

Then he stopped short as reality hit him.

What he was doing was making it easy for Hagbarth and the others.

They weren't likely to shoot him. Why would they bother, when shooting him meant they would have to explain away the bullet holes? While if they simply left him alone he would die of the cold. He could hear what Hagbarth's semi-pious explanations would be: "I guess the poor son of a bitch must have done something stupid that caused the accident, you know? And then he ran away, probably trying to hide, maybe in shock or something, and then he must've got outside somehow. It's really too bad, and I'm going to hate having to tell his wife, but, Jesus, look at the damage the bastard caused!"

So hiding out here was no good. To have any chance at all of surviving, Giyt needed to get back to the warmth inside.

He looked around wildly, each breath a separate hurtful thrust of pain in his nostrils. Instinctively he had been running back toward the rocket port, so the building that was just ahead of him had to be where Mrs. Threewhiteboots and her mate were overseeing the instruments at the plenum.

There had been an outside door there too, he remembered.

There was, and just by the door, parked, was a Centaurian hovercar. He tried the door of the car, but it was locked, and his fingers were getting numb.

Perhaps the Centaurians could help? If he could get the door to the plenum open from outside . . .

As it turned out, he couldn't. There was no external handle on the door, and not even anything for him to grip and try to pull it open.

But when he had hammered on it long enough, freezing, despairing, it opened a crack and a long Centaurian snout poked inquiringly out to peer at him.

It was hard enough for Giyt to try to explain what had happened, his limbs numb, his teeth chattering. It must have been even harder for the Centaurians to comprehend him through the vagaries of the translation program. But Mrs. Threewhiteboots was quick to figure out what he was trying to say. "Damn right," she said. "Something require being done. Never liked that stinky Large Male Hagbarth—no offense other Earth humans, all right? So okay, we hide you someplace. Warm you up. Come."

As it turned out, not all the tiny doors along the corridors were for Petty-Primes; Mrs. Threewhiteboots held one open while her husband scuttled ahead, clucking and mewing to the chorus of tinier clucks and mews that came from inside. A door that was built large enough to allow passage for a Centaurian was not meant for humans, but Giyt somehow managed to bend his stiffening body low enough to squirm through.

At least it was warm inside the Centaurian lounge. It was dimly lit, and it also smelled quite horrible, likely because of the half-dozen pups that were squirming around one of those elevated Centaurian sleeping pads. "New litter," the female said proudly, cuffing them out of the way. "Exceptionally handsome lot, don't you agree? Now you come closer here, I hug you to defrostedness."

Her fur was soft, her body blessedly warm. The pups didn't like the idea of this alien monster preempting their mother's embrace, but the male spoke sharply to them and they curled up sullenly against Giyt's back. When he tried to talk Mrs. Threewhiteboots shushed him peremptorily. "You get blood running again, then have conversation. Not yet." But then, as he felt life returning, he felt also a nearly overpowering urge to drift off to sleep. He resisted it; his story could not wait. Haltingly he told Mrs. Threewhiteboots what he wanted to do.

"You bet, sure," she said. "Show proof of total iniquitousness of other large males six-species gathering, good idea. So we take you to rocket, all right, let damn ugly Large Male Hagbarth try to stop us."

"But he has a gun," Giyt remembered to say between bouts of yawning.

That produced a considerable silence. Then Mrs. Threewhiteboots murmured something to her mate, who turned and pushed his way out of the door. "Hate damn guns," she said morosely. "That make things tough, right? But we do best we can. Mr. Threewhiteboots go check things out. Now you sleep a little, understand me?"

It was an invitation hard to refuse. Against his better judgment Giyt let his eyes close. Perhaps Mr. Threewhiteboots would come back with help. Or perhaps he would raise the alarm, and the several dozen other persons in the polar complex, human or otherwise, would turn away from the broadcast of the opening ceremonies long enough to overpower Hagbarth's few and convoy him to the rocket, and then to the Hexagon to show his chiplets to the council meeting. . . .

But perhaps Hagbarth would not want to be overpowered.

And he and his bullies did have that gun.

The gun made all the difference.

Of course, Giyt reasoned, it would make no sense for Hagbarth to start a shooting war here and now. Everything was against it. Hagbarth wasn't ready for anything like that. Especially right now, with the six-species council in session, and capable of summoning quick reinforcements from the parent planets. Most of all, Hagbarth's illicit armory had vanished with the explosion of the Kalkaboo bombs; that was another reason why this would not be a good time to start his putsch. Shooting anybody would certainly not be a sensible thing to do.

But, on the other hand, who had ever described Hoak Hagbarth as sensible?

A sudden twitch of alarm from Mrs. Threewhiteboots made Giyt open his eyes. That was a strange sensation, for what he saw was no different either way. Eyes closed, eyes open, there was only blackness. Was this what blindness felt like?

But it wasn't his eyes that were at fault. "Is power out," Mrs. Threewhiteboots said worriedly. "Power never out. Is bad thing. You stay here inside lek where no one can see, Large Male Giyt, I look."

That was an order he could not obey. As she peered out of the door Giyt was shoulder to shoulder with her. Power was out, all right. The principal illumination in the corridor was from one distant, palely glowing panel of green emergency lighting on the ceiling. He could see the plenum at the end of the hall, but the brilliant readout displays were gone, leaving only one fast-moving line of symbols on one wall. There were brighter moving lights just beyond there, too. Someone—no, several someones—were there with pocket torches. And he heard voices.

One of the voices was raised in anger, and it belonged to Hoak Hagbarth.

Mrs. Threewhiteboots moaned something, then reared upright to peer down the hall. Something small was skittering rapidly toward them. It turned out to be her mate, who leaped into the fur of her back, chattering at her. She listened for a moment, then turned and shoved Giyt back inside. "They coming, maybe! Go in! Close door!"

The power was out, and so were communications. Mr. Threewhiteboots (his mate explained to Giyt) had gone to the communicator; but that was when the power went—shut off, most likely, by Hagbarth himself to make things even tougher for Giyt. While Mr. Threewhiteboots was trying to get the emergency circuits working to sound the alarm, two large Earth-human males had come in. "They asking you, Large Male Giyt," the female reported. "My husband hear you name, but nothing else; he not have translator. They talk at him, but he not understand nothing. Then they point stinky gun at him. He run."

"Hell," Giyt said. Communications dead, access to the rocket blocked: Was there any way out of this? He thought rapidly. "Are they still there?"

"Think not. Don't want to look. You want?"

"No. Well, maybe I do, but not right away. They won't stay around. Then maybe I can—"

But he stopped there, because he knew, before he said it, that they would never let him get to the rest of the complex. They would let no one in or out until they had made sure Giyt was not still inside.

Then he remembered what was parked by the outside door.

He took a deep breath, then opened the door a crack, listening. The Centaurian pups were whining softly, but he heard nothing else, and it was dark outside. When he poked his head out there were no lights.

There would be no better chance than this. "Mrs. Threewhiteboots," he said, "do you have a keycard for the hover? If I could get around the outside to the rocket pad—"

She made a snuffling sound that might have been amusement. "What you do with keycard? You think you driving Centaurian hover?"

"Maybe you could tell me how to do it."

"Maybe you being very ridiculous, Large Male Giyt. Never happening; driving instruments quite complicated. Also what you think those large males do, they finding us here and you gone? No, not giving keycard. Driving vehicle own self, most fearfully."

Mrs. Threewhiteboots delayed only to scrabble in a compartment for a body-shawl and a set of flat disks like snowshoes. When she had strapped them to her little feet she muttered to her husband, and the two of them led Giyt to the door.

The hovercraft started quickly and moved easily over the drifts. It took only a few minutes to reach the rocket launch pad.

And then they stopped, looking at each other, looking

back at the dome they had left. There were more of those handheld lights moving around outside that door. They undoubtedly belonged to some of Hagbarth's people, searching for them. If they went back there, they would be caught.

But there wouldn't be much point in trying to do that, anyway. The pad was empty. The suborbital rocket itself was gone.

XXVIII

With heartfelt sadness I have to tell you all, dear friends, that there isn't any doubt any more. Our mayor, Evesham Giyt, was definitely lost in that terrible explosion at the Pole.

So, folks, I think it's time for us all to show what big hearts we have here in Tupelo. Never mind that the explosion was his fault. Never mind what it's going to cost us all—many months of lost production, and I don't even want to think about how much money. Say nothing mean about the dead and gone, folks, no matter how much of a mess the guy made. Probably he just didn't know any better, maybe. So let's forget that part of it and just give our deepest sympathy to his grieving widow—who, you know, is probably going to be leaving us herself before long anyway.

—Silva Cristl's broadcast

When Rina was awakened from a restless sleep with the word that Giyt was missing and presumed dead, she didn't believe a word of it. Wouldn't believe it, because it was just too unexpected and far too awful for her to accept. And then, when she accessed the Earth-colony news channel, she had no choice but to believe it, because the scenes of destruction from the Pole were too terribly convincing to be denied.

In the view from outside, the Earth autofactory dome was

split completely open, oozing black smoke into the dark polar sky. In the view from inside, everything was simply wrecked. Rina sat quietly in front of the screen, sometimes remembering to eat a bit of the breakfast she had absently made for herself, sometimes simply sitting motionless, not even thinking. When the news items began to repeat themselves she switched randomly to other files, her lessons, her household reminders, sometimes Giyt's own files . . . but that was painful; because he wasn't there. She was a practical woman. She always did her best to be prepared for whatever future needs and problems might arise well in advance, so that she could deal with them when they came. But she had not envisaged any future for herself that did not include Evesham Giyt there to share it.

Lupe was the first to arrive at the house. "Oh, Rina, hon," she said, her voice as mournful as her face, and stopped there because she had nothing to add. She sat quietly next to Rina, holding her hand. Then it was Matya, with the younger children, the others busy getting themselves off to school. Matya was more businesslike, and full of news. The six-planet meeting was convening early to discuss the accident. The loss of life, at least, had been small—two eeties missing and supposed to have been caught somehow in the blast. And Giyt. The suborbital rocket had made an emergency flight to the Pole, bringing twelve Earth firemen to help control the damage, and was already on its way back for more. The economic consequences for the Earth community were worrisome; until the autofactory could be rebuilt everything would have to come by portal from the home planet. As would everything needed for the rebuilding; the Earth delegation had already sent a message back to Earth to say what had happened and that emergency help was needed.

Rina listened politely to everything Matya had to say—having, of course, already heard it all for herself on her screen—until Lupe finally gave up trying to force food on her and Matya insisted that she go back to sleep. It was easier to pretend to obey than to argue, but Rina knew that sleep was impossible.

Well, not quite impossible.

Rina had taken it as given that she would lie wakeful in the bed that still bore traces of Evesham Giyt's friendly male odor, while horrid thoughts recirculated through her brain. However horrid, they needed to be thought anyway: Should she stay on Tupelo? Go back to Earth? Bear the child that was just beginning to stir inside her? Abort it?

All of those unpleasant thoughts had subsidiary thoughts, just as unpleasant, that followed instantly from the first: wondering about what life would be like as a single parent (or about what childless life would be like if she aborted the one thing she had left of Evesham Giyt). And what should or could she do about Hoak Hagbarth?

They were ponderous thoughts that would keep anyone awake, one way or another. They were all attempts to discern whether she had anything left that was worth the trouble of going on living for. They didn't do the job, though. Willy-nilly, she drifted off, and the first she knew that she had gone to sleep after all was when Lupe touched her shoulder to wake her. "It's Mrs. Brownbenttalon," Lupe whispered. "She just wants to pay her respects."

Actually the Centaurian female had brought more than sympathy. She hadn't come alone; with her was a nearly grown female, painfully lugging two large packages wrapped in green fabric. "This shade of green our frequency devoted to sadness," Mrs. Brownbenttalon explained. "Contents of package food and drink. Hey, everybody know have no time for cookery with death in family. You meet my third daughter, Miss Stubnose? You say hello, Miss; good, now go back home." She crawled up onto a couch and acknowledged introductions to Lupe and Matya. "Yes, very sad happening," she agreed. "Have serious pain in abdomen, right here where husband mostly hang, for you, Mrs. Large Male Giyt. You main husband damn good son of a bitch. You know I also lose close family members in cataclysmic event?"

That took Rina by surprise. "You did?"

The matriarch bobbed her long snout mournfully. "Esteemed wife of male littermate Mrs. Threewhiteboots gone missing, perhaps caught in blast, also said secondary husband of same. No trace found. Damn Hagbarth claims must have been trespassing in Earth factory at accident time. Untrue. Mrs. Threewhiteboots never waste personal time in dumb Earth human factory."

"Oh, I'm sorry."

"For what? It not you guilt." Mrs. Brownbenttalon sighed. "Simply accident, surely. Reason I sorrowing, six babies of littermate's esteemed wife now orphans, very sad. But," she added emphatically, "remember I still friend; you need any kind help you ask."

"Thank you," Rina said. "I think Lupe's making tea. Would you like some?"

"Earth tea?" Mrs. Brownbenttalon pondered for a moment. "Sure, why not? Only why is Earth female Lupe waving at you in this fashion?"

The reason Lupe was trying to attract her attention turned out to be something on the kitchen screen, and when Matya turned on the one in the living room, the face that appeared was Hoak Hagbarth's, being interviewed by Silva Cristl as he got off the polar rocket at the pad. " . . . total devastation," he was saying to the interviewer. "No, we don't know *what* the hell Giyt did, but somehow he blew up the whole damn factory; God knows how long it'll take to get it running again. And it's dangerous up there, so Chief Tschopp has ordered half the fire company to the Pole to prevent any further loss of life. Giyt? Oh, he's dead all right, missus. He probably got blown up in that blast, I don't know if we'll ever find the pieces. But if he didn't, maybe he staggered out into the snow and then just froze to death." He shook his head. "The damage is just unbelievable, but you know what is the worst part of it? It's the way he left his poor widow and their unborn child—"

That was more than Rina could take. "Turn the bastard off," she said, her voice shaking with anger at the man. But the fury she felt had one good quality. It told her that she did have one definite thing to go on living for.

Her plan was simple. If she couldn't bring Giyt back, at least she could avenge him. When she was finally alone she considered how to set about it.

What was hard to see was just how to go about doing that. Giyt, damn the dear man, had not left a clear record of what it was that he knew or guessed. There were any number of items in his files that provided clues: the tabulation of chiplet imports paired for some reason with the shipping records of finished products; a log of failed attempts to access the ongoing processing data from the Pole; scraps of files that might have meant something, but without Giyt there to explain their relevance were simply puzzling. There was even a just-arrived packet of data from Earth that was directed to Evesham Giyt himself, but how useful that was going to be was dubious, because of course it was encoded. Perhaps there was something interesting in that, provided it wasn't just a financial statement from one of Giyt's half-dozen money dumps.

The trouble was, Giyt wasn't there to provide the key.

It was high noon, then it was dark, then it was light again. When Rina could not stay awake she slept for a while. Then she got up and made the bed, so that company wouldn't think her a slob. And there continually was company, usually Lupe or Matya coming by every few hours and staying until she somehow managed to get them to leave again, usually by pretending to be sleepy—and often enough by actually going to sleep. And getting up. And making the bed again. And repeating the process. She picked up things in one place and put them down in another, made herself meals but couldn't always make herself eat them, switched on the news channel, and for lack of anything more useful to do, watched the unfolding stories: raucous times at the six-planet meeting as the eetie delegates joined in deploring the sloppy precautions the Earth humans had provided at the Pole; warnings that there would be shortages of some consumer items until new shipments could be received from Earth, coupled with appeals to refrain from buying anything not urgently needed during the emergency. She watched only as long as her interest was held—not long—and then she turned the screen off again.

If she had some technical help, she thought, absently rubbing her belly, she might be able to piece together whatever it was that Giyt had learned.

But help from whom? Was there anyone she could trust? Or would anyone she asked for help be just as likely to be part of the problem?

But she could not let Hagbarth get away with whatever he was up to.

So Rina faced up to the fact that if anything was going to be done, she would have to do it herself. She sat down before the screen again and attacked the problem of decoding the data packet from Earth. Although she hadn't had much recent practice, it was like riding a bicycle, she found. Once she got started she remembered the skills Giyt had taught her. She set up a program to try every possible password, feeding in every word she could imagine Giyt including.

It took a while, but the program ultimately produced the password, which turned out to be "I guess I love Rina."

She cried at that, but only for a bit. Then grimly she began to study the packet.

And it was all there.

Ex-Earth was a front for an American expansionist conspiracy that reached up into high levels of the administration. They were planning to take Tupelo over. The autofactory at the Pole had been secretly manufacturing weapons.

Rina sat back, considering. Then she called Mrs. Brownbenttalon. "It seems that I do need help," she said. "Can you get me into the meeting?"

It was the first time Rina had been in the Hexagon since it was rearranged for the six-planet conference. The six little platforms for the members of the Joint Governance Commission had been replaced with a cluster of seats (or pads or trees) to accommodate the high officials from the home planets; there were from six to a dozen members of the appropriate species in each position, with most of the floor space given over to their staffs and experts. It was *crowded.* And as they were all talking at once, it was also hopelessly noisy. Rina's translator button struggled valiantly to render scraps of the other languages into English for her, but it was unequal to the task. What came out was a sort of chowder of half sentences and expletives, and she finally took the thing out of her ear. It eventually took the best efforts of the chief Centaurian delegate, Mrs. Oneeyewanders, a female so august that she had not one but three husbands scuttling about in her fur, to restore something like order. When she screeched for quiet the rumblings of the crowd simmered down enough for Rina to finish her testimony. And all the while, there were the Hagbarths standing in the little cleared space next to her, giving her poisonous looks, shaking their heads in the simulation of reproof.

Poisonous looks were all they could manage. It had not been smart of Hoak Hagbarth to send all his fellow conspirators in the fire company to the job of cover-up at the Pole, because the ones that were left behind were not part of the conspiracy. Behind the Hagbarths stood a pair of the brawniest fire police left on the island, and neither of the Hagbarths dared move.

Then Rina accessed Giyt's decoded packet from Earth, and everyone was still, or nearly still apart from indignant whisperings to each other, as the record unrolled.

When it was over, Dr. Patroosh was the first to speak, glaring at Hagbarth. "You *scum,*" she said.

Then the Swiss delegate chimed in—speaking in French, Rina guessed; but her translator had not been equipped with French-language capability and so she could make nothing of it until the New Zealander spoke up. "I agree completely," he said. "We will all transmit this complete record to our governments at once."

"But it is all lies!" Hagbarth burst out. "She made it all up! Are you going to take the word of a whore against me?"

It didn't do him any good. They *were* taking it; the evidence left no room for doubt. Rina got the button back into her ear again in time to hear Mrs. Oneeyewanders speak up for her; so did the Slug, on what grounds Rina could not imagine. Then the Kalkaboo piped up: "Exists here no problem believing statement of Earth-human female. Can make factuality check, surely. Immediately we can order stop to present clean-up at the Pole, then quickly dispatch six-species delegation up there for total discovery of truthfulness."

It was the most sensible thing Rina had ever heard from a Kalkaboo, and it had its effect on Hoak Hagbarth. The man wilted before her eyes. He gave Rina an imploring look, while his wife, sobbing, clutched at his arm. But if he wanted to speak he had no chance; the whole assembly was talking at once again.

So it was over.

The accumulated fatigue of the last few days struck Rina then; she looked around for a place to sit down, failed to find one, squatted on the floor, her head bowed. It was a moment of triumph, but she couldn't feel exultation. It only meant that now she had to face up to the real questions of life continuing without the presence of Evesham Giyt.

She didn't even notice that the assembly had quieted until one of the fire police poked her. She looked up.

The Principal Slug had slithered his way to the delegates' platform, clutching his pocket screen; he was showing it to the Slug delegate, who looked, and raised his forebody to speak. As Rina hurriedly replaced her translator he was saying, "—interesting news from ship terminal at dam. Unscheduled robot sub has arrived at terminal with passengers. They are three. Are hungry, cold, very, very dirty, but not in the least dead."

XXIX

URGENT. ACTION REQUESTED.

Access attached files 1 (data secured by Evesham Giyt) and 2 (statements of Hoak Hagbarth and Olse Hagbarth at interrogation by Inter-Species Conference).

Urgently recommend immediate full-scale investigation of Extended Earth Corporation and all persons named in accompanying files. If allegations in attached files are supported, further recommend indictments for conspiracy to initiate military action on Tupelo, in violation of existing compacts. By unanimous decision of all five other species involved, all sessions of the conference are suspended until this matter is resolved.

—TUPELO DELEGATION DISPATCH TO UN

As their boat raced across the làke to the dam, Lupe on one side of her, Mrs. Brownbenttalon and her husband on the other, Rina at last let herself cry. Mrs. Brownbenttalon examined the process with interest. "Leakage from eyes indicates sadness, I have information," she called over the whine of the motor and the rush of the air. "This leakage not necessary, Mrs. Large Male Giyt. You husband alive okay; he remember robot sub can take home as easy as rocket, only slower. Like I say, he damn good son of a bitch; smart, too!"

At some point, Rina told herself, she should explain to

Mrs. Brownbenttalon that there were such things as tears of joy. Not now. Now she was fully concentrated on peering ahead at the dock area, looking for the person she most wanted to see in all the worlds. There were Delt technicians supervising the hoisting of cargo from the base of the dam to the lakeshore; there were Slugs watching the proceedings with a proprietary air—well, the ship terminal was in Slugtown. But it wasn't until the boat had actually pulled up to the shore that she saw the hoist coming up again, and this time bearing two figures—well, three if you counted the little one poking his snout out of his Centaurian mate's fur. Beside her Mrs. Brownbenttalon squealed and rushed to greet them, but not so fast that she beat Rina to the scene.

And then they had each other in their arms—Giyt shaky, dehydrated, dirty, but entirely *alive.* "Shammy, Shammy," she whispered in his ear. "You scared the shit out of me."

"I'm sorry," he said, sounding as though he meant it. "I couldn't figure out any way to let you know I was all right without letting Hagbarth know, too. Now let's get back to town. They were making munitions up at the Pole! I've got evidence that'll prove it—"

"I turned it over to the council already," Rina told him.

"—and I have to get it to the six-planet meeting right away . . . You *what*?"

His mouth fell open as Rina explained what had happened. Then he shook his head, looking at her wonderingly. "Jesus, woman," he said. "Looks like you're perfectly capable of getting along just fine without me."

"Why," Rina said with satisfaction, "I actually never doubted I could. I just don't want to."

•

ABOUT THE AUTHOR

A multiple Hugo and Nebula Award–winning author, Frederik Pohl has done just about everything one can do in the science fiction field. His most famous work is undoubtedly the novel *Gateway*, which won the Hugo, Nebula, and John W. Campbell Memorial Awards for best SF novel. *Man Plus* won the Nebula Award. His mature work is marked by a serious intellectual agenda and strongly held sociopolitical beliefs, without sacrificing narrative drive. In addition to his successful solo fiction, Pohl has collaborated with a variety of writers, including C. M. Kornbluth and Jack Williamson. The Pohl/Kornbluth collaboration, *The Space Merchants*, is a longtime classic of satiric science fiction. *The Starchild Trilogy* with Williamson is one of the more notable collaborations in the field. Pohl has been a magazine editor in the field since he was very young, piloting *Worlds of If* to three successive Hugos for best magazine. He also has edited original-story anthologies, including the early and notable *Star* series of the 1950s. He has at various times been a literary agent, an editor of lines of science fiction books, and a president of the Science Fiction Writers of America. For a number of years he has been active in the World SF movement. He and his wife, Elizabeth Anne Hull, a prominent academic active in the Science Fiction Research Association, live outside Chicago, Illinois.